MAKE HER

A DARK BEAUTY AND THE BEAST FANTASY
ROMANCE

TRANSFORMATION TRILOGY
BOOK THREE

CASSIE ALEXANDER

1

LISANE

For one perfect moment, I was in a unicorn glade, astride one of the proud beasts' backs, smiling down at Rhaim and ready to pledge the rest of my life to him.

I didn't know how to quantify the way that I felt, but I also knew I didn't need to because I knew he felt it too. Something had changed between us last night, vastly for the better. I could tell in all of the actions he'd taken with me this morning, how he felt free to touch me now, but was gentle when he did so. How he teased me, while still giving me a smile.

Finx could create webbing from himself to use to bind things together, and while what Rhaim and I had was not so literal, we had somehow done the same. There was a thread racing from my heart to Rhaim's, growing tighter by the moment, and I knew that it was love.

Then my father came to kill him.

I felt the portals opening around us, only I didn't know what it meant, as Rhaim swept me off of the unicorn and tried to hide me behind himself, and as they were talking, I realized the truth, though I made Rhaim repeat it in my horror: my father had known where I was all along.

And now?

Everything was through.

We were completely outnumbered, and there was only one way for me to save Rhaim's life from my father and his guards.

"Don't hurt him!" I shouted, stepping away from his protection. "I'll come out!"

"Moth," he growled and reached for me, but I yanked away before he could catch hold.

I had to deny everything between us.

Vehemently enough that everyone would believe it.

Even him.

"How dare you?!" I shouted at him, backing up, as tears started streaming down my face, feeling the thread between our hearts grow taut. "Everything was a lie, and I was your joke! And to think I almost let you ruin me!"

I watched my words hit Rhaim like so many blows. "Do not say those things, Lisane," he pleaded.

"Or what?" I asked him, begging him to understand, to know that I would choose a life without windows for a thousand years, as long as I knew he was safe. "Or you'll torture me more?"

"Stay by my side and we can fight or flee, but do not abandon me like this," he growled, obliviously.

I ran for Jelena and she caught me with open arms. "I could never love you!" I shouted back at him, knowing I was lying. "I could never want to be with you!"

And then I plucked my father's ring I'd found among his treasures from a pocket and threw it at him. It was the only clue I could give him that I was doing this intentionally— that I had figured out some small piece of my own captivity the prior night and that it hadn't mattered to me.

Because every moment of this morning among the unicorns, here, with him, had been true, and I would treasure the memory of it for the rest of my candle-lit days.

Jelena grabbed me, and then my father did, and I could feel the thin thread in my heart begin to fray. "I never want to see you again, beast!" I screamed, sobbing, and I saw Rhaim surging forward on instinct, changing into his monstrous form to take me back, even if it cost him his life. "Live with the knowledge of my hatred in your heart!" I shrieked to repel him—and it worked.

He stopped—mid-step, mid-change—and the thread between us snapped.

Rhaim didn't dare take my love for granted, even though he ought.

Even though I knew I would love him helplessly, until the end of the world.

I stepped into the cold dark of Castillion's portal, knowing I would never have my freedom again, but at least Rhaim was alive, hearing him, still half a beast, broken-heartedly howling my name.

RHAIM

Lisane was gone.

Of her own volition.

And I was alone like I would always be until she someday took pity on me and came back and killed me.

Or maybe I died, dreaming of her face.

Because I didn't know what was left for me now.

I fell to my knees in the middle of the glade, all of the unicorns scattering as I panted, unable to manage the intensity of my pain.

Lisane was gone, and at no time had I even begun to plan for this possibility, the one where I gave my heart to a girl and she tore it to pieces before disappearing. I had been hurt by innumerable creatures while learning their ways, been pierced and poisoned, bitten and burnt, but nothing I'd ever encountered had ever destroyed me so utterly as this: my little moth, fluttering away.

Denying me—and everything we had.

Had I been a fool? And Lisane the world's most impressive actress?

Or had the sudden realization that I'd played even a minor role in her kidnapping truly turned her against me?

I didn't know, and I couldn't hold back my base nature any longer. I couldn't stand to be a man if it meant hurting like this.

Let *him* be in charge of me.

Let *him* be the one in agony.

Because I—I did not want to feel anymore.

Or ever again.

I went wild and shifted, letting my beast take me over.

LISANE

We stepped out of Castillion's portal in a group, the mage, my father, Helkin, Jelena, and me, into a small bedroom, with a cot for a bed and cushions, a tiny desk, and bathtub— it was well-appointed for a cage and wrapped in dark red fabric at every turn.

"Take the girl and go," my father commanded Castillion. Castillion gave me a complicated look, and then grabbed Jelena. She squeaked in protest, but went along with him, through what was a fabric door, and I realized we were in a tent. I got a clear flash of the outer world, a place with other tents beneath a bright blue sky—before the tent's heavy protective fabric fell back into place.

When would I see the sky again?

And—how far away was Rhaim?

"Oh, my daughter," my father said, giving me a look of pure relief. He stepped up to hold me again, pressing me against his furs, where the green gemstone he wore, Love's Lost Tear, that symbolized our country, Drelleth, was fittingly crushed against my heart. I stiffened in his arms, fighting not to struggle until I couldn't stand it anymore.

"No. Don't touch me," I said, freeing myself, stepping back with wild eyes. I knew I needed to pretend to hate Rhaim for Rhaim's sake, but that didn't absolve either of them from what had happened in the least.

Helkin made a pained sound, but my father held up an understanding hand. "You've been through a lot, Lisane. I know. "

"How could you possibly?" I sputtered.

"I got your letter. "

I blinked and swallowed, spotting the line of lighter skin on his hand from where his ring had been. "You," I began, then the words drifted away, while I was stunned, fully realizing the depths to which I'd been betrayed.

Castillion was alive.

And I?

I had been given to Rhaim.

So of course he'd delivered my letter.

Why wouldn't he have?

Why didn't he tell me?

"What was your bargain with him?" I demanded. I needed to know. My father said nothing, so I turned to my brother, who turned red like I did when stressed, but he followed our father's lead.

"Everything's going to be different now, Lisane," my father went on, brushing past my demand. "And better. We saved you. I'm sorry we took so long. "

"Saved. . . me?" I repeated slowly. "You've damned me, more like. "

Because now I would know what I was missing, for the rest of my life. I could still hear the echoes of Rhaim's beast's howls in my soul.

"No, Lissy!" Helkin interjected, using the name he'd used for me all of our childhood. "We all saw you on the unicorn. There are a hundred different men and mages who will attest to it. Your honor is still, somehow, amazingly, intact. And we'll find you a match—"

"You. . . will find me a match?" I said, repeating his words again, as my voice went high. "You gave me to him!" I said fiercely, and looked between them, for shame or—or—or—*something*—that showed that they had even an ounce of remorse at my betrayal. And while my twin brother's face was still red, I could see the line of muscle clenching underneath his jaw, rather than apologize. "You just handed me over," I said, to myself, since they didn't care. "None of you told me where I was going, or why, or what would be facing me when I got there. "

When I thought back to how lost to me everything had seemed in Rhaim's dungeon—and how badly I felt, knowing Castillion had died—the abuses I had suffered, thinking I had no other choice—and how much worse things could have been, had Rhaim been a different man.

It did not matter how their decision had turned out.

They never should have made it without telling me.

I shook my head wildly, breathing hard.

"Lissy—" Helkin complained, stepping forward again, making me step back further.

"No, Helkin—let her be," our father said and then gave me an exasperated sigh. "It wasn't a decision I made easily, Lisane. We needed his help in the war. "

"He. . . helped you? When?" I asked, but I didn't need to, because I suddenly realized what had happened. I remembered all the times I'd tormented Rhaim for his inaction. . . not knowing that when he went off to "study" he was truly here.

Fighting the Deathless with my father's men.

Getting injured. Repeatedly.

Just like I had seen, his cuts and tears and bruises.

Because of the deal he'd struck for me.

Why couldn't Rhaim have told me?

"And you couldn't have warned me?" I asked.

"Would you have gone quietly if we did?" my father said, in the same clipped tone of voice I'd heard him use against my mother. When he had decided something was final, no matter what—like the time when he decreed Helkin would leave chambers and spend his nights in the castle above, leaving her and I behind, not long before the Deathless' first attack.

I knew my brother blamed himself for not being there to save her—*and maybe I did, too.*

I certainly blamed them both for this.

"I hate you," I said softly. The words tumbled out of my mouth before I could stop them, but I wouldn't have even tried. "I hate you both. And I will never forgive you and I will never let you give me away again. "

My father's expression was implacable. "Your hatred will fade in time, Lisane, and you will do what your kingdom requires. Until then, these will be your chambers," he said, gesturing to the tent we were in. "You will stay here, well-guarded against any who might try to take you, and protected from the Deathless until other arrangements have been made. "

"Arrangements that I will have no say in?"

My father gave a settling sigh before answering. "I know what's best for you, Lisane. "

I inhaled to fight him, because I knew that was a lie. But to argue more was pointless. If I raised my voice, I would only become easier to ignore. And I would not gain control of the situation by begging for it, or pleading, as my childhood had proved.

I could not demand power from a man who believed my life was of no consequence, who had already shown himself to be callous and cruel, far beyond whatever I had *ever* thought Rhaim capable of being.

So I said the only thing I could. "Yes, Father," I agreed, mimicking his tone of voice. If he bothered to notice, he showed no sign, before turning and walking out the door. Helkin stayed behind for another moment.

"I told him not to," he said, defending himself.

"But you didn't stop him," I said. "And? You didn't warn me. "

"No—but the guilt from that wracked me every day, Lissy. It was why I sent Vethys to save you, without telling him," he said, looking to where our father had stood. "And then that monster killed him, and very nearly started a different war—if Vethys hadn't been the fifth Ker in his family—"

Helkin kept talking as I put my hands to my face. "That. . . monster," I whispered, remembering when Rhaim had saved me from being pulled aboard the airship.

"And when I'd heard that he'd bitten you," Helkin went on more loudly, putting a knuckle to his teeth. "I will find him some day, when this war is through, and I will make him pay, I swear it. "

I knew *I* was better suited to hurting Rhaim than Helkin was, though I could hardly tell him that.

Nor could I tell him the reason that I'd gotten bitten—or what it'd subsequently allowed me to do. "Please," I said instead. "Just—stop doing things for me. Especially ones you don't bother to tell me about first. " Helkin looked hurt, but that didn't stop me. "I don't want your help. I don't want anything from you anymore. "

I realized the words were true as I said them.

The only thing I wanted was what I'd had, for a few brief moments, among the unicorns.

Something I likely would never have again.

I put a hand to my heart, where I thought I could feel it breaking, as Helkin shook his head to deny me. "You're just tired, Lissy—you'll feel differently once you've rested. You need food, and water—I'll send in a maid—"

A stranger looking at me with wide eyes might make me use up whatever magic I had left. I frowned, and Helkin tracked it.

"What about the girl from town?"

Jelena? "Only if you promise to ask her first," I said. "Promise me. "

"I swear I will. " He leaned in, trapped between decorum and attempting a hug, before giving up. "I'm glad you're back, Lissy. And at least you're above ground, now," he said, trying to say something to lift my spirits.

"I am," I agreed, with a sigh.

Just not as high as I once had been, on top of a unicorn.

Helkin left quickly after that, and when he did I saw the temptation of the outer world—and guards outside I did not recognize—before the tent's flap swung into place again, sealing me away. It might as well have been made of stone.

I sank to the cot and put my elbows on my knees, absorbing my new reality.

I was trapped in chambers, I had no idea where Rhaim was or if I would ever see him again, and I was still to be given away.

And my brother—without any thought to what *I* might like or want or hope for my future—was *glad* I was back.

I had the wisdom to stuff a pillow on my face first before I screamed because I didn't want anyone else to know how badly I was hurting—not that anyone would care.

But I had to protect Rhaim, even though I was pissed off at him.

Funny how loving him, and knowing he would hurt me, had trained me to hold both feelings in my heart at once.

And then I felt a tapping on my boot.

I moved the pillow aside, saw a disembodied black paw swiping at me, and almost screamed again, this time without the pillow. "Finx!" I hissed, the second I calmed down, as he crawled out, and pivoted quickly, back and forth, looking around the tent. "How did you—"

"I jumped through the sky hole with you!" he quietly exclaimed.

I swept him up off the ground at once and hugged him to me. "I'm so happy to see you. "

"You are?" he asked, wriggling around so he could focus most of his eyes on me. "You seemed very mad at Rhaim, earlier. "

"I had to act that way, to save him. But I was never mad at him—well, maybe now, a little," I said and softly sighed. "But I was never, ever mad at you. "

"Good. Because he told me to make sure I went with you. " He brought up his pedipalps to gently tap the likely darkening circles below my eyes as I closed them and errant tears leaked out.

I heard the sound of the tent flap opening as someone came in unannounced—and found Jelena there. She took Finx and I in, her jaw dropping as she gave a great inhale. I waved a hand to stop her at the same time as she closed her mouth hard enough to clack her teeth before quietly hissing, "Are you okay?"

With Finx still in my arms, I prayed he had the wits not to talk to her. "Not really. "

Her expression was still curdled, staring at Finx. "What is that?" she asked, pointing with a shaking hand.

I held Finx protectively. "He's my pet, from the beast-mage. He made the dresses I gave you. "

Finx waved one of his many arms hello. Jelena's eyes widened, but then she managed to give him a low wave back, slowly. "Your brother told me to come in here," she said, peeling her eyes away from Finx at last.

"I figured if I'm to have a maid, it might as well be a friend— if that's what you are. "

"I don't know, am I?" She crossed her arms. "I didn't even know your true name. "

I winced. "I'm sorry. I had to lie. I couldn't very well tell you this was my life," I said, then despondently looked around the tent's four close walls.

"Well it explains why you weren't very good at laundry," she said with a snort, before taking Finx and me in again. "But the rest—I don't understand. I saw him *bite* you, Lisane," she said, now using my real name for the first time.

"I know. " If only that hadn't happened, maybe Rhaim and I would've gotten a few additional sweet days—and my "honor" wouldn't have been intact anymore, to be so readily bartered away again.

"But then I saw you on the unicorn. "

I nodded, then could tell she was waiting. "So?" I prompted her.

"When you were bitten, I thought the worst of him, and feared the worst for you—but if I had known when we came for you, we'd find you there, with him, like that. . . I don't know that I would have said a thing. "

I gave her a tight lipped smile. "I would have assumed the worst and done the same as you, if our situations were reversed. "

"Then was your anger at him true?" she asked, her brow furrowed with concern for me.

I liked Jelena, and I wanted her to be my friend, but I also knew the realms I had to move in now. "It was as true as it needed it to be at the time," I said, circumspectly, as I set Finx down and stood to walk over to her. I was exhausted, and my heart was pained, but the most important thing was that Rhaim was still alive.

Her eyes narrowed at me perceptively. "Did you manage to do *any* of the things I taught you with him?"

I bit my lips not to laugh, remembering. "Some," I said, giving her a bittersweet smile.

She harrumphed at that. "Then I will stay and be your maid, until you get a chance to do them all. "

I reached and quickly took both of her hands in mine. "Thank you. "

2

RHAIM

I didn't know how many days I had spent as my beast when I next woke, lying in close-cropped grass, staring up at a moonlit sky.

I was in front of my castle; there was blood beneath my nails and fur stuck between my teeth. My beast had either exhausted himself, or decided it was time for me to deal with the consequences of my own actions, not *him*. I sat up slowly, feeling the weight of my sorrow fight against me.

I should have killed Jaegar and Helkin when I'd called a convocation and had the chance. But then that would have only lost me Lisane another way.

And if I had fought that day with the unicorns to keep her. . . while I had what felt like an infinite amount of rage inside me, I surely would have died, beast or no.

I breathed unsteadily, creeping up piecemeal to stand, feeling uneasy on what should've been familiar feet.

The only thing I was sure of was that I would see her at least one more time.

I had to.

It was fated.

I arched my back, coming into my own body again, raking my hands through my hair, and when I was finished I caught a glimpse of something gleaming in the grass. I knelt down to inspect it—it was Jaegar's ring, which Lisane had thrown at me, who knew how many days ago. It wasn't spelled to shift with me, like my leathers and piercing, and my Beast had just left it behind.

I picked it up, wondering when she'd found it—I'd tried to hide it exactly as hard as she'd tried to hide her journal, which was to say not very.

But she'd brought it out of the castle with her, and had it on her that whole lovely morning that she'd spent with me.

If it had been weighing down her conscience then, she hadn't let on when she had nuzzled up and kissed me. And I knew I hadn't tasted a moment of remorse—*or hesitation*—on her lips.

Had I been naïve? Wrapped up around my little moth's finger like the ring I held?

I weighed it in my hand. Lisane was a smart girl. And perhaps, at the moment when her father had arrived, she'd been smarter than me.

Maybe throwing his ring at me to catch was her way of telling me she'd already guessed some of what he'd told her.

And, perhaps, that she'd already forgiven me for my part in it.

I wouldn't know until I managed to talk to her again, and with Jaegar having nearly every mage that wasn't throne-sworn on the continent in his service. . . that did not seem likely.

But I thought I still had one friend. . .

I portaled to Filigro's, once again landing on his pavilion before dawn.

This time, I ran up to the doors of his cave—and found him waiting for me, behind a half-closed door. "I don't want to talk to you," he announced.

That set me back. "Why not, old man? What have you heard?"

"That you lost your mind, and bit the girl in public. "

I winced, wishing my beast had known better in the moment, and that somehow Lisane had been less tempting. "Only because it needed to be done," I said, a weak defense without telling him the truth.

Filigro twisted his beard into a knot with one hand, making to shut his door with the other. "No. Don't tell me any more. I don't want to know, and it won't change a thing besides. "

"Filigro," I pleaded, after catching the door on instinct.

"I already know what you want—for me to go and deliver some message for you. I can't, and I won't. " He grunted with the effort he was using to try to close his door, but my strength was far beyond his.

I hadn't even thought that far ahead yet. "I just wanted you to see if she was well. "

He paused and stared at me with his white-blind eyes. "And you say you do not love her. "

I closed my eyes and shook my head. "I was wrong. "

Filigro stopped trying to push the door closed and groaned, so I finally let it go. "I told you to stop, Rhaim. And I gave her books to scare her off—"

"It didn't work. " I licked my lips, considering, and then decided to come clean. "I had to bite her. I needed her to help me. "

His hoary eyebrows furrowed. "What do you mean?"

"It's the price of her magic, Filigro. She can't access it unless she's been hurt—and using it hurts her further. But she was the one who stopped the Deathless that day. Not me. "

He pushed his way outside with me, instead of letting me come in, and settled his back against the door.

"Do not say these things to me," he begged.

"It's true!" I declared. "I was there! I saw it myself, through my beast's eyes. "

"Rhaim, listen to me. " He stepped forward aggressively and took my shoulders in his hands to shake them. "Never tell another mage you've done this. "

"Why not? She—she could actually help her father's cause, rather than her talents being wasted in a cave somewhere!" I protested, trying to read his face. "She didn't catch on fire, Filigro!"

"Of course not, you fool!" he shouted, releasing me, and raking his hands through his beard again. "None of them did!"

I scowled at him, trying to understand. "What?"

He made a sound of deep frustration and banged a palm on the door behind him. "Women who learned magic didn't spontaneously catch on fire—"

"Of course not. No one does, because its ridiculous," I interrupted him with a growl.

"—they caught on fire because we burned them. "

I took one step back, stunned, and then made fists on instinct. "What did you say?"

"That I have been alive for a very long time, Rhaim," he snapped. "And not all of those years were kind to me—or I to others. "

My beast rose up to ride beneath my skin. "Speak more plainly—*now.* "

"Bah!" Filigro said, pushing past me to storm down the path to his garden, with its many cliffside graves. "I tried to tell you to step away! I tried to help you protect her! If you'd even managed to sleep with her, you would've made her life inestimably easier, but no, you had to go and show her unicorns!"

"None of that is fire," I snarled, stalking after him. "Explain yourself!"

Filigro walked right up to the edge of a curved bluff of stone and then appeared to look over, even though I knew he couldn't see. "One of the mages of my generation had the power to see the future. Or, *futures*, I should say," he said, correcting himself. I stayed a few steps away from him, lest I be tempted to do some violence, as he continued. "His gift was complicated, like many of ours are, and not all of his futures came true. But one thing he felt for certain was that there would be a day the world could end because of a woman using magic. "

"Merely *could?*" I practically shouted at him.

"I know how it sounds," he complained bitterly. "You may mock us now, Rhaim, but you weren't there. We. . . we believed him. "

"How long ago was this?" I demanded.

"Millennia. Back when I was very, very young, barely Ascended myself. But I still clearly remember the chaos his visions caused. Up until then, there were numerous women among our ranks. But then. . . after. . . " His voice drifted, with memories or guilt; it didn't matter to me.

"How many?" I needed to know.

"Before the flames? They made up roughly half our ranks. "

"You murdered hundreds of women? On the word of just one man?"

Filigro turned his head to roll white-blind eyes at me. "Many of his futures did come true, Rhaim. Give us credit for testing him, at least. "

"I will do no such thing!" I closed the distance between us, coming close enough that I knew he could feel my presence and the heat of my breath.

Filigro held his ground, despite the cliff he had to know was nearby. "I was doing my job. I was protecting the world. "

"If protecting the world requires the slaughter of innocents on a maybe, the world can go fuck itself," I snarled. Every piece of my body was ready to change.

"Oh, really?" He twisted to plant a finger on my chest. "One life? A handful of lives? Even hundreds? Against an entire population? I don't feel comfortable balancing those scales, Rhaim—do you?"

"I will do whatever it takes, to keep Lisane alive," I swore.

"So somehow her innocent life is more valuable than others?" Filigro mocked me. "I see. "

I seethed with impotent rage, and my beast was totally willing to fling him over the cliff's edge, if that was what Lisane's safety required. I asked the only question that was important to me. "And what will you do, now that you know of her powers?"

Filigro stroked a hand through his beard and gave a mighty sigh. "She has nothing to fear from me. I've lived long enough now that I think maybe the world deserves to end. Or at the very least, I understand that it's no longer my job to try and save it. "

I stayed close, weighing his intent, wondering if he knew this was how he died, and if so, if he would betray his knowledge to me in these, his final moments.

"I stopped caring centuries ago, Rhaim," he said simply. "Your Lisane isn't the first girl I've known to learn magic, and for all I know, she may not be the last. If I have learned anything in the intervening years, it is that the future is far murkier than it seemed when Vizaveth was extoling the virtues of feminine flammability. "

That didn't absolve him. "I am disgusted by you. "

"As well you should be," he said, and shrugged. "I am not proud of my past, but it happened nonetheless. Better that you know it now than not. "

If I had ever thought less of Lisane for her father—how should I feel now, knowing this, about the man who'd practically been mine? "Why did you never tell me?"

He seemed to stare across the vast crevasse in front of him for a time. "Guilt?" he finally answered. "Shame? Finally having a black-and-white understanding of the world shaded in by life? And because up until you *kept* the girl, I never had a reason to—and by then it was too late. " He sighed and set his shoulders with a thoughtful nod. "So—I will go see her, for you, on your behalf. "

"The fuck you will. " I swept up the front of his robe in one hand without thinking, instantly ready to send him over the edge, plummeting to his death.

He swatted at my arm in annoyance. "Let go of me, Rhaim. This is not how I die. "

"It is if you plan Lisane harm," I let my beast growl, through me.

"On the contrary," he protested. "Somebody needs to go and tell her to never use her powers again—because doing so would be as good as setting herself on fire. "

Losing her to Jaegar was one thing, but at the thought of my little moth being murdered—I could only barely rein my beast back. "Who would dare?" I demanded, shaking him, as my jaw began to sprout fresh teeth.

"I can't say, Rhaim! Teachings get handed down, generation after generation, and not even I know the heart of every mage!" he shouted fearlessly. "But there is no safe place for her now, as she is—as you have been fool enough to make her. Do you understand me?"

I kept him hovering near the precipitous edge a moment more, then hauled him back safely to stone. "Yes," I said bitterly, letting him go.

He straightened out both his robe and his beard with his hands. "Good. "

I hulked in front of him, pulling my beast back in. "I don't trust you anymore, old man. And if even so much as a strand of hair on her head is snapped—"

"You don't need to trust me. You only need to acknowledge that you have no other choice. "

My chest heaved with my impotence. Jaegar's mages would know instantly if I portaled myself anywhere near his camp, and there would be no excuse for my presence there—they would attack me to protect Lisane, on sight.

And I had already told her to trust Filigro. . . even if I no longer did.

"I know you are ready to die, but if you hurt her," I warned him, "there will be no stopping me. I will take out an entire generation of mages in retribution, and their blood will be on your hands."

"My hands are used to blood, Rhaim," he said, scoffing lightly. "Luckily for you, however, I find the thought of more exhausting."

I forced myself to step back then, giving him room to portal, but he didn't do so, he just walked past me back to his mountain home. "What are you waiting for?" I demanded as I followed.

"A ride. I've never seen Jaegar's war camp—it didn't exist before I went blind."

I folded in on myself, groaning. "I can take you near there then."

"And have all my further interactions there be suspect if someone senses you? No. I'll just wait. Mages—ones who don't threaten my life—come by fairly frequently. I'll portal in with one of them."

"Filigro," I growled. Now that my mind was made up to risk this, and I knew the danger she was in—

He waved his hands in my direction, batting down my concerns as he opened up his door. "Things will be all right, Rhaim. Or as okay as they can be." Then he paused, before going inside. "When I see her though—what do you want me to tell her, from you?"

I paused. In my rush to act, I hadn't taken a moment to consider what to say before coming here. And at the thought that it might be my last contact with her prior to whatever interaction we had before I died, I wanted to tell her everything.

That I loved her, and I would be proud of her, even unto death.

"Tell her," I began, ready to say as much—but I then realized it likely wasn't fair to burden her with what she meant to me. She had the whole of her life ahead of her, and I. . . I did not. "Tell her I said, 'I am sorry,'" I told him, hanging my head.

Filigro waited, then asked, "That's it?"

"It is. " I took a step back. "Filigro," I started, either to beg him to speed or to threaten him again to help Lisane, I didn't know. I was full of the need to *do something* and inaction was exquisite torture.

"It is all right, little beast," he said, and I knew he was absolving me—even though it was he who had acted criminally in the past. "I may have hidden things from you, but you have always smelled the same to me. I always knew who you were, as both a man and a friend. "

"We are not friends anymore, old man. "

"Eh, you're not in a position for it to matter much. " He stepped forward and clapped a hand on my shoulder. "I wish I could've saved you from this. The world will be a darker place without you in it, and I am saying that as a blind man. Go home, little beast. Live what time you have left sweetly, and know I will pass your words on to the girl, and tell her enough to keep her safe. "

I shook myself free of him, and didn't say a thing as I portaled away.

3

LISANE

Jelena spent that first night with me on the cot—she offered to sleep on the floor, but I knew from the dungeon how much that hurt. Plus, I didn't plan on sleeping much besides.

No, I stayed up most of the night, her on one side, and Finx on the other, listening to her snores and feeling him stir restlessly, as I tried to come up with plans that would somehow change things and lead me back to Rhaim.

There was no guarantee of how long my family would keep me here. My father was a forward-thinking man—I doubted he would have brought me back, if he didn't already know who he would give me to next, and I knew Vethys had brothers, and there were definitely other eligible Kers.

I was unwilling to admit how hopeless the situation was, because the further and longer I was away from Rhaim, the harder it was to imagine a life without him. I would've given anything to get the past day back and change everything in it somehow.

And by dawn, I had a semblance of a plan.

The second Jelena went out to get us food and water the next morning, Finx waved me closer with a pedipalp. "Can I talk now?" he asked.

"Yes," I quietly whispered. "And thank you for not talking earlier. "

"I remember what you said about spiders here. And I met a few under your cot when I was waiting to talk to you yesterday. You're right, they're very underwhelming. " He sounded disappointed, while I glanced back at my cot in horror, then I shook my head.

"Never mind that now, Finx—can you do me a favor, before she gets back?"

"Certainly!" he said with a bob.

"I need a piece of webbing, this size," I said, drawing out a square on the ground half as big as my cot. "Make it thin enough to fold a hundred times? But also, if you can, make it so I can use it like paper. "

He bobbed again, then scratched his back with several legs in thought, before embarking on creating it for me. He was finishing it when Jelena came back, carrying a basket and a water bag.

"What's—" she began to ask, as I quickly put my finger to my mouth to shush her. I was certain the guards outside could hear almost everything. "The reason you're up already, princess? I would have thought you'd like to sleep in. " She covered for herself, setting the food down on the small table I'd been given, and coming over to see.

"Oh, thank you for bringing me food. I'm so hungry," I lied, while gesturing her over to the ground, then whispering. "How big is this place?"

Her eyes widened. "Very. "

"How far away did you walk? How many guards or mages were there?" I used my hands to illustrate possible perimeters on the sheet of webbing.

"Why?" I closed my eyes rather than answer her, and when I opened them again I found her giving me a serious look.

"Because you mean to escape," she answered her own question, barely daring to mouth the words.

I swallowed, then admitted it. "Yes."

"To go back to your beast?"

I shook my head quickly. "That would condemn him." All I knew for sure was that I couldn't stay here—and I needed to leave before I was given to someone else.

She nodded and went over to the cot, poking the cushions industriously, until she'd evacuated a downy feather from one. I watched her snap it halfway down the spine, then thread the feathers through the broken piece, till she'd made a tiny quill, and then pick up what apparently was a lidded mug of coffee out of the basket. She dipped the quill into it and painted a little brown square on Finx's web.

"Here we are," she cheerfully said aloud, tapping her quill on the map, before re-dipping her quill, sketching several more tents, and then taking a sip of coffee, before offering the mug to me.

J elena was on a mission after that—I sent her roving far and wide—and she'd come back and count out how many tents down she'd made it, and what their positions were over the next few days. She hadn't been joking; the camp was almost a city now, on a wide plain, at an intersection of several roads and with a river nearby, all of which were used for transporting men and supplies.

In the interim, my father sent me bribes—probably as often as he could track Jelena down to deliver them. I'd been given gifts of fancy dresses to wear—though I only wore them when Jelena had taken my "boys" clothes to wash—delicately carved animals like I'd used to play with in my youth, and necklaces strung with fine stones.

The most galling of these presents was an empty journal and a writing stick.

Even if they had not conjured up memories of the life I'd lived with Rhaim—what did he think I had to write about here, with nothing to look at except for these four walls?

It made me wish that I could catch them on fire. . . and someday I intended to.

I just needed to talk Finx into continuing my experiments in secret.

"This seems like a bad idea," he said when I'd explained to him what I needed, on the sixth day after Jelena had gone out.

"It very well could be," I confessed, rolling up the sleeve of my shirt to show my skin to him. "But it's the only way I can gain magic."

He spun back and forth between me and the tent's door, then began rubbing his back furiously with his hindmost set of legs, making himself shed fine black hairs. "But what if someone catches us?"

He'd seen what'd happened to Rhaim for biting me, after all. "I will defend you with my life, Finx. I swear."

He made a dancing move then, zipping quickly from side to side. "But I don't want to."

I sighed. This was what I'd been afraid of. "I understand." Maybe I could talk Jelena into stabbing me with a paring knife.

And as if to prove Finx's worries right, my brother finally came in. He paused for a moment, clearing the webs that sealed the door closed with disgust, which gave Finx a chance to run beneath the cot, then he looked at me, sitting on the sturdy fabric floor of the tent, in the same pants and shirt I'd been stolen in, and sighed. "I thought you had a maid?"

"I do. " I stood, dusting my hands off, beginning to tense. "To what do I owe the honor?"

My long hair was in its braid behind my shoulders, which gave Helkin the opportunity to see my ears and the hoops I'd pierced through them. "You need to take those out. "

"Why?"

"Because they mar your perfection. "

I rolled my eyes so hard they may have seen my own brain. "I do not want to. "

"Do not make things harder on yourself. " He clucked.

"Harder on you, more like. Let us not pretend that I am the one keeping myself here," I said, falling into the one chair my tent possessed.

"You don't have any other choice," he said, like that was true. "It is the consequence of your station. "

"A station I never wanted nor required. " I felt myself filling with an empty rage then, no less potent for not having magic to attach itself to inside me.

Helkin gave me a profoundly lost look. "You wouldn't talk like that if Mother were alive. "

I sat up suddenly. "Because Mother would've never let Father give me away to the beast, and you know it! Yet somehow you, her son, stood idly by. " The thought of it made me want to spit at the ground at his feet. "How crucial was he? How many Deathless did he kill?" I pinned Helkin with my eyes. "Just how much was I worth, brother?"

He grit his teeth before answering, then I watched himself forcibly calm. "I know your captivity was hard on you. Father told me about your letter. "

My letter. In which I'd illuminated everything I'd suffered at Rhaim's hand.

I stood up very slowly. "It was better there than here. "

"You can't possibly mean that," Helkin said, curling a lip in disgust.

"I can. At least the All-Beast owned his cruelty towards me, and never tried to wrap it in a glove. " I picked up one of the dresses I'd been given off the floor, wanting to wind it around his neck. "Don't you dare for one moment think that what you are doing is kinder. "

"Lisane—" he protested.

I threw the dress at him, rather than listen to more of his ignorant lies. "Why did you even come here?" I shouted.

"Because!" he shouted back.

I was not cowed, I only wished that I'd managed to talk Finx into biting me. I stared straight at him, demanding that he take full responsibility for whatever he'd say next.

"Because," he repeated, at a lower volume. "Father's announced it. Your courtship begins tomorrow, and seven days from now, you will be officially unveiled. " My jaw dropped in horror as he continued. "Three of the Seven are in talks with him—who would have thought?" he said, beaming with patriotic pride. "So many horrible things have happened to get us here, but Drelleth's sun is rising, at long last. "

I rocked slightly where I stood, feeling my blood pounding in my ears at being given away again.

No, that was the wrong word for it.

I was to be *sold.*

"It's just like you always wanted, Lissy," Helkin said softly, trying to encourage similar kindness from me.

What would I be worth this time? Soldiers? Cows to feed the camp? The addition of more mages to his cause?

My brother was right, there was a time when I'd been sad I wouldn't be unveiled. When I'd been promised to Vethys, there'd been no point, because I was already betrothed—so not having an unveiling was something I'd felt the lack of, before, in my pre-Rhaim life, knowing I had so few things to look forward to, or back upon.

But now. . . the Kers would want to see me.

And they would decide if I was *pleasing*, to them.

The thought of being paraded in front of them made me want to retch. . . but I also realized I would never have a better opportunity to ruin my prospects in front of a crowd.

Everyone knew mages were barren.

So if I couldn't get Jelena to stab me, I'd race outside and make my own guards take me down.

I would get magic in me one way or another, between now and the night of my unveiling.

"Right?" Helkin asked again with hope.

"Yes," I said slowly. "It. . . is. " I exhaled roughly through pursed lips—I would have to pretend to be on board with this plan for the next week, because if I didn't behave, my father might summarily hand me off again, and if he did, who knew if I'd ever escape? I couldn't very well talk some Ker's mother or sister into pricking me with sewing needles once in chambers, nor would I get very much magic in me if they did. "Can you get me my favorite perfume?" I asked. "The one that smelled like honey?"

"Of course. " Helkin's expression slid to relief immediately, happy to have "me" back again, not realizing that it was only the slimmest version of myself standing before him because he could no longer comprehend my entirety. "That was Mother's favorite too. "

I hugged myself. "I remember. " After she'd died, I'd spent the next month sleeping in her bed, trying to breathe the last of her out of her sheets.

And Helkin. . . had abandoned me.

We'd been so close, up until Father had taken him up into the castle—and then after our mother's death, he'd left me entirely alone, no matter how many messages I gave to maids and mages to give to him. At first I thought they weren't getting passed along, but then I realized he was possessed of his own two feet.

I'd been so mad at him for so long because of it. And Father would only come by seemingly to torture himself—he would stand in the center of the main chamber without talking, and stare at the ground where the Deathless had come through, as though he could wind back time with his eyes.

"You know, you look like her, Lisane," Helkin said, breaking our thoughtful silence. "Like the portraits of her in the palace, from when she was younger. "

I remembered those, too. Oddly, in all of them, the painters had taken the liberty of placing her outside. "Thank you. "

Helkin looked pained, then said, "I think that's why he doesn't come to visit you. "

I knew he meant our father. "Why?"

"Seeing you hurts him. "

"Hurts. . . him?" I asked archly.

Helkin heaved a sigh, to be facing down the angry version of me again. "You don't know what he's done for you. For all of Drelleth—"

I stared at him like he had grown a second head. "And when exactly did he give you to a beast?"

My brother gave me a wounded look that he had no right to have. "We have all made sacrifices. " Then he turned curt, in imitation of our father. "I'll see that you get your perfume, and anything else you need to prepare. " He looked around the chaos of my room, which echoed my despondence. "Did you need more maids?"

"No—just the one is fine," I defended Jelena. "She's excellent with hair. "

"If you say so. " It was clear he didn't believe that, but he wasn't willing to risk further discussion. "Stop wearing pants, and take out your earrings—please. "

I grimaced, but nodded. "All right. "

He nodded back, then left.

I waited until the fabric door had fallen back into place to sink back down to the floor, and Finx emerged not long after. All eight of his eyes followed the path my brother had taken, and then he whirled back to face me.

"Show me your arm," he hissed.

I did so without questioning and bit my lips.

He ran forward and crunched his fangs into me—the same ones that crushed bugs and killed birds. I felt them pierce the skin and then slide in, tearing flesh, and I swallowed a startled yelp, as blood began to trickle down. Finx disengaged his jaw from me carefully, and began panicking right after.

"Did I hurt you?" he whispered in his most quiet voice.

I didn't answer, I just nodded, tears welling from my eyes. He'd been a hundred times more direct than Rhaim ever was, up until his beast's bite.

Finx quickly patted himself all over his body with his hindlegs, setting off a wave of fur. "Did it work?"

We both watched as the wounds slowly, slowly closed.

And inside of me, I felt the beginning of my powers stir.

There was hope for me, yet.

I rolled up my other sleeve to offer my other arm. "Do it again. Please. "

4

RHAIM

I walked into my castle and found it empty.

I had known that it would be, but I wasn't prepared for how much finding it that way would hurt.

How could I have been?

I had never been in love before.

I had cared for people, I had experienced friendship in all of its many forms, and I had had more than my fair share of sex when I had desired it.

But I had never had my vision of the world narrow down to just one person. I could so easily hear the echoes of Lisane's throaty laugh in the halls in my mind, and close my eyes and remember the way her eyes could go from innocent to hungry. I scented both her and the smoke we'd shared in my library, and I'd never manage to use my healing bath again without remembering being face down in her sweet, pulsing cunt.

I had known my death was entirely dependent on her.

But I hadn't realized how dependent I had come to rely on her for living.

Because what was here for me, without her, now?

I wandered through the rooms Lisane had been allowed to be in, her bedroom, her bathroom, the library, and the stable, knowing I should have broken open all the other doors. I shouldn't have hidden anything from her, ever—from the miscellaneous closets that held rarely used items, all the way down to the darkest depths of my heart.

And then I reached my bedroom, where our sheets were still tangled, and I could still scent her in the air.

My beast, which I had assumed I'd exhausted, stepped forward inside of me again, raging anew.

But there was nothing either of us could do now.

Nothing but think.

And possibly. . . plan.

I roughly shoved my beast back inside myself and he let me, knowing that solving the problem of returning Lisane to our arms would require more than brute force, and I started to pace with intent.

5

LISANE

Courtship gifts began arriving the very next day.

The guards outside the tent wouldn't bring them in—they couldn't breach the door; it was against protocol—so it was up to Jelena to do so, and she was overburdened by them every morning: armfuls of carved wooden boxes, silk pouches, and dyed leather satchels embossed with artful stamps.

Inside of each of these were assorted displays of wealth. Some were obvious, faceted jewels set in rings and brooches —many of these were in teardrop shapes that mirrored the stone my father wore. I was also given soft fur stoles, and shoes of fine silks made for someone with much smaller feet than mine. Other gifts were more obscure—one silver tin held a gift of what looked like cheese, but both Jelena and I were afraid to eat it. Another box was entirely full of blue butterfly wings, and I didn't know what to make of that. I suspected they wanted to show me their country's natural bounty, but what did it matter, when even if my father did choose to sell me to them I would hardly ever be outside?

I opened that box for Finx when Jelena was gone, in case he knew more about them then I did, and he reached in to stir the wings with a disconsolate forepaw. "They cut out all the good parts," he complained. I turned a little green, but petted him nonetheless.

At least I hadn't been given moths.

After several days of presents, it looked like we were stuck on Darkest Day inside my tent, despite the brief flashes of bright sun I got through the tent flap when Jelena came inside.

"Who knew there were this many eligible Kers?" Jelena muttered, bringing in the morning's lot. "How many of the Seven is your father trying to sell you to?"

I flipped through the growing pile of handwritten notes on the pile on my desk while frowning. "Three, I was told. "

Jelena made a thoughtful sound then, before picking up a new note attached to a rather large fabric and ribbon-covered square. "Make it four. " I had learned that Jelena couldn't read, but she was more than smart enough to recognize each country's stationary flair.

I bit back a growl and turned it into a sigh as she handed the newest letter over. "The Ker of Calraith sends his best regards and wishes me good health on this auspicious day," I said, reading the letter aloud for her dryly. Perhaps Rhaim and I had floated over Calraith before. In the sky, borders felt imaginary.

"That's longer than most," she said, unlacing the braids of ribbons around the object itself.

"Better handwriting, too," I said, adding it to my stack. To anyone else, it might've looked like I was saving them for later, but for me, they held the possibility of future kindling. I'd taken to sorting gifts according to what I assumed their flammability might be, and had arranged them in a spiral about the tent's floor accordingly, the boxes and ribbons they'd come with too.

Maybe this was why women who learned magic burned.

To escape.

A gasp from Jelena stopped me from thinking about setting everything on fire. "Oh my," she said, peering into the fabric case at whatever was inside.

"What?" I asked. I stood and crossed the tent to her, as she finished freeing the object.

It was a portrait of me, atop a unicorn, wearing a flowing dress much like the one I had on now. I noticed Rhaim was nowhere in the painting—and neither were any of my father's mages or guards.

"Well that's highly inaccurate," I muttered, taking it from her.

Jelena's lips twisted to the side like she had eaten something sour. "By now, people who weren't there think the unicorns were coming to rescue you from him. "

A bitter taste flashed across my tongue. "You're kidding," I said. There were at least a hundred witnesses to my retrieval, so there was no excuse for people not to know the truth—

"I wish I were," she said, with an apologetic wince.

My fingers curled around the frame's wooden edge. "These aren't even truly *for* me—they're for my father, my brother, or to impress one another. None of these men know me in the least, nor do they really care what I think of them. "

Because if they did. . . they would be afraid to be in my presence: there was magic in me now, that Finx had put there.

I only had to be good for a few more days.

I knew I could manage it—I had no choice.

"I'm allowed to see her," announced a stranger's voice from outside the tent, talking to the guards. Jelena looked at me, and Finx ran from where he'd crept out to inspect the painting back to underneath my cot. The guards complained, as the stranger continued. "Your wife wants to leave you. She's sleeping with your neighbor, the one with the apple trees. And as for you—the man who shares your tent is in love with you. He is a good match, and you should tell him so. "

Jelena and I both stepped back, as seconds later, a mage in robes, with a very long, white beard, stepped through the fabric door.

"Who are you?" I said, pulling Jelena behind me, protectively.

The stranger had white-blind eyes and took deep, almost distrustful, inhales before speaking next. "I am the mage Filigro. I was told you'd be expecting me. "

My heart flung itself into my throat, and I turned to look at Jelena. "Remember the item we talked about getting yesterday? Go get it—tell Helkin you need them immediately. "

She squinted her eyes in question. "Are you sure?"

"I have no interest in her honor, girl," Filigro assured her, waving a dismissive hand. "But please hurry—my appearance must be brief, as I cannot spell the guards outside to lose too much time. "

Jelena nodded quickly and danced out.

"We're alone now," I said, once the tent's flap had fallen back into place because I thought he couldn't see.

"She's gone," the mage agreed, then took another sniff of the air. "But he's not. "

Finx crept out from underneath the cot again. "Hello, old man," he whispered.

A warm smile cracked the mage's face. "Hello to you, too, my eight-legged friend. "

If he and Finx knew each other. . . I felt better already. *Unless* — "Nothing's happened to Rhaim, has it?" I asked, taking a step forward.

If it had—if my father had gone back to hunt him down and kill him—the magic Finx had already imbued me with sprang to my hand, and the mage's head snapped up, as if sensing it.

"Calm yourself," he commanded, and I did so, slowly. Filigro nodded at that. "He's the one who sent me. " He made his way further in and sat on the edge of my bed. He seemed to have no problem finding it.

"Is he. . . all right?" I asked, biting my lips after.

"Depends on your definition. " Filigro sighed, and then gave me a prim look, his lips set into a thin line inside his beard. "He'd be better off if he never met you—but that's not your fault, not entirely. Your father is a stubborn man. "

"And you're here to take me away?" I asked quietly. A hopeful *Back to him?* went unsaid.

"Oh no. No no no, girl. No. This is your life now," he said, twisting his head as if to look at my four fabric walls. "I'm here to tell you you'd best get used to it. "

I gawked at him. "Is that really what Rhaim sent you to say?" My voice rose higher as I said it.

"No. *He* told *me* to tell *you* he was 'sorry'. "

I frowned at the old mage, even though he couldn't see me. Rhaim wouldn't have abandoned me—it wasn't in his nature. My time at the unicorn glade would've set him back —but I knew he wouldn't have given up on me entirely.

"He also told me to tell you to quit using magic," the mage went on.

"You're lying. "

The older mage took a deep inhale and appeared to study me. "No. I am not. He requests that you do that, because he wants you to be safe. "

"Safe," I repeated, and huffed. "There's no such thing. "

"There's alive, and then there's dead, and he'd prefer you'd choose the former. "

I squinted at him. "I'm not afraid of Ascending. " And Rhaim knew that—which made me question why he'd sent Filigro here.

The old man clucked. "But you should be. The pain is almost incomprehensible and, once you gain the knowledge of how you die, it is not so easily forgotten. Especially because your death will probably be at a fellow mage's hands. "

I took a moment and stared at him, blinking. "Knowledge? Of how I die? What do you mean?"

"When you Ascend," he said curtly, then it was his turn to squint. "Did Rhaim teach you nothing of being branded by fate?"

"No," I said truthfully.

Filigro began what I assumed was cursing, only with words I'd never heard before.

Rhaim had told me he'd kept parts of other mage's journals hidden from me, because he didn't want me to know mage ceremonies. . . but I had assumed he would stop, once I'd begun my apprenticeship.

I just hadn't had a chance to read a single journal after that, though, what with my training, other than the one this mage had sent me to warn me off of training. . . and I did not have any to read here.

"Is that what happens?" I pressed.

"If he didn't—"

I cut him off. "Would it kill a mage to just tell me the truth for once?" I hissed.

Filigro cursed again before answering. "He must have had a reason. "

"Perhaps he did. But he's not here—so—what is yours?"

The old mage pulled a handkerchief out from somewhere and furiously blotted his brow, shaking his head in a profound fashion. "What you are is not allowed, girl. Not ever since the olden days. If men find out you can do magic, they will do anything to stop you. "

"Mages, you mean," I corrected him, licking my lips thoughtfully.

"Oh, no, men too. Mages are probably the most open-minded of the lot. You think your father would let you go now? Or any of the Kers lined up to take your hand?" he said, and scoffed. "But you can't overturn all of society just because it displeases you. And *Rhaim* wouldn't want you to take that risk. "

He said Rhaim's name like his opinion ought to have special meaning for me, and it did, but. . . he wasn't here, was he?

And if my options were literally dying, or just *wishing* I was dead, I would opt for the former every time, something I was sure Rhaim knew. "If I don't Ascend, do you know what will happen to me?" I asked the mage in all seriousness.

Filigro made a dismissive sound. "You will become a queen. You'll have servants and children and a husband who dotes on you. "

"Do you think I want any of those things? Or rather—do you think I want any of those things, at the cost of my freedom, until the end of my time?"

One of his furry eyebrows rose. "I fear I know the answer. "

"Then it seems you do. " I stood, noisily, so he would hear me. "You should go. "

"Rhaim—" he began, but I cut him off.

"I have strong feelings for Rhaim, yes," I whispered quietly. "But I also have strong feelings about windows, and sunlight, and moonlight, and grass. I want to touch snow. I want to ride horses whenever I like. I want to learn how to swim, if it pleases me. I want to count the stars at night. And while Rhaim may want me to be safe, he knows all that about me, too. So thank you for coming here, but you may tell him that I am also sorry, because none of those things can happen until I am free, and as I will never *be* free without the ability to portal—my studies will continue. Please go. "

He didn't move a muscle. "You're as stubborn as your father, girl—mark that I did not want to tell you this," the older mage said. "But if you won't behave for your own sake—you must do it for Rhaim's. He is close to his death. I can smell it on him—and I suspect it has something to do with you. "

A hand raced to my mouth in horror. "Why would you tell me such a thing?"

"Because if you use magic, he will feel compelled to save you, and doing so would surely hasten his demise. "

I knew it was true—the sound of his beast's lost baying at the unicorn glade haunted my nightmares every night. Given the chance, he would have fought to the death for me, my heart knew it. "Tell him not to, then. Tell him I hate him. Tell him if I ever see him again, I will never forgive him. "

"Would any of that work on you?" he asked, without giving me time to answer. "I think we both know the truth. So promise me you will behave, Princess of Tears, lest you give your heart more reasons to cry. "

My mouth opened and I took in a breath. . . then I paused. "Did he tell you to tell me that?"

Filigro shirked back. "No. What of it?"

"Rhaim *knows* me. " I put a fist to my stomach for strength. "Is the death fate shows you always accurate?"

"Yes," he said, emphatically.

"Yet he didn't send you here to tell me *not* to do a thing. "

He glowered, the beardless skin of his face reddening. "He shouldn't have to! You should be possessed of sense!"

I shook my head at him. "He sent you to warn me, maybe. . . but only *told* you to *tell* me that he was sorry. "

And Rhaim had a very long list of things to be sorry for: not telling me how I came to be in his possession, what happened to mages when they Ascended, and now, this, the story of his own passing, which if he had known was upcoming, he should have shared with me the second our feelings crossed.

But instead of any of that. . . he was apologizing for a fate that neither one of us would be able to avoid.

I had risked everything to save him once already.

I loved him.

But he knew, and I knew, who I was at heart.

"Then tell him I love him, instead. "

Filigro swept to standing. "I am not your messenger, girl. "

I ignored him utterly. "And I will always love him. And no matter what happens I am certain of his love for me. But I cannot go below ground again, nor can I idly wait for another man to rut me. Tell him that I am his, and his alone, but I do not need his help—he has given me the strength to find my own way," I said, walking for the tent's door. "You need to go, now. For all I know, he dies because they catch you whispering to me. "

I put my fingers on the fabric door for the first time and opened it.

One of the men who I presumed was supposed to be guarding me was having a heated conversation with someone nearby, and beyond him, across a muddy road, was everything that I longed for, the city my father's encampment had created, in all of its squalor and its glory, beneath a blue sky and a blazing sun.

Then I looked back for the mage—and he was gone.

Of course. Going home, Filigro didn't need to use the door.

He knew how to portal.

I let go of a small breath.

Then someone I didn't recognize came running up, a handsome-looking man, with tan skin and blond hair. He stopped a safe distance away, just as I was about to step back.

"Princess?" he asked, upon seeing me—and I watched his gaze roll up and down my body. "I see now the portrait I commissioned didn't do you justice. "

I swung the tent's door halfway closed, hiding myself in shadow. "Are you from Calraith?" I asked, and a bold smile lit up his face.

"Did you read my note, or did someone else read it for you?"

My hand tightened on the fabric. "I can read. "

"Do you enjoy it?"

"What do you care what I enjoy?"

"Because I might desire to have a conversation with you. "

And then Jelena returned, brushing past him, and finally attracting the attention of the guard, who caught me on the edge of sunlight. "Princess!" he exclaimed, urging me back with his ceremonial shield.

I let the door fall shut behind Jelena.

"I got what you asked!" She held out the scissors I'd told her to get from Helkin. "Who was that?" she asked, looking behind herself.

I took them from her hand. "The Ker of Calraith," I said. "Go chase after him. Tell him I do like books, very much. "

"Really?" she asked me. I nodded. She shrugged, then ran to do as she was told.

Because as far as gifts went, books were far more flammable than portraits.

6

RHAIM

The actual idea of how I would turn my fortunes around came to me rather easily, but the implementation of it was a bear—and not the kind I could easily tame with my magic.

I needed someone's help on the inside, and there was only one mage left I would reluctantly trust with my life, so I portaled a safe distance away from Jaegar's encampment and plagued it with fleas, trusting that eventually one of them would hop on Sibyi.

After I'd figured out where he was, I kept a discreet group of creatures at the ready around him, much as I'd kept an eye on Lisane when she was outside of town prior, until I caught him holding a portal open for a group of soldiers to pass through, giving a dragonfly, a toad, and a shrike all the chance to see what was on the portal's other side: a pine forest near evening-time. It was nothing after that to give him a head start, and then portal in after him, waiting for him to finish dealing with a commotion of Deathless, before sending snakes in to draw arrows on the ground near his feet to my location. I smiled to hear him groan when he realized they were there, and what they meant.

"I've got to go relieve myself—I'll be back in camp shortly," he said, funneling the soldiers he brought with him back through an open portal, until we were alone, which was when I stepped out from behind a tree trunk and he whirled on me. "Rhaim. " He said my name like it was a curse. "Talking to you is as good as treason. "

"Says the man who wrote to me in the sky. "

He took a deep inhale and released it in a rush, his thin lips turning prudish after. "Did you really bite her?"

There was no point in denying it. "I did. "

"Why?" He gave a disgusted shudder. "Could you just not hold your beast back any longer?"

I shrugged bodily, unwilling to divulge Lisane's secret to anyone else. "It was a mistake. "

"I'll say," he said and stabbed the end of his cane between his feet.

"And how are things going for the war?" I asked.

He eyed me dourly. "Don't pretend you give a shit about it. "

"Fine," I said, shrugging, and asked what I wanted to know. "How is she?"

"I wouldn't know. I haven't even seen her. She's guarded night and day, and it's not like she ever gets to come out. "

And at the thought of my beautiful little moth, trapped, something in my soul started howling. "Does her tent have windows?"

"No. Why would it?"

"Because if she's not safe in the war camp, with a hundred mages around her at all times, plus Jaegar's protective ring of them, guarding the camp from the Deathless themselves— when will she ever be?"

"Never," Sibyi said with a groan, then caught the way I was looking at him. "Because, unlike you, they probably know it's not good for her to get used to freedom. "

A snarl rose up in the back of my throat. "I should've left you in that cave. "

"I'm just being rational, Rhaim—"

"Cruel, more like," I corrected him with a growl.

"You can't change—*well*—everything! Not without some dastardly, or highly foolish, plan. " And then he realized he was alone in the forest with me. "Oh—*no*. Whatever you are thinking now, keep it to yourself. " He immediately reached a hand back to create a portal as I stalked forward to stop him.

"Have you heard of yllibrium?" I asked him, and his hand's spinning slowed, pausing the sensation of building magic.

"The metal that neutralizes magic?" he asked and started shaking his head right after. "It's imaginary. "

"What if I told you it was not?"

"Pah," he said, expressing his disbelief. But I could see the curiosity that tortured all of my kind gleaming in his eyes, bright as a cat's near a campfire, so I continued, telling him something I had never told another man or mage.

"It's only exceedingly rare—but I've gone out of my way to gather it for centuries. I needed it to more easily study magical creatures during my career. "

He took a moment to consider this, and his hand stopped spinning entirely. "How much do you have?" he asked with caution, and I knew I had him.

I gave him a wicked grin. "Enough to get myself into trouble," I said. "The Deathless have to have some magical component to them—otherwise, how do they keep working? If I didn't believe in magic, then I'd have to believe in gods, and I'm really only up for one kind of miracle at a time here. "

He squinted at me and he sucked his lips. "Oh. So *now* you care about the war. "

"I do. "

"Because you think if you solve the Deathless, you'll get your woman back. " Sibyi stared me down, daring me to contradict him, and when I didn't he pitched his voice lower than it'd been before. "Rhaim, that's insane. You think you're better than the world's best mages and scholars, who've been working on this problem now for years?"

"No, I don't. But I have reason to want it more. "

"Rhaim—" he said, twisting away, reaching behind himself again.

"If they're so smart, why haven't they solved it yet?" I asked, as the portal behind him opened. "Is it because the Deathless are an abstraction for them? Even for you? You're out here putting out fires, but you don't know why they're burning, and you're only nominally concerned about the damage they do. " He paused in front of his portal, but he didn't turn around, so I continued. "You care because you've been told to attend, and you're young enough for that to still mean something to you. But I care because if I don't manage this feat, I will never get her back. "

"Oh, Rhaim," he said with vast disappointment, but he let his portal close nonetheless. "Jaegar still has pride, you know."

I shrugged and said what I hoped would be true. "If I solve the Deathless then I can steal her away and no one would dare come for me." I took a step nearer him, momentarily transported by imagining the moment. "And—what's more —it wouldn't be stealing. I guarantee you, if Lisane were given free will, she would run to my side."

All sorts of emotions warred across his face, before eventually landing on concern. "Why did you bite her, then?"

"My beast knows she will be the death of me." As it was a truth Sibyi had already guessed at, it was safe for him to know. "But everything in me that's man..." Words failed me in the moment, thinking of my moth. Adoration was too slight, and love felt too cloying. Want—too selfish, need— too trite—and lust, too narrow. "She is the only creature I will never tame. Not because I cannot, but because I would not."

"You're an idiot and a fool." Sibyi rocked back, and I feared I'd lost him, until he went on. "And also the most violent man I know. Luckily your temper is matched only by your intellect." He shook his head like he couldn't believe what he was going to say next. "How do you envision this working, then?"

"No one will trust me unless I bow—and that's when I will need your help. To make sure they use me, rather than just give me punishment. "

Sibyi made a thoughtful sound before eyeing me like Lisane sometimes did, when she knew she was right. "So it seems then that I *am* your friend, after all. "

I snorted ruefully. "It does seem so. "

Sibyi dramatically clutched a hand to his chest, "Did it kill you to admit that?"

"My soul is dying, even now," I said, grinning at him. I put my hand out for him to take, and he swung his down so that we shook one another's forearms. "But before it extinguishes all the way, let us see if we can't stop the Deathless first. "

7
LISANE

B y the night of my unveiling, I had done all I could to prepare to escape.

Thanks to Finx, I was empowered, and thanks to Jelena, I had memorized a map of the encampment, and we'd chosen a location near my unveiling tent for her to go and hide my "boy" clothes for me.

The dress I'd chosen for the occasion itself was white satin, which Finx had covered with skeins of webbing until the top of it was pearlescent. It had wide shoulder straps, and a ribbed bodice, that pinched in and then led out to a perilously large skirt. It'd been the most structurally sound of all the dresses—the one most likely to keep me standing if somehow, like sweet *Lirane,* I fainted from the attention— and with Finx's help, I'd stashed whatever items I felt I might be able to sell later underneath in pouches, in its many, many underlayers.

After that, I'd carefully applied visible jewelry from each of the countries that had "honored" me, and let Jelena paint my lips and cheeks again with berries, trying not to let memories of what had happened with Rhaim the last time we had done so distract me.

I planned to tolerate my presentation for as long as I could— long enough to make sure it was night out, certainly—and then perform some magical display.

Either I would use enough magic to Ascend and portal away immediately thereafter, or I would publicly ruin myself in front of all interested parties, because what Ker would want to be married to a barren mage? And given the slimmest chance for chaos after my performance, I would rip my dress's laces out, take out the scissors that were also hidden on me and cut off all my hair, and run away in an underslip that we had dyed dark with coffee, with my bags of gemstones, until I could reach the stash of clothes that Jelena had hidden for me.

One way or another, by the end of the night, I would be free —and then, someday after that, when I was sure it was safe, I would find my way back to Rhaim.

"I'm sorry if this hurts," Jelena apologized, digging jeweled hairclips in close to my scalp.

"It is no matter," I told her, forcing myself not to grimace for her sake, feeling small jolts of power accumulating with each new pinch.

I ate a tiny nervous dinner, hoping that it would be my last one inside these fabric walls, and then paced as much as I was able to until Castillion arrived. Like my father, Castillion had avoided me ever since my return, and, like my father, I was unbearably mad at him.

Especially because he appeared to be the same man I had known my entire life, considering how magic made mages age more slowly. This version of him had been my guard as a child, taught me my first magic, and had watched me grow up. The only difference between today and any other day between us was that he had on a slightly nicer vest than normal—he'd always eschewed shirts, seeing as when he would use his magic, he would ruin them.

As he entered, he acknowledged Jelena with a curt nod. "You have done all you need to do tonight. Go," he said, holding the door open so she could leave. She looked back at me once, knowing all the details of my plan except for anything to do with magic, then did as she was told. The open door behind her gave me a flash of a graceful carriage waiting outside, before leaving the two of us alone, and then the mage turned to me. "Your father and brother are busy entertaining the Kers, princess, so I have been sent to collect you. "

I couldn't help but remember the last time I'd been in a carriage with the man. "I grieved for you," I told him.

Castillion gave me a weary sigh and briefly directed his gaze at the tent's floor. "So I was told. "

By who? I almost asked, before realizing I knew the answer. *Rhaim.* I swallowed. *My beast had so much to answer for.*

"Was anything true?" I asked Castillion, meaning the day that I'd been given over. I remembered him bursting into my chambers, telling me that the Deathless were on their way and that I needed to evacuate the castle immediately. I hadn't grabbed any of my belongings. We'd been in such a rush—and I had been so innocent—that I hadn't thought to wonder why we didn't portal, or why the carriage I was loaded into had all its curtains drawn until it was too late, and my next memory was of waking on Rhaim's dungeon's floor.

"The danger was always real, princess, as you yourself know," he said, giving me a look that urged me to remember my mother's passing. "And that morning, one of the mages guarding the castle died suddenly, endangering it. While the Deathless didn't attack at that very moment, they certainly could have."

"But... they didn't?" I asked, needing to hear the truth.

Castillion looked like whatever he would say next pained him. "Your father didn't just send you to the beast to bribe him. He sent you to him because his castle flies. There was probably no safer place for you on the entire continent."

I felt my brow rise as my nostrils flared. "Discounting the man himself, inside."

Castillion bowed his head slightly. "I did not agree with your father's choices, but I do as I am told, princess."

I gave a bitter laugh. "You would think that'd mean we had much in common then, Castillion."

And once again I found myself wanting something that I knew I would never get from him—or from my father or my brother, either.

Just one moment of acknowledging the possibility that they could have been wrong.

I was wracked with longing for Rhaim, not only because my body craved his attention, but because he managed to leave space for doubt—which had made every single moment I had had with him more true.

"And will you be drugging me this time?" I asked Castillion, not archly, just daring him to be honest.

He held his hands in front of himself, illustrating their current emptiness, before giving me a soft smile. "Not unless it is required. "

I could tell that he was teasing, perhaps, or that he meant for that to be comforting, but it was rather the opposite. And at the thought of that happening, of my father deciding where I was going again without informing me, and me never even getting a chance to do magic *or* run. . . my blood sank, and I swayed, just like poor Sweet Lirane, ready to faint in horror at the thought.

"Princess?" Castillion asked, moving quickly to my side. "Are your ties too tight?"

"No," I said, clenching my hands in and out of fists to recover.

Castillion eyed me like he didn't believe me and gave me a moment to collect myself. "The Kers are waiting. "

I reached for the combed veil Finx had made for me that matched my dress and set it into the rest of the elaborate series of braids and clips already on my head. It was made of sheer silk that came down to my hips on all sides of my body, which made it just as hard for other people to see me as it was for me to see them.

"Let us go to the carriage," Castillion said, opening up the tent's fabric, finally letting me outside.

8

RHAIM

"I can't believe I get to see inside your castle," Sibyi said after I'd taken him back via my portal chamber. He was now clapping his hands together like a child impatient for a surprise in front of the door to my laboratory.

I'd waited a week to summon him, after gaining his promise of aid. I'd spent it taking apart the cage I designed to be used for magical beasts, re-spacing the bars such that an average-sized Deathless wouldn't be able to fit through—which left me with an extra bar of the stuff to forge into what I knew I required.

"I'll expect the same from you in the future, you realize," I muttered, moving past him.

Sibyi swung one arm in a dramatic flourish as I finished unlocking my door. "You will always be welcome in the Lightning Palace. Once I build it, that is. "

I eyed him with a snort. "If you call it that, I will refuse to visit. " Sibyi chortled, and then we were in my laboratory. He gasped audibly and then began wandering around, touching everything, staring like his eyes were mouths and he needed to eat up everything he saw. "Take your time," I told him. "I want you to be able to get back here. "

This stopped his impromptu tour and he turned toward me. "Why?"

Because I had also spent the intervening week in heavy thought. "If I die, this place is yours. "

He puffed his chest out. "And what if I call it the Lightning Palace, then, eh?" he challenged me, before roughly exhaling. "No, really, Rhaim, I know you're a fatalist—and also that this plan of yours is absurd—but let's at least pretend we might succeed. It's no fun if we don't. "

"It's not that," I said, leading him to the staircase.

It was that the hope I held inside my heart was beginning to feel flammable, and once I set it aflame, I wasn't sure I would be able to return. Better to keep it tamped down, because any moment I spent thinking about Lisane and my future, was one less I had to secure it in the now.

I opened up the stable door for Sibyi, and he walked in, wrinkling his nose.

"What is that scent? Hay? Horse? Goat?" he asked, looking back at me for answers.

"All three," I said, glad his nose was unable to make out the finer memories the room held for me: the shining ambition of one perfect apprentice, and the eager way she had ground her cunt against my boot.

"And this is made of yllibrium?" he asked, walking up to the cage that was in the center of it.

"Yes," I said, pushing down intrusive recollections, just in time to watch him shove his hand between the bars. "Don't!" I shouted at him, but it was too late—Sibyi jumped back just like the cage had burned him.

"What—is—that?!" he complained, shaking his hand with regret.

"*That* is what it feels like to have your magic stolen from you," I said, coming up beside him. I had first read about yllibrium in some of the oldest of Filigro's journals, during my first long stay in his caverns in my youth. All knowledge of it had been lost, or perhaps purposefully destroyed or hidden by earlier mages.

Then centuries later I'd heard stories from townspeople in an obscure village I'd set down near, of objects called hurt-stones, that sometimes children found on the bank of the Orine River, and used to chase each other around in games.

Not all of the stones the children used hurt them—and not all of the children were hurt, all of the time—but some of them did, and were: stones with an actual quantity of yllib-rium in them, and children who had enough latent magical ability to feel it torn asunder by the rocks. Often their own parents didn't believe them though, and I did nothing to discourage that while I was there, scouring the riverbanks for rocks that looked like they had the correct crystal forma-tion, once I thought I'd discovered what it was. An additional confounding factor was that they only worked in relation to one another. Just one wouldn't hurt you; you needed to be in between them, so that they could create a field of depowerment.

It had taken ages to accrue enough to use, to figure out how to impregnate it into metal, and longer still to figure out how to use it "safely."

"It doesn't hurt normal creatures," I told him. "But for ones such as you and I—and like the Deathless, I am hoping—it's like getting your spirit ripped out." I set a hand on the cage's thick wooden top. "It doesn't do permanent damage, though."

"How would you know?" Sibyi asked me in disbelief. Then his lip curled in horror. "Wait—you've used this on yourself, haven't you?"

"I have tested it extensively. " So much so that I'd decided not to actually use it on any magical animals. Research was one thing, torture another.

"Rhaim, you are almost literally playing with fire here. " Sibyi's eyes went even wider than they'd been inside my lab. "The Kers cannot be trusted with this. "

"Oh, I know. And which is why I've never mentioned owning it before, to anyone, nor will I now—nor will you. "

He made a face. "Stop telling me secrets, I don't like it—"

I cut him off. "Learn this place, Cloudmaker. You'll need to be able to portal here as well, if things go according to my plan. "

Sibyi frowned, but took a moment to scan the room, committing the place to his trained memory. "Your plan, which is?" he asked when he was through.

"To capture one and study it. The Deathless are possessed of some mind, even if we cannot fully understand them. Maybe if we separate one from its magic or maker, we can figure out what purpose it serves. "

Sibyi circled the cage warily, before looking over it at me. "And what if you put one inside and it just explodes?"

One of my eyebrows cocked up. "There is that."

There were many things against this plan, and not much to recommend it. But it was the only thing I could think of that might work—or at the very least, get me close to Lisane, one last time.

If I couldn't figure out how to cage a Deathless—I'd never be able to free Lisane from hers.

"Rhaim, that's horrible," Sibyi said, focusing on the cage again, which he was staring at as though it'd done him wrong.

"Yes," I wholeheartedly agreed.

I knew because I'd made a collar for myself out of the extra bar.

9

LISANE

Aside from her actual pledge ceremony to my father, and my and Helkin's date of birth, my mother's unveiling ceremony had been the happiest day of her life.

I knew because she'd told me about it repeatedly, what it was like to be dressed in her finest silks and jewels and then taken to a building her father had specifically built for the occasion. She'd been snuck in through the back, so that she could surprise the Kers who had come to vie for her hand when she was finally unwrapped like a present.

She'd told me more than once how lovely it'd been to be put on display and adored, and laughed about one Ker's interest in her ankles, and another's in her teeth...

But *she* had been kind.

She had been innocent.

I was neither. Which made me doubt my ability to carry out my plan, because if someone asked to see *my* teeth at the ceremony tonight, I would bite them for having asked.

The carriage stopped, and Castillion came around to help me out of my seat, which was good, because I couldn't see much through the veil. He took my hand through its silk and carefully led me around another fabric structure, a tent easily ten times the size of my own as I counted steps, until we reached what I assumed was the rear of it, and I was allowed inside.

"Will you be all right standing, princess?" he inquired.

"Of course," I said, then watched him use his magic to cast light about the room, before walking about to strike the lamps.

I can do that, too, I longed to say. I wanted to show him everything else I knew—I wanted him to treat me like an equal. But there was no place for that here, tonight. . . yet.

"Do you remember when you taught me to do that?" I asked him, wondering if the moment had meant anything to him, when it had meant everything to me.

I heard him snort. "How could I forget, princess? And your mother got very mad at me that day, I'll tell you. She knew eventually you'd get up to trouble, holding light and reading books at night. " I could hear him smiling, and because he couldn't see my face, it was easy for him to think that all was forgiven. "I'll go get your father," he said and moved away from me, past where I could see his shadows through the silk.

I used the moment I had alone to assess myself. I still had magic in me. There was still hope. And whatever pain was coming up, I would be able to endure.

Then I heard the familiar sound of my father clearing his throat before I saw his outline coming near.

"I would see my daughter," he said, his voice warm, as he lifted the silken veil that separated us. He was wearing the many ornaments of his office for the occasion, including Drelleth's teardrop shaped throne-stone, in an ornate gold setting, rather like I imagined a dragon's eye to be. He was crossed by a wide leather strap, and his eyes traced my face like he had forgotten what I looked like.

"Now?" I asked him. "But not yesterday? Or the day before that?" I was embarrassed by how hurt I sounded. But it was possible for me to be two things: both mad at him and injured that I had been abandoned, again.

"I have my reasons, Lisane, and lest you forget, I am running both a country and a war," he said calmly. "And there will be plenty of time for us to catch up in the future—once yours has been secured. "

I bit back what I wanted to say on my tongue—*A future I had no interest in*—but he seemed to sense it nonetheless.

He took hold of my chin. "You will favor Ker Zesh from Streon. " Streon was the Third country of the Seven, I knew. "He is wearing red tonight, and he is the most appropriate choice for you. "

My eyebrows rose. "By which you mean strong enough to be tactically useful, but not enough to threaten Helkin?"

The corners of his lips crinkled into a painfully familiar smile. "You were wasted in chambers. "

I hugged myself tightly—the way I used to want him to hug me. "We agree on that at least. "

He kept my face looking up at him, pressing his thumb beneath my chin. "I know we've had our differences, Lisane. But I wouldn't have given you to the beast were I not certain you'd survive him. "

"But you didn't know for sure," I said, begging for him to admit just one moment of uncertainty.

He only lifted one shoulder a fraction of an inch. "I knew he was violent, and I am sorry that you suffered. But his aid in battle was remarkable—and his aid in killing Vethys, and thus freeing you from your pledgebond, was even more. "

I blinked and gave a soft gasp. It'd never even occurred to me that my father'd given me away to take my former suitor off the board.

"What I want you to know though, Lisane, is that I was always going to come for you. " He let go of my chin and gave me a warm smile that hurt me worse than my magic ever had. "I—as would any Ker—knew the beast mage wouldn't be able to get you with child so your light would've only been slightly dimmed. And I knew that when I rescued you, I would find you a better match. So here we are tonight," he said, tilting his head to the thick fabric wall behind him. "What I didn't know was that somehow you would manage to keep your honor," he said, shaking his head from side to side and beaming at me with unrestrained pride. "They're already calling you the Unicorn Queen. "

I swallowed. "He could have eaten me," I said, with reprobation.

And there were times when I had wanted him to.

"But he didn't. " My father cast a quick glance at my shoulders and neck. "Although, where are your scars from his bite?"

"He used magic to heal me," I lied.

"I will give him credit for that at least," he said, letting me go and stepping back. "Is there anything you want to tell me?"

Not to sell me again? That I wanted my freedom more than I wanted my life? But as he looked at me expectantly, I knew he was waiting for a response. "Should there be?"

He gave me an indulgent look then, one he had often given to my mother, and put his hand against the heavy green stone he wore. "I'm not a fool, Lisane. And because of your recent history—I do understand why you want to run. "

"What?" I blinked, trying my best to seem innocent.

"Show me your shoes," he said, glancing at where my skirts met the ground.

"Father," I protested, indignant before I had the chance to be horrified.

"Show me your feet," he calmly commanded.

I reluctantly lifted my dress to show him the same boots Rhaim had given me. "I didn't like any of the others," I huffed, because it was true. . . and because I couldn't run with just silk slippers on.

"Then you needn't wear any at all," he said, like it was eminently reasonable. "Remove them. "

"But no one can see them, and these are comfortable," I tried.

"Enough to run in?" he asked, then tugged up the leather band around his chest, swinging a satchel forward, opening it to pull out my hidden clothes. "Your friend may be true, but a master in spycraft she is not. "

My heart leapt into my throat with fear for Jelena, as I felt my magic land in my right hand like the hilt of a sword. If any of his mages had been near, they might have known it. "Is she okay?" I demanded.

"Of course. " My father seemed wounded by my vehemence. "I did consider punishing her, but I instead decided to appreciate how loyal she is to you. She will serve you well at Zesh's court. "

He made everything sound so perfectly magnanimous, like he wasn't ruining my life, as he continued. "You know, when I went to your mother's unveiling, I was expecting nothing. I was the next in line to rule our small country, and her country's position was even more perilous than ours, stretched out as it was across a long chain of islands. "

Islands I had only heard of.

Islands I had never seen.

I could point to them on a map, but that was all.

"My own father discouraged me from going," he went on, "saying that any merger with them would only lessen our own safety. But I disobeyed him, and had Castillion portal us over, just in case. And while I had been to many unveilings, I had never once felt tempted, until I saw her. She was so beautiful and seemed so delicate and kind—I knew at once that I would have the sweetest daughters with her. "

"More girls for you to forget?" I asked him.

He made a sad face, and tried to reach out and touch my hair, then realized the elaborate contraption it was in and gave up before doing so. "More for me to remember," he gently corrected me. "And after I'd seen her, I knew I had to have her. I went home and made my father give her country half our harvest to secure her father's favors. And we were very happy, for a very long time. "

Until she died, trapped behind a door, locked from the outside, my soul longed to scream.

"So I want you to trust that you don't need to run, Lisane," he continued. "And know that I will never give you to a monster again. So take off your shoes," he said, then added a soft, "Please. "

I had no choice. I tucked toe to heel twice and kicked them off, stepping back to reveal them. He nodded at this. "Be gracious and genteel tonight, Lisane. Make your mother proud," he said before dropping a kiss on my forehead, then hiding me with the veil again, and offering me his arm. "I hear Ker Zesh's mother and his sisters are lovely, too, and their chambers are quite spacious. "

It didn't matter to me.

Because I would never meet them.

10

LISANE

I could hear the ends of conversations winding down as I entered a dimly lit room.

"She was more of a slave," I heard my own brother tell someone.

"Or maybe he only mates with beasts?" suggested a man I did not know.

I made sure to keep my spine stiff, and my shoulders straight.

I was meant to be a mage.

And because of that, there was nothing that could ever ruin me.

"The main course, at last," said a masculine voice as my father led me along. Other men chuckled, and one of them burped. I fought not to give a disgusted shudder.

"Kers from all countries, may I humbly present to you my daughter, Lisane—your future Unicorn Queen. "

My father took the front of the veil that obscured me and lifted it up, blocking them from my view, before stepping aside.

I was on a small stage set in front of a banquet table. The flickering lamps in the tent illuminated several men sitting in front of empty plates, spaced out evenly, each flanked with throne-sworn mages standing behind them on either side. One of the men was my brother, another the man who'd sent me the books, and the others I did not recognize.

And the walls of the tent behind them were painted with a herd of unicorns. Some chased one another, others had lowered heads to graze on painted grass, and others bucked and battled, rising up on hind legs to cross their horns like swords.

If I were not here under the current circumstances, I would have loved it.

"As beautiful as promised," said a nondescript-looking man, dressed in red, with grease stains shining on his chin.

Zesh. It was all I could do not to use magic in that very moment to escape him.

But my father's attention was on another. "Ker Vorsha?" he said in surprise. His name, even I knew—he was a Ker of Rabel, the First and most prosperous of the Seven countries, and first in line for its throne. He was thin, and all dressed in black, in very tailored clothing, and he had a long face which wasn't helped by a short and pointy beard. "When did you get here?" my father asked him.

The Ker stood in acknowledgment. "Mere moments ago. I had my mage portal me in outside. I didn't think you'd mind my addition to your group," he said as he sat back down.

"Not at all. Of course you're welcome here—though may I ask as to your current wife's health?"

The man grunted. "She died in childbirth earlier tonight, and took the baby with her. "

"Was it a boy?" another of the Kers asked.

His thin lips pinched. "Does it matter? It's dead," he responded coolly.

My father turned to me again, tilting his head at the newly arrived Ker's chair. My target for the evening had been changed, and a now-familiar acid began rising in my throat.

Was he, or was he not, a monster? And how lovely were the chambers his newly dead wife had slept in?

I doubted my father knew—all he cared was that an alliance with Rabel would see Drelleth safe, should the wars with the Deathless ever end.

I nodded subtly to let him know I also understood—because it didn't matter who I was assigned to charm, as I was going home with no one.

"Won't you sit down, Lisane?" my father asked, gesturing behind me with his hands.

I could hardly move in the dress I wore, much less do anything as prosaic as sitting. I still tried though, perching on the seat of the chair behind me, realizing as I did so that it wasn't a mere chair: it was a throne.

Decorated with unicorn horns.

They comprised the armrests of the chair, their formerly sharp tips filed down to softer blunts, and they were arrayed behind me in an ornate fan, looking like the rays of the sun behind my head.

I gasped in horror at how many unicorns they must have killed for them, while the horns themselves glinted and gleamed.

"She's still pure! You owe me a hundred dramiers, my friend!" one of the men present said to another.

He made a noise of complaint, and twisted back to a man standing behind him. "And it's not magic?" His mage silently shook his head. He then pounded a fist on the table, making the silverware near him jump, before reaching into a pocket on his vest to pull out a unit of his currency.

"Say something, girl. I would know if I'd find your voice grating," another of the men commanded me.

I waited a for tremulous moment, torn between incaution and playing along. "I suspect that finding me grating would be more a problem with your ears, than my lips," I said sweetly, with a smile just for him.

Another of the Kers snickered, I knew not which, but it didn't matter, as another one piped up. "What skills have you?"

I named the only one I could, wringing my hands into fists on my thighs. "Needlepoint. "

"She helped make that dress," my brother cheerfully recommended me. He knew I'd been given dresses and fabric, but he didn't know about Finx, so no wonder he'd assumed. Any man buying me for my dressmaking skills would've been sorely disappointed.

"And what is it you enjoy?" asked the Ker of Calraith, who'd sent me books, and already knew as much.

The stars at night. Grass beneath my feet. The feel of a horse's mane in my hand. "Reading," I said softly.

"Histories? Legends?" he pressed.

"What does it matter?" another Ker chastised him. "Are you good with children?"

My father rested his hand upon my shoulder again. "Of course she is. "

"Let her speak for herself," the same Ker complained.

"Do you truly want a woman that prattles?" another Ker asked him. "Because I don't. "

"I have no fear of that," Vorsha said.

"Had you no sisters, man?" Zesh asked him with a laugh.

"I did. But I know how to make a woman quiet. "

His voice was dark, and it made me nervous. I quickly regathered myself to continue though. "I was told not to speak, lest I upset you," I said in the same obsequiously reasonable tone my father was so fond of using with me. I felt his fingers claw my shoulder a bit upon hearing it.

"Upset us, how?" the Ker of Calraith asked with bafflement.

"By making us curious how useful her tongue was," the man who'd bet against my virginity said, and then guffawed.

"Just so," I said, leaning forward to agree with him slightly. It was time to send my future up in flames. "Because how else are you to guess what I'll sound like when I'm moaning another Ker's name?"

This set back many of the men present, my father and brother included. Zesh slammed his fist on the table with a grin, while Vorsha continued to appraise me silently.

"Lisane," my father warned, gravely.

"I have always been only as proper as necessity requires," I said, pretending to give him a bashful look. "Because I believe a unicorn horn arch absolves me of all else. " Then I twisted to face the men gathered before me. "Did you think I was only possessed of my mother's famed looks, and had none of my father's fire? If you wanted something docile, I am not so. But if you want someone to bear you strong boys with eyes that burn like mine do, come closer and make your case. " I somehow managed to cross my legs beneath my skirts, letting the bare toes of one of my feet pop out from beneath the ocean of fabric. "Who would you rather come home to, after a battle? A limpid lily, or a thorned rose?" I asked them. "If you find me uninteresting, by all means, there's the door," I said, pointing at it with beringed fingers, "but know that I'll be keeping all your jewels. "

Some of the Kers present were horrified, while others of them grinned, and I didn't care about any of them at all, until Vorsha of Rabel stood to speak.

"I'll be honest with you, Jaegar, I find your attempts to ingratiate your country into our number irritating, no matter our loose alliance with you now. " My father stiffened beside me as the Ker went on. "But seeing as your Queen of Tears managed to not only birth one but two children successfully, at the same time, I am, perhaps, shallowly interested in your progeny. "

My eyes found Helkin in the crowd, at the mention of our mother. He looked angry—*on my behalf?*—and I watched him set the line of his jaw.

"It's a shame she's still a virgin, Vorsha," the betting Ker said. "Because if the beast had stretched her out with his cock first, you'd be sure there was plenty of room for your upcoming baby's head. " He looped his hands above his own head like he was emerging through them, with a surprised face as he cleared them, followed by a chortle.

Vorsha turned to glare at him, while I became more and more certain that I would rather die.

Even if I had sworn to Filigro not to use my magic, and meant it—Rhaim would've never expected me to stand for this.

So I would do it now.

I slowed my breathing, concentrating on sending the magic in my belly evenly to either hand, ready to send out a wave of power strong enough to knock all of them flat, so that there could be no doubt as to who had used magic and why.

If there was any justice in the world, doing so would earn me my mage-mark at once, and I would be branded here in front of them, Ascended, and able to portal.

But even if the world were as unfair as I feared, I would still make myself unweddable, and perhaps if no Ker wanted me, I would finally be free.

I inhaled deeply, and several of the nearest mages looked over at me in confusion, feeling the change in me, before everyone with magic in the room felt someone else's magic entirely from a portal opening, right outside.

Each of the mages present moved to protect their wards, and Castillion grabbed hold of Helkin's arm and stepped him up to the stage beside me.

And then I heard a roar from outside, followed by another, and another, and I knew that Rhaim had come.

I stood up at once, and it took everything in me not to run to his side.

11

LISANE

Castillion unsheathed a metal spike the length of his arm from his hand, while other mages raised up flames and acrid clouds of poison, readying to protect themselves from whatever onslaught Rhaim was about to bring, as the flaps of the tent at the front of the room parted to let him in.

"All-Beast!" Castillion called in warning, as the bear Rhaim was riding pushed through, with Rhaim briefly ducking down. It was a massive creature, its shoulders just as high as the shoulder of the piebald workhorse Rhaim had ridden in town, and each of its paws was bigger than the dinner plates that were still atop the tables. A phalanx of other creatures followed him, the lions I'd heard roaring, snakes as round as his biceps and as long as the tent, and a flutter of ravens and vultures, which took up spots in the corners, tilting their heads back and forth, so they could see everything with unfriendly eyes.

"Castillion," Rhaim said, dismounting from the bear with ease, landing casually with a bounce.

He'd spoken to the mage, but his gaze was just for me. I swallowed and stepped back beneath the weight of it, the throne catching me behind my knees, remembering what it felt like to have all his attention on me, as he thrust himself deep inside.

"I want a place at your table tonight, Jaegar," he announced.

One of the Kers laughed, several sputtered, and I could feel the anger radiating off my father. "I should have you killed on sight!" he growled.

"Why?" Rhaim asked, as cocky as ever. "For doing as I was asked? And not taking advantage of her, no less," he said, rolling his eyes up and down my body. Helkin moved to shield me from his eyes.

"You bit her!" my brother shouted.

Rhaim shrugged. "You knew I was savage when you sent her to me, and you sent her nonetheless. "

Castillion stepped up. "I should pierce you where you stand, for ever having touched her. "

But my father held him back. "Why on earth would I give her to you, All-Beast? You have no country to claim, and you've made no offers of courtship—not that I would've accepted them besides."

Rhaim bowed his head in acknowledgment of that fact. "You will give her to me because within a month, I will have solved the problem of the Deathless for you."

My jaw dropped. Was such a thing possible?

Did I dare have hope?

My father put a surprised hand to his chest, covering the green stone there with his palm. "How?" he demanded.

Rhaim licked his lips. "I cannot tell you yet," he said. "But it is a thing that will happen, I swear it, if you give me a month of your time."

My father stepped forward and off the stage, heading for him. "You forget, I don't trust you."

"I didn't expect you would," Rhaim said, coolly. "Which is why I bought this." He tossed a circlet of dull black metal out into the middle of the table.

None of the Kers knew what it was, that was clear, and none of the mages either, which was more curious. But I caught them looking to one another—they knew it must be an object of some power—and the boldest of them went to touch it.

He cursed, dropping it immediately, and gave Rhaim such a look.

"It is yllibrium," Rhaim confirmed with a nod. This sent a commotion through the mages in the room that the rest of us didn't quite understand. "If you leave me to my own devices to perform my research, I will let you collar me in trade. It will hamper my magic, but not my mind."

One by one, throne-sworn mages leaned in to whisper furiously at their Kers, and Castillion was no exception, hopping down to my father's side.

"I won't be able to portal," Rhaim continued. "And I will need some aid—I'll need access to the Deathless to study them. Research materials—and whatever else I require." He swung his head around to include everyone in the room. "All I ask for is a month of your time."

"And just what happens if you solve this problem for us?" Zesh asked.

Rhaim's eyes focused on me again. "I get the girl."

"And what happens if you do not?" Vorsha asked imperiously.

Rhaim produced a key from somewhere upon his person. "The collar has a lock. " He tossed it out onto the table as well. "If I cannot solve the Deathless, I will become your loyal servant, until the end of my time. "

I was suddenly in danger of fainting. The bodice that bound me was too tight, and my blood was thundering in my ears. Rhaim had just as much as admitted he didn't have an answer yet, and the price he would pay for failure was too great for me to bear.

I knew what it was like to be trapped in a cage.

I would never, ever, send anybody else—much less the man I loved—into one.

"Father, you cannot agree to his terms," I told him. But my father was surveying the other Kers present, weighing his options with them, without a second thought for me. I rose up on my tiptoes, leaning over Helkin's shoulder to shout, "I still hate you, beast!" willing Rhaim to change his mind.

Rhaim gave me a wicked smile, and spoke in the growl that bypassed my ears and went straight to my cunt. "As well you should, princess. And know, too, that if I am given you, I will never show you kindness again. The things I will do to you will make the unicorns weep. "

I rocked back, panting, knowing he would make good on his promise.

And knowing that I wanted that.

Utterly.

"I say give the mage a chance," said the betting Ker. "Not because I think he can manage it, but because I'd like to see him try. "

"I'll take that bet," Zesh of Streon said. "This time though, for five thousand dramiers, and twenty casks of wine. "

"I need an heir—and I don't want to wait," Vorsha stated, looking directly at my father.

My father swept forward, picked up the key, and considered things, giving the impatient Ker a cold look. "Then perhaps you should've been more polite, earlier," he said, then tapped the key against the gemstone on his chest, before looking to Rhaim again. "You get two weeks, All-Beast. " I watched Rhaim's nostrils flare slightly, but he gave nothing else away. "And after that," he said, raising the key up as if to toast the other Kers present, "you will become part of my daughter's dowry. "

"Father," I hissed. "No—"

"Done," Rhaim accepted with finality. He glanced to me a final time, but I couldn't offer him any public kindness for what he'd done. Then he turned on his heel, and he and his animals surged through the door.

Castillion lunged forward to pick the collar up the second he was gone. He cursed the moment his fingers touched it and then contrived to lift it up on one of his spikes, but he couldn't do that, either; any time his magic tried to enter the interior of its ring, it disappeared. In the end, he wound up carrying it outside suspended on two mundane forks with their tines speared together.

"What have you done?" I whispered, falling back against the unicorn throne.

"What Drelleth requires," my father answered me, not realizing I'd been speaking to myself.

My veil was replaced, and I was bundled up into my carriage after that, but not even the distance or the doors could block out Rhaim's subsequent roars.

12

RHAIM

Physical pain meant nothing to me.

I had been trampled before, tusked, and gored. I knew what it felt like to have almost every bone in my body broken, some of them simultaneously, like the time a falling bull had crushed my leg, and I did not even scream once then, just told the bull it needed to fucking move off of me, and cursed myself for thinking racing it was a good idea.

I let my creatures turn back to dust once they were outside with me, so that I stood alone.

"Get down on your knees, All-Beast," Castillion demanded, handing the dangling collar aside. I did as I was told, knowing if I fought, they would doubt my intentions.

I didn't know most of the mages who circled around me— they were throne-sworn, and had not participated in the war effort. They passed the collar from man to man, each of them unable to believe that it existed, until it had hurt them, too, eliciting yelps of fear and surprise.

"Where did you get this from?" one of the mages demanded. He'd been standing behind Vorsha of the Seven.

"Many, many years ago," I said calmly.

"I asked where, not when," he growled.

I gave him a toothy grin. "Your mother gave it to me when I was done fucking her. Said I was the best she'd ever had. "

He took the metal ring, howled in pain, and hit me upside the head with it before dropping it with more curses, and I laughed.

Another reached for it, picking it up carefully from the outside, with the fabric of his skirt. "If you break him, he cannot stop the Deathless," this one complained.

"Like he could manage it besides," the one who hit me snarled.

"I might," I said, running the back of one hand against the swelling bruise beneath my jaw. "So collar me already. My hourglass sand is pouring. "

It was so much better that all of them were out here, with me, and better yet when I felt the horses that drew my moth's carriage trot away.

Because I knew Lisane's body like I knew the lines of my hand, and when I entered the tent I could read her like my own writing.

My little moth had been about to do magic on them.

I had only barely saved her.

Had Filigro lied and not warned her about the possibility of a true death by fire?

Or, more likely, had his warning gone unheeded?

I didn't know—but she was safe now, for half a month, at least.

Castillion regained the circle, now that his king was safely away, and came to stand in front of me.

The look he gave me then was of deep disgust before inhaling roughly and spitting on my cheek. "That is for *ever* touching her," the Spiked One hissed.

I waited for a long moment before wiping his spit away and answering him. "When I am done here, when the matter of the Deathless is solved, and when I am finished painting my cock with her virgin blood—my beast will come for you, Castillion. ”

Castillion's jaw ground, and he put his hand out. Another of the mages present carefully handed the collar over to him, and he gritted his teeth through the pain of holding the thing, unlocking it with the key Jaegar had given him, leveraging it open so that it was ready.

“No, All-Beast. You will never be free again. Offer your neck. ”

I reached up to pull my hair forward, and bowed my head down, feeling the agony begin as he let go of either side of the collar and it slammed shut.

Grooved foot met grooved foot, I heard the mechanism locking, and the yllibrium engulfed me.

I knew the pain meant nothing long-term. . . but that didn't mean that the experience wasn't excruciating in the now.

The absence of magic flowed through me like a poison, burning every piece of me it came across, like it was sucking out my soul. My beast rose up in me, fighting for his life, making me slam my fists on the ground and repeatedly bellow, until the yllibrium had ground him down, too, and only what was pathetic and human in me was left, with a dull and echoing ache.

But I knew what to do with that.

Having already had my heart ripped out—losing my magic hurt nowhere near as badly.

And the only thing worse than what I was suffering currently would be losing my Lisane.

I stayed hunched over on the ground, breathing until I could manage movement, and stumbled to stand. Most of the mages around me took a step back then, eyeing me wildly. "I was promised help," I told them, my voice torn from roars, "and access to subjects for testing. "

Sibyi came running up, his jaw dropping in feigned horror. "Rhaim? What happened?" I had already made an extra key for my collar and given it to him, on the chance that the Kers decided to waste my sacrifice entirely.

"What happened is your friend's a fool," Castillion informed him, without looking away from me.

"I will solve the Deathless, or die trying," I told him.

"Well," he said, offering me his staff for me to lean on. "Hopefully only one of those is true. "

LISANE

Rhaim had come for me and inadvertently ruined everything.

I rode back to my tent in a state of shock, the gemstones I'd hidden in the pockets of my skirts grinding against my thighs with each bump the carriage wheels took.

He'd come for me.

He'd risked everything for me.

Right down to his very life.

I didn't realize tears were seeping from my eyes until their cool drops fell from my chin and landed on my chest.

I loved him, I loved him, I loved him, I thought, with each fresh jolt, and all I wanted to do was unleash enough power to shatter this entire carriage around me—maybe even all the tents and people surrounding me too—and race back to his side.

But I could not—not as long as he was chained, and someone else held his key.

And to think that his servitude might be part of my dowry—I leaned forward, clutching my hands to my stomach, and I would've thrown up, only there was nothing inside me. Just a rush of acidic bile that wouldn't leave.

The carriage shuddered to a stop and I didn't wait for any of my minders—I ripped my veil off and ran back into my tent, not caring who might see.

RHAIM

Sibyi did the things that I could not, magically hampered as I was. He created a bivouac for us, at the base of nearby mountains, far enough away that anyone who wanted to see what we were doing would have to portal in.

Which meant that we were also too far for me to be tempted by Lisane, seeing as I could no longer create a portal with the collar around my throat. He kept hopping back and forth to the war camp, making plans, accruing supplies, and securing help all night, while I was left guarding the cage, and praying to gods that I did not believe in, that my absurd plan would somehow work.

And the first mage he came back with was Wyrval the Green, who quickly took me in. Wyrval was as lean and tall as the trees he controlled, his eyes were the color of willow leaves hit from behind by the sun, and his beard and hair had a mossy tinge to them. "You do not look healthy, Rhaim," he said, in a sonorous voice.

"I do not feel healthy, either," I agreed, with a snort. I'd done my best to stay awake and begin setting up the things that Sibyi brought, but the entire time it'd felt like the collar was tugging me to the ground.

Wyrval frowned at me, then crossed his arms, considering the cage. Prior to me offering myself over, I'd flown my castle nearby, and shoved the cage out the hole that was conveniently still in my library's wall, before hiding my castle back where only Sibyi could find it. "No good can come of that," he intoned.

"I know. It's why we brought you first. " Wyrval cocked a brow at me in query. "There are very few mages who can help protect it like you can—and also who might want to. "

"Indeed. "

Because it didn't take much to imagine the Kers, who were already argumentative, figuring out a way to use the bounty of yllibrium the cage represented on each other's mages rather than the Deathless. Humans could touch yllibrium perfectly safely, which meant they could take the bars I'd created and reforge them into chains, or maybe powder them into a fine dust they could blow into an enemy mage's lungs, where the element could never be escaped.

And I read as much in Wyrval's eyes when he again looked to me. "I hope you are not making a vast mistake here, All-Beast. "

"I hope that as well," I said, sincerely. "Will you help?" Rather than answer me, I heard a sound like kindling catching fire—and saw cracks appearing in the dirt and rocks in an equidistant circle around the cage's base. Thick green vines looped up from these and began growing all around the cage like a set of hands erupting from the earth, holding it without touching it. "Thank you," I said quickly, with deep relief.

Wyrval jerked his chin at me. "Fuck the throne-sworn. With the exception of Castillion, they don't know what it's like to have been fighting these things. And, I must admit, I'm exceedingly curious about how all this will turn out. " He watched his vines until they bowed over the cage's top and twisted shut against one another, trapping the cage itself inside his magic, where it would be protected. "Although I must ask, is one woman really worth this much hassle?"

I put the fingers of one hand through the collar I now wore and held on. It couldn't hurt me anymore than it already had. "Yes," I answered, without reservation.

13

RHAIM

The next two days passed the same—Sibyi accrued a group of people he felt were trustworthy to our smaller camp, and Wyrval used his grand magic to protect both the cage and the camp itself. By the end of the second day, we were ready to begin.

We set up a portal frame for Jaegar's war tent to speak through, so that other mages could tell us where the Deathless were going to appear, and once we had that information, Sibyi pulled me through a portal he created with him to where the fighting was taking place.

Where I. . . was next to useless.

Even without my magic, I was still strong; the muscles I possessed in one form didn't depart in the other.

But it meant that I did have to fight the creatures personally, and they were their normal, somewhat breakable, selves.

I cornered one, ignoring the rest of the fighting around me, and tried to grapple with it. It bit my forearm—and where it bit me, it hurt. I swung at it without thinking and knocked it down onto a stump, where it immediately began bleeding out. "Fuck!" I cursed, watching the thing die.

Sibyi came up beside me, discerning the problem at once. "A bag?" he asked. "Maybe leather?"

"Perhaps. "

But I was unable to make things out of nothingness anymore —and because Sibyi's magic was not in working cloth—any time we tried to catch one of the creatures, it was like being too rough with firebugs as a child: there was a thin line between catching light in your hand and your palm being smeared with bug guts.

When the last of the creatures died, as the eruption faded, Castillion immediately portaled near.

"Oh, dear. Did all of your test subjects die?" he asked, feigning solicitousness.

"Fuck you, Castillion. "

He laughed and made a show of portaling off.

By the next time we went out, we had quickly procured a large leather bag, and managed to wedge a Deathless into it without breaking it. We were just about to attempt to portal it to our small camp, but then the other mages present settled the eruption, and I felt the thing I held inside the bag collapsed, disassociating from its magical source already.

I unlaced the top of the bag quickly to look in, and saw the Deathless inside melting down into its component fluids, which I knew would then sublimate away. I howled in irritation, and then started to pace, until everyone else had gone and it was just Sibyi and me.

"All right," I said, turning to him with a decision. "We'll need to capture one, and then transport it to our camp and cage it, before they finish killing the rest of them, or flatten the eruption itself."

"And just have mages and soldiers watching things get worse, until we let them know it's worked?" Sibyi asked, with a hint of disbelief.

"Something like that," I muttered, moving to sit on my heels. I played a hand through the dirt, like I would have when I was empowered, wishing for something, *anything*, to answer me, so that I would not feel so helpless.

He cleared his throat. "You realize we don't even know if they'll survive *being* portaled, right?"

"Yes," I said grimly. "If they don't. . . then we'll just have to hope an eruption occurs near our campsite, and that we could trust the mages present to sustain things for long enough for a physical transfer to occur. "

"Hmm. All right. I'll go tell the others what it is we need to do next time. " He created a portal behind himself and hopped into it, abandoning me. Half a minute later, he returned with an apologetic wince. "Sorry. Habit. "

I only shook my head slightly as he made a portal back to camp, big enough for both of us to go through.

After that, for two days, there was an odd gap where no Deathless appeared. It was like being on a triple-sailed warship, and experiencing windless doldrums out at sea. I made Sibyi bring me scholars then, with their papers and their theories.

They, at least, were as eager for me to be successful as I was. Not all of them had even seen a Deathless in person, although those that had frequently bore deep personal grudges against the things, like my Lisane, because the creatures had disrupted livelihoods and murdered kin. And some of them had been quite thoughtful in their research, which I found admirable, seeing as they only possessed one life's worth of time to do it in.

They'd created maps out of the locations of attacks, and crossmatched these with the time of year, or the ambient weather, trying to see if there was some cyclical nature to the Deathless that we hadn't cracked. I poured over their efforts with my fresh eyes, hoping to see something that they had not, but in the end, I found myself frustrated anew, because every day I had not accomplished my task was a day closer to losing not only myself, but Lisane, for good.

"How do you feel?" Sibyi asked from behind me as the second of these useless days drew to a close, and I found myself pacing around the empty cage with an empty heart.

I shook my head at the ground. "Soul-sick. "

"Hmm. Perhaps you're just hungry?" I turned toward him, and saw he was holding a plate full of food. "You need to eat. "

"Eating is not research, and it also is not science. "

He came to stand beside me, facing the cage, trapped as it was in Wyrval's vines. "You're human now, Rhaim, or something akin to it. " He swung the plate in front of me again. "Your brain needs food, even if you think your body doesn't. "

"Pah," I disagreed, but still took it from him, eating with my fingers rather than taking a step away.

I was awakened in the middle of the night the next night by the sound of fire catching.

I leapt out of my bed half-dressed and ran outside—my tent and the cage were away from the rest of the camp, at my request—and I found two throne-sworn mages I barely knew, Neth the Slicer and Shael the Fire Soul, destroying Wyrval's vines.

I accosted them at once. "What are you doing?" I demanded, as I ran to block the yllibrium cage with my own body. Sibyi was gone, and with him, my collar's spare key. I watched the last of Wyrval's protective wooden circle blacken and dust, as Shael shot fire from his chest at it—and around Neth's feet were what I assumed the shreds of Wyrval's body, which appeared an odd mixture of burned human and charred botanicals. "I will call a convocation!" I threatened.

Neth looked over at me, now done with his slicing. "How?" he mocked me.

I tilted my head. They had not thought this through. "How will you take the cage without touching it?" The only reason I'd been able to manage its creation is because I'd individually picked up the hurt-stones, and been able to walk them into my castle.

"An army approaches," Shael said, finishing his chore, closing his shirt over his still gleaming chest.

"You would trust it in human custody?" I asked him archly. "And you think I'm a fool. "

Neth brought a hand up, but Shael slapped it down. "If you kill him, we won't know where to get more. "

I took another step forward. "If that's the only thing that's stopping you from killing me, don't bother. I will never tell you. "

"You shouldn't tempt me, All-*Man*," Neth sneered. "Plus if no one knows where to get more, think how much this amount will be worth?"

And just then, the ground cracked. I hadn't gotten a sensation of it happening beforehand, and neither, seemingly, had they. If the Deathless erupted here, it would make my life easier—but I wouldn't be able to stop them by myself, collared like I was—

Then lashes of green vines roped out and caught Neth the Slicer's hands.

Wyrval.

I jumped back to what I hoped was safety as the vines dragged Neth down to the ground and bound him there. Shael ran over to him, ripping his shirt open to use his fire-magic, but then stopped himself—there was no way for him to burn Neth free without burning the man, too.

More vines whipped out, a veritable tangle of them, and soon Shael was dealing with his own bindings, screaming as he was dragged to the ground, facing up, the fire from his chest beaming a panicked beacon up into the night, followed by his screams.

Wyrval was slowly pulling both of them apart and I couldn't have stopped him even if I'd wanted to. They screamed until fistfuls of vines punched into their faces, choking them, and then their terrified writhing slowed. I watched in equal parts fascination and horror as Wyrval's magic crushed them, pulled them apart, and possibly ate them, giving them exactly what they deserved.

After that, a tremendous oak tree shot up, almost instantly shading the cage and my tent beneath its boughs, and a figure stepped out of the trunk, appearing as tree-like as it did, before resolving clearly into someone more human.

Wyrval held up a fire of his own in one hand. "Everyone always thinks they can defeat me with fire. " He walked over to the two mages who I assumed were dead. "But green wood doesn't burn well, asshole. "

I walked up, feeling an unfamiliar sensation in his presence: awe.

"I take it you knew you didn't die tonight?" I asked.

"Not here, not now. " He pointed up to the heavens, which were obscured by the branches of the oak he'd created. "Not beneath this sky. "

"Well then," I said, wondering how the other two mages had seen their own deaths coming. Shael had lived a little bit longer than Neth. "He probably saw himself die under a tree. Since there wasn't one, he thought he was safe. "

Wyrval grunted at that.

"And the Slicer. . . " I sat down on my heels. Wyrval had rammed vines through the throne-sworn mage's eye sockets. "Maybe he didn't see his death at all. Maybe he just felt an eerie painful dark. "

Wyrval chuckled. "I hope so."

I stood up again, and toed Neth's head with my unshod foot. What remained of it began to crumble into dirt, leaving only a knot of the oak tree's roots behind, in the same shape as his skull had been. "It is so unfortunate that I find myself unable to call a convocation," I told Wyrval, with feigned dismay.

"Truly," he agreed. "If you'll pardon me though, it seems I have an army to convince to turn back now."

"By all means," I said, as he began to create a portal behind him. "And, Wyrval!" I called after him, right before he was about to step through. "Thank you."

He turned back to give me a toothsome grin. "You are most welcome."

14

LISANE

Not knowing what was happening to Rhaim was torture, and the sound of him being collared haunted me. I knew it worried Finx, too, because he was quieter now, and restless when he slept by my side.

Jelena passed along any gossip she heard in the camp—about a crazed mage, his promises of defeating the Deathless roundly scoffed at—but I couldn't send her asking questions with intent. I didn't want her in any danger, and I put nothing past my father anymore.

So the only thing that felt true was the growing dread that was gnawing at my insides.

Whatever magic Finx's bites had given me had faded, and I didn't dare to ask him for more, for fear of what I might do with it.

I had to give Rhaim's plan—such as it was—a chance to work.

And me outing myself to an entire camp's worth of soldiers and mages was not part of Rhaim's ploy.

After seven days, though, when there was just a wisp left of power in me, I ran out of resolve—and for the front of my tent, to peek through the fabric door.

"Go get Castillion," I whispered, to one of my guards. I used the end of my magic like a bee might sting—a singular jab of command, towards ends profitable to me—and I felt it, same as he did, a short sharp poke in an uncomfortable place.

But then he ran off to do as he was commanded.

Hours later, Castillion came as called, boldly stepping into my tent, his bearing tense. "Princess?" he asked. "One of your guards said you needed me."

I made a show of wringing my hands. "Tell me how the Beast fairs."

The mage made a soothing gesture in my direction. "You needn't worry about him. He has not made any progress yet. You're safe."

There were so few things I could say, without giving away my true nature. "Are you. . . sure?" I asked, sounding exactly as frightened as I felt, only for vastly different reasons than the simple mage assumed.

"Absolutely," Castillion said with finality. "He has set himself upon an impossible course. " Then he arranged himself more casually before continuing, stepping one foot out and letting his shoulders fall slightly. "If you're worried about him being part of your dowry, however. . . you will be in chambers. You would never see him. And, frankly, I don't think most of the Kers would care to keep him close. Wounded dogs are dangerous and need to be put down. "

"Put down," I repeated, softly, all of the air leaving me like I'd been punched.

Castillion nodded. "Please do not let his fever dreams trouble you, princess. It wouldn't matter if your father had given him a month or a million years. He will never be able to claim you. "

I forced myself to nod back, as Castillion took his leave of me, without asking the next question that came readily to mind.

How could Castillion be so certain?

RHAIM

I spent the rest of the night beneath the tree's swaying branches, with my back against the cage, only dozing the most minimal amount. When Sibyi returned, I told him what had happened.

"No," he gasped, looking at the tree, and the knotted roots, for signs of destruction.

"Yes," I refuted him, standing. I'd already known I wasn't going to go out of my way to anger Wyrval, and the events of the prior night had only solidified that.

"Most impressive!" Sibyi muttered.

"I'll say. You can tell no one, of course. "

"Obviously," he agreed. "So Ker Zesh doesn't care if we fail. "

"Or, he doesn't want to lose his bet," I said, knowing Sibyi hadn't been there for that portion of the evening. "Although I suspect he may be feeling differently this morning when he realizes his two closest throne-sworn mages haven't returned. " I'd never been tempted to put myself in the service of a king, and I couldn't really understand the motivations of those that did. I suspected they just liked someone else telling them what to do—or having someone else to blame for their shortcomings. "But let's carry on as if nothing had happened, today. " I couldn't afford to get distracted by internecine wars between the Kers—it was another morning, which meant I was another day closer to winning or losing Lisane.

"All right, then. I'll go and wait at the war tent until they know of an eruption, and see if I can't convince them to wait for us to cage a Deathless before putting an end to it. "

"Please, do. "

When the Deathless attacked again, the places they were in were too populous to risk waiting for a transfer—or so Sibyi was told by Castillion, for an entire extra day. I was ready to shove the Spiked One into a bag and throw *him* into the cage, when we finally got the opportunity to capture one, as the creatures finally manifested someplace more desolate.

Other mages managed to keep the things at bay without winning, while Sibyi and I carefully gathered a test subject into the leather bag, and then other mages set up a series of portals for us to transfer through.

That a Deathless would even survive the portaling was the first hurdle—but I assumed they must themselves be coming up from some sort of portal in the ground, and not growing out of them wholly, like perversions of plants.

So we caught one, bagged it, and then Sibyi portaled us through to where the cage was, and Wyrval granted us access to it through his branches. "I would help you, but—" he said while watching.

"No, I understand," I said, carefully bringing the ensnared Deathless forward. The thing was moaning and moving inside of the leather.

"It didn't explode," Sibyi said. "That's saying something. "

I grunted a response, and took it up the small steps to the cage's top, where I removed the lid, then placed the Deathless inside gently, tugging free the lacing around the top of the leather. The creature clambered out of the leather bag, and I managed to close the cage without hurting it and. . .

"The eruption?" I called out to Sibyi, through the portal he was holding open, back to where we'd come from, without me taking my eyes off of the thing.

"Finished!" he shouted. "And our captive?"

I stared at the creature moving aimlessly in the cage. "Still alive!" I shouted back. Somehow putting it in the cage had freed it from the rest of its brethren that had rejoined the ground.

Sibyi whooped and then ran up to join me. "You realize no one's managed as much before?"

Of course I had. *But.* "It took eight days. " Which only left me six days, to unravel the rest of the creature's secrets.

"You'll manage it," Sibyi said, resting his hand on my shoulder. "I have faith in you. "

"I hope it's not misplaced," I muttered—and was vastly disappointed, when I accidentally killed the thing the next day.

I'd just been meaning to get a sample from it, to give to the scholars to do simple tests on, but after I'd pricked the creature's bloated arm, all of the fluids in it started pouring out, and there was nothing, absolutely nothing, I could do to stop them. Being magically suppressed inside the cage had made the thing even more fragile.

I cursed and watched the creature die a second, more final, death, and then thought about ripping the cage apart with my bare hands, and keeping going, clawing my way into the center of the earth in my irritation.

"Rhaim," Sibyi said, trying to calm me.

I shook his attention away. I didn't have time for his sympathy, or my own despair. "Help me to get another one. "

"Of course. "

After we procured a second, I was afraid to let anyone touch it. Scholars came and scholars went, proposing ideas one after another, which I mostly ignored, concentrating my will on the creature, like I would've any other beast I'd wanted to tame in my uncollared life.

I watched the way it moved, suddenly turning, from east to west, and all points in between. I couldn't tell *why* it moved though. It didn't seem to be following any senses—seeing as it wasn't using sight to see, or ears to hear, or even a nose to scent things. I used the scholars like a living shield to tempt the thing, wondering if it were more inclined to go to a grouping of two of them, rather than three, or perhaps the opposite, based on sensing greater heat. . . but whenever it moved, it did it for its own obscure purposes alone.

"You've seen them in action, Rhaim," Sibyi said, on my second day with the thing. "They're like birds in the air or fish in the sea."

"But even those have purpose. You forget—I know," I said, tapping my temple with meaning, before beginning to pace. "Creatures move towards pleasure and away from pain. Seeing as we're not torturing this one. . . what *is* its goal?"

"To torment you?" Sibyi guessed, giving me a look.

"You are not funny," I growled at him.

"No, I know, Rhaim—and if there were any justice in the world, capturing one for *anyone* to study should be accomplishment enough. The scholars appreciate you, at least. "

"And I will appreciate their appreciation, when I am trapped in some Ker's dungeon shortly, thinking of said Ker mounting my Lisane. " I ground my teeth together, my mind going dark at the thought.

"Rhaim," Sibyi began, his tone more kindly.

"I need to think, Sibyi," I growled, as courteously as possible. "So please, fuck off. "

The Cloudmaker snorted and stepped away, sitting down with his back against the oak's thick trunk for a nap.

15

LISANE

I knew Rhaim was failing when my courtship gifts renewed.

Not all of the Kers still wanted me, after my little show at my unveiling—I had frightened off the Ker of Calraith—but the ones who did were highly interested. Especially Ker Vorsha, who seemed to want nothing but a replacement for his recently dead wife. His gifts began as odd, and then quickly became frightening.

The dresses he sent were too big for me, plus they all had a light lavender scent, like they'd been worn by another woman—something confirmed when a half-filled bottle of lavender perfume was delivered, too. He sent an ornate silver hairbrush, the back of it set with gems in the emblem of his kingdom, but the bristles had someone else's blonde hairs streaked through it.

I couldn't figure out if he wanted me to *be* her? Or if he was just showing off how lazy he could be, knowing that my father's mind was already made up for him? I didn't know—I didn't *want* to know—but Jelena, Finx, and I all found it very strange.

And the night before my final day of "freedom," I got the strangest gift of all. I was pacing my tent, laced into a soft pink dress that looked far more peaceable than I felt when one of the guards called for Jelena. She stepped out and brought back a small, black lacquer box, handing it over to me. None of Vorsha's gifts had come with stationary—they didn't need to; they were always wrapped in black—until this one. There was an unsigned note tucked beneath, that I unfolded.

". . . because you are mine," was written on it in script. I recognized it as just one half of the vows one said when one was pledged, and I read it aloud for Jelena.

"I don't like that," she said.

"Me either. " I undid the latch with my thumb, folded the box's lid open, and inside, on a bed of black velvet, I found a silver bit, like one might put into a horse's mouth.

Which had been visibly scratched, I assumed, by human teeth.

Jelena and I both stared into the box in horror, while Finx ran around our feet, sensing our mood. I turned to her. "Go get my brother. " I hadn't sent her on a single errand after my unveiling, but now I had no choice. She nodded her assent and raced out the tent's heavy fabric door.

I stood stock still until she returned, and Finx went to hide, knowing Helkin could come in at any moment. And when Jelena came back, he was hot on her heels. "What's the meaning of this?" he asked me.

"Leave us," I told her.

"I'll be right outside," she said, and left, as I shoved the box with the bit in it into Helkin's hands.

He inspected it with his eyes and frowned, then shook his head. "It's a game. Nothing more. "

I stared at him, experiencing new levels of betrayal. "How do you know?" I asked him. "Did you ever meet his wife?"

He made a face. "I never had reason to—"

"So for all you know, she was bound and bridled in her chambers her whole life. "

"Ker Vorsha is from the First of the Seven countries, Lisane— we hardly made his acquaintance until now!" Helkin protested.

"And he thinks so little of you, that he sends me this," I said, snatching the box back from him to throw across the room. "You do understand, none of these gifts have ever been for me!" I gestured at the piles of them that I'd accrued. "They've all been for you! And that one is no different," I said, pointing to where the bit had fallen out of the box on the ground. "It is a message, and I cannot believe that you are too foolish to see it. You would let him take my honor, not realizing that by bridling me, he means to bridle our entire country!"

Bridled. . . and *ridden.*

"Lisane," he said firmly, trying to calm me. "That will not be. "

"How do you know?" I demanded.

"I just do," he said. "We will handle things for you. "

"As you did when I was with Rhaim?" I challenged him. I didn't think my family had known my condition the entire time I'd been there.

Helkin's eyes narrowed slowly. "You mean the beast. "

"He knew my name and I knew his," I spat. "He could have killed me a hundred times over, and you wouldn't have been the wiser. "

"Father has a plan, Lissy," Helkin said, in a fair imitation of the man. "It is already in action. "

"Oh, I know he does," I growled at him. "It's just that—" I began, and then stopped.

None of my father's plans had ever involved me.

When Rhaim had said my entire life, the only thing that counted was what was between my legs. . . I hadn't wanted to believe him.

Because I knew of all the rest of me. My sweetness mixed with bitterness, my hopes, my yearning, my strife.

I couldn't imagine not mattering—I had a life, and it should have had value—yet it was clear that I did not.

A voice I didn't recognize began outside. "Helkin, you're needed—"

My twin brother looked imminently relieved to have a reason to go away. "We will discuss this later, Lissy. "

"I only have one day!" I shouted at him, but then he was gone, and it was too late.

Jelena stepped inside immediately, giving me a pained look. "I'm so sorry, Lisane," she said, engulfing me in her arms.

I hugged her back, gathering my strength again. "Me too. "

Who knew when the Kers would give up on Rhaim? Would they even give him the full benefit of tomorrow?

And what would happen to him, with his collar on, when I outed myself as a mage?

I didn't know, but I couldn't go with Vorsha. I just couldn't.

It would have been one thing, were it Rhaim asking to tame me—because first of all, he *would* ask; he would never force or assume. If *he* were to send me a bit as a gift, I might think it a piece of play, because he would never want me to set it into my mouth, were I not ready.

But most of all. . . he knew I didn't want to be gentled.

Nor did he, in turn, want to gentle me.

Hurt me, maybe.

Yes.

But he would never quench my spark.

I pushed Jelena away from me. "You are fired, Jelena. "

"What?" she asked, looking alarmed.

"You cannot be my maid anymore. Where I am going, you cannot follow. " I didn't want any blame to fall on her shoulders when I escaped with my magic—and if for some reason

I didn't make it, I didn't want her trapped with me, with that evil Ker either.

"Lisane," she began to protest.

"Fall back on your old ways. " I knew she had other ways of making money—and I moved to rustle through all the jewelry I'd been given. "Take this," I said, handing her over a spill of rubies on a necklace. "And this, and this," I said, giving her brooch after brooch.

"Lisane, no!"

"You are not coming with me," I said with finality, grabbing her hands and making her hold the pieces. "I will not accept your service anymore. Take as much jewelry as you can carry and escape, tonight, while it's dark. Get as far away from here as you can. "

Finx looked between us—and then quickly knitted her a spider-silk bag.

RHAIM

Trapped inside its cage, the Deathless was freer than I was, because it didn't care what happened to it.

It appeared to have nothing to gain, and it seemed to have nothing to lose.

And it didn't sleep and it didn't eat, and so for three days, I didn't either. I spent all of my remaining moments watching it through yllibrium bars and doing calculations.

Did it cue on sight, like a hawk? Did it only see speed? Did it experience time differently than I did? Did it want to move towards water, or away from the sun? I couldn't understand its movements or its reasoning, no matter how elegant my tests were or how many of them I ran.

And then that night I had to deal with Castillion.

"Any luck?" he asked, stepping out of his portal, into the ring of light I'd illuminated with a torch because I had no magic.

"Who showed you how to get here?" I growled, moving to stand between him and the cage.

"You're not the only one with friends," he said simply, then took in both my wild appearance and the intact creature. "But the answer is no, isn't it?"

"I have another day. " I chose not to look at him, and stared into the yllibrium cage instead, willing its occupant to give me his secrets.

"A little less than a day," he corrected. "I collared you the second hour of night. It is almost the fourth now. "

"Leave the mage be," Wyrval said, appearing from nearby his oak, where I hadn't realized he'd been standing. "He still has work to do. "

Castillion ignored Wyrval utterly and spoke only to me. "Jaegar has chosen your replacement, you know. Ker Vorsha, First of the Seven. " I saw him put an apparently impressed hand to his chest out of the corner of my eye. "I know, I couldn't believe it either, a country such as Drelleth being elevated so, but—"

I reached out and grabbed the corners of his vest, nearest his throat. "Do not say another word. "

Spikes shot out of all of him, all pointed at me, like he was one of the spine-backed rodents I knew of—only all of his were made of metal. "When you're done here, All-Beast—when, in twenty-two hours, you have given up all hope—I will come for you and use your collar to chain you like a dog. " He cast his gaze around and scoffed. "Your last free time here would be better spent creating leather padding for yourself, for when you are dragged behind her bridal carriage. "

"If I do not accomplish my goal. . . I will see you then. " I let go of him without turning, and his metal spikes withdrew. He snorted, and stepped away to portal himself back home.

Wyrval turned to me once the other mage was gone. "You have given this the effort of a great mage, Rhaim. I know. I've been watching you. "

I shrugged. It didn't matter. I hadn't succeeded yet—and my glass was running low on sand.

"But tell me," Wyrval pressed, "if you do not manage to accomplish this. . . will you really let men enslave you?"

"Yes," I whispered. *Even though Sibyi had an extra key.*

Because there was no way I would be allowed to be around Lisane otherwise.

I would keep my word, and my collar, until my little moth had the decency to kill me.

16

LISANE

"Did you want me to bite you, princess?" Finx quietly asked the moment Jelena was gone.

I sank down to the ground beside him, the pink silk of my dress, pooling on the ground.

The truth was, I didn't know.

When I thought about my future and how angry I was, it felt like if I had enough power I might take the entire war camp off the map—so much so that it felt like the ground was shaking around me.

I wanted to give Rhaim all the time he was allotted. . . but I also couldn't stomach leaving my future in someone else's hands.

I nodded sharply, where Finx could see it with all eight of his golden eyes, and I quickly pulled up the sleeves of the dress I was in. "Do it," I whispered, and he ran forward, crunching his fangs into me.

I bit my lips not to cry out, and saw blood leak out of the wounds. Finx extracted himself carefully and then watched me.

"Two or three more times," I told him.

He danced from side to side a little. "What if I just do it one more time, but *very* hard?" he asked.

I wiped the tears leaking from my eyes away with my free hand as I snorted. "Finx—" I began to complain—and then Jelena burst back in.

I swept back up to standing, well aware of how bad things must look—the wounds on my arm were almost healed, but there was no denying the spatters of red blood on my dress's skirt.

"There's Deathless!" Jelena said, her eyes white with terror. "Here!"

"What?" I said, lunging toward her, for her protection.

She shook her head and pointed behind herself. "I saw them —I was on my way out of the camp, like you told me to go— and then the ground moved—"

"I know" I agreed with her. Because I could feel them now, and maybe I had earlier, when I thought it was my own desires shaking the earth. . .

I heard distant screams, soldiers yelling, and then from closer, "Fall back! Fall back!"

One of my own guards entered, and luckily he was so terrified he didn't see Finx zip away. "Princess, we have to move you, now. "

"Why?" I demanded. Was Rhaim somehow behind this?

"Two mages at the edge of camp got into a fight with one another and died—and everyone else is out handling other infestations. We're stretched too thin. "

Jelena looked to me. "They were coming up from beneath your unveiling tent. "

I blinked, realizing what that meant. They were near my father's tent, in the camp's center. The guard came nearer, knowing it was his duty to move me—but also knowing that he wasn't allowed to touch me, to make me go. "We're reforming north of camp—we need to leave, princess. "

I gave a soft gasp. I knew from Jelena's map that the population south of the war camp were the ones that served the soldiers. The butchers, the bakers, the armorers—who were themselves, unarmed. "And what happens to the south?"

This time of night, how many people were asleep in their tents, after a long and hard day?

"They'll make do. " The guard came forward, his hands up to grab me, and Finx ran out from underneath the cot to hiss at him, throwing his first two sets of legs up in the air, and the man was momentarily stunned.

I took advantage of it. "This tent is on fire. Go get water," I said, while willing him to do so with all my heart. I believed in the fire, I could see it all around me, rising up, feel its heat burning me, and wished the same for him.

He yelped, and ran out of the tent as though he himself were aflame.

Jelena looked at me, wide-eyed, gawking around, unable to understand why the guard had just run. "Is it?" she asked, her terror compounding.

"Not yet," I told her. "But it will be. "

17
LISANE

I grabbed a small bag of things—more useful than the gemstones I'd sent Jelena off with—and then she and I ran outside and into the general chaos, with Finx at our feet.

"I still want you to go," I told her.

"Where?"

"North. Where it's safer. "

"And where will you go?"

"It is better that you don't know," I said, and squatted down. "And Finx—I want you to go with her. "

He looked up at her, then back at me. "Why?" he asked, the first word he'd ever spoken in her presence. She gasped and threw a hand across her mouth.

"I'm going to go do magic. I'll be in enough danger—I won't be able to protect you. "

"I am me!" he huffed, throwing his arms up again, and showing me his claws and fangs and underbelly.

"And you are my best friend. You both are," I said, looking up at Jelena. "I can't have anything happen to either of you. "

"But what if you get trapped again?" Finx protested.

"There are plenty of things in this world that want to hurt me. I'll make do. Stay with her. Please. "

Finx reluctantly walked over to her feet, while Jelena looked nervously at him. "And what will you do?" she asked me.

I rose, looking back at the tent that had trapped me for almost a month. "First. . . I'm going to give this thing windows. "

I turned and ignored them then, hoping that they would do as they'd been told—and knew my doubt about them doing so, which must've been a familiar refrain for Rhaim while he was training me. But I concentrated all of my attention on a spot on the wall, imagining the point of my stare burning like the sun, feeling my own eyes almost go blind for a time while I was staring at it, until the magic caught and the fabric flared.

"Yes," I hissed, and then turned, to run to the center of camp.

I was buffeted by the chaos, which was a good thing. A man's bag caught me in the shoulder, a woman's basket hit me in the stomach, and a small child ran into my knee. I paused at that and wanted to make sure they knew where they were going, until another adult picked them up, hopefully their mother.

I used the cacophony of all these much smaller blows to let magic build in me, one slight at a time until I encroached the area where soldiers were grappling with the undead things.

"Get back!" one of them shouted at me in warning—and I was sure he didn't know who I was.

How would he?

He'd likely never seen my face.

After this, though. . .

I spotted the tattered remains of my unicorn tent in the background, as a Deathless turned toward me. I angled around it, running through a group of them, dodging their reach, until I got inside.

There was a hole rent into the earth where the table had been, like a giant had reached down and clawed the soil up, and it was out of this gaping gash that the Deathless were somehow both forming and emerging from.

I didn't have much in the way to personally compare them to, only things that I had read about in some of Rhaim's books: they were like underground rats being pulled up into daylight, or maybe like the ants of a nest that someone had kicked. Their foul presence made a mockery of the unicorn paintings on the walls. I drew to a halt, thinking quickly.

When I'd stopped the Deathless with Rhaim, I'd had a vast bank of power inside of me from his bite. I'd demanded that the ground flatten, and it'd done so, just as I'd told it—flattening me, along with it.

But now. . . I quickly scanned the environment for something I could use, as many of the things drew near and—I found it.

My unicorn throne.

It was still here—likely meant to come with me as part of my dowry, so I could sit on it, horns agleam, one last time, as I was presented as a queen to my new people before my pledge ceremony finished and I was in chambers and it would never shine again.

It would do.

I put my hands out, focusing all my concentration upon it, as the Deathless blocked me, the ones I'd run past returning for me, fresh and easy meat, and new ones focusing upon me the second they'd left their grave.

The throne was *mine* and it would *give* and do as I asked of it.

I heard the sound of something snapping, like twisted wood, as I felt the claws of a Deathless on my back. I gasped in pain but did not lose my concentration—because that gasp would be my last inhale.

The throne shattered, pulled apart by *my* will and *my* desires, until all the horns that had comprised it were hovering aloft, where my magic could send them out like arrowshot.

The Deathless in front of me were pierced first, a unicorn horn drilling them through, the twisted alabaster length spiraling between ribs to come out the other side, now stained black, as the creature fell to the ground.

Yes.

I envisioned it happening. . . *everywhere.* All of the Deathless in this tent with me—and all of the ones outside too. I heard the wet sounds of their flesh being punctured, and the pink silk of my dress was spattered with their dark ichor.

And the cost of this magic was my breath.

I felt it leaving me, as each horn sought Deathless out, performing aerial turns like ivory hummingbirds—like I was blowing them along. I knew I couldn't stop—if I did, I didn't have enough magic in me to start up again.

A horn slammed through a bleary eye and out the back of one's skull, another was railed through its chest, and I didn't even know what was happening to the Deathless outside, only that I *willed* their destruction.

Fighting them opened up a vault in me to memories long since hidden—my mother's surprised shouts, her herding me into my room, and then her terrified screams.

Answered by mine, from behind my locked door.

What I would have given to have a skill like this then, when I was fourteen.

So I didn't care if I suffocated now, as I sank down to hands and knees on the floor of the tent.

All I needed was for all of them to die.

I heard cheers from outside, just before I imagined myself turning blue. Then the ground shuddered and the hole into the earth that'd been torn through the tent's floor went away, leaving only a small seam of mounded dirt behind.

My magic stopped, unicorn horns dropped out of the air, all around me, and I could breathe anew.

Panting, I slowly rocked back, and looked behind me to the tent's entrance, where the same guard who'd told me to get back earlier was standing in awe.

I had no idea how much he'd witnessed—but he knew I was here, alone, now.

Alive.

"Tell everyone who asks that I truly am the unicorn queen," I told him, and collapsed.

18

RHAIM

I stayed up until the last hour of my last night of freedom—and when Castillion didn't appear to collect me and gloat, I panicked.

"Why are they not here for me? What has happened to her?" I asked Sibyi.

The other mage held his hands wide. "I have no idea. Did. . . you want me to go see?" He looked between me and the cage. "I don't want to miss saying goodbye to you, Rhaim. "

"Say goodbye to me now then—and go look for her," I growled.

Sibyi's thin lips pressed together, then he nodded, created a portal, and disappeared.

There was nothing for me to do after that but pace around the cage. Had they taken her early? Was her freedom already stolen?

Or had something worse happened to her?

My mind, which I'd been channeling towards solving the Deathless for fourteen days and now three hours, went wild with agonizing possibilities.

All of the ways that her family, or the Kers, or other mages, could hurt Lisane—and none of the ways I could save her, being helplessly trapped here.

I walked up to the cage with the Deathless in it, took hold of the bars, and shook it, shouting—and the foul creature didn't even run away. It merely moaned wordlessly, senselessly, back.

And then I heard the sound of a footstep behind me—someone stepping out of a portal, and I turned.

Lisane was there, wearing a dress that was spattered with blood and possibly more, her hair wildly tangled, and she took me in, saying my name softly. "Rhaim. " She took a hesitant step forward. "You look how my heart feels. "

"You're here," I whispered as her mood changed, and she rushed up with one fist held high, before stopping.

"I didn't save your life just so you could throw it away again!"

I swept her up in both hands, spinning her before setting her down as Sibyi emerged from the portal with a cough loud enough to be noticed.

I glanced over at the other mage, who pitched an object to me. I caught it without thinking—it was my collar's extra key.

"If they come for you, you deserve a chance," he said.

"Thank you," I told him, meaning it sincerely.

"You tried, Rhaim. I wish it had worked. " He looked between the two of us. "And whatever this is, now. . . good luck. "

My gaze was pulled back to Lisane.

I didn't need luck anymore, now that my little moth was back with me.

19
LISANE

I'd woken up in an unfamiliar tent, with none of the trappings that my prior one had had—there wasn't even a cot, and I was on the ground. I cast a tiny light in my palm to look around.

How long had I been sleeping? And what had happened in the meantime?

I stood and ran for the door—and found it sewed shut.

My prison had gone from metaphorical to actual, which meant everyone knew what I was now.

A mage.

I stood and inspected myself, still in the same dress I'd ruined. I hurt. . . but that could've been just from sleeping on the floor.

I hadn't Ascended. I had had no visions of my own death, and there were no mage-marks on me.

My hands curled into fists so hard that my nails cut my palms.

Hours passed by, I was sure of it—and I knew *someone* was going to have to do *something* with me.

They weren't just going to leave me here, *surely.*

But the echoes of my confinement in Rhaim's dungeon were familiar.

Which meant my father was still deciding *what* to do. . . even if I hadn't been given to a Ker.

I bit my lips to stop from laughing out loud, worried if I did so that I would sound mad. If I had at least messed up that portion of my father's plan—

A wisp of smoke drifted up into my line of view.

Was I truly to be burned?

My jaw dropped in horror, and I scooted away from it, as it thickened and writhed up. I stood and ran, ready to beat my fists against the door, hoping that someone would hear me scream or see me punching out.

Then I realized I didn't *smell* smoke.

I turned, casting more light now, watching the smoke coalesce into the form of a being—and I realized it wasn't really smoke at all. No, it was more like condensation—a thick fog.

And it began hissing at me.

"Are you the princess?" it whispered.

It was clearly from, or the product of, a mage.

I had no idea how to answer it, and crouched defensively instead. "Are you here to kill me?" I asked.

"The opposite, in fact. Rhaim needs you."

I stood straighter then. "Tell me something he would say," I breathed.

The human-sized mass of fog scoffed. "He wouldn't. He's too proud," he said, and that did sound accurate. "But when the mages and Kers didn't come for him, he told me to come ask after you, so I did, and now I know you've done magic—magic he likely taught you." The fog-form shook its head deeply. "In any case though, I know whatever information I have to tell him, it will not be enough. I'd rather just take you to him, than play his errand boy."

I took a step nearer the presence. "You can portal me away from here?"

"Yes!" the fog said brightly. "I've always had storm-sight—where I could see what it looked like beneath strong enough clouds. But now I have a storm-form!" he said, illustrating himself with one hand. "Cleaved off a little bit of cloud, and concentrated, and—"

I almost laughed. Listening to him talk, it was like he'd been lifted off the page of so many of Rhaim's journals.

"But you can't tell anyone—this is too powerful—they'd try to blind me. Which. . . I might be able to make myself eyeballs out of clouds, then. " The living fog appeared to consider this. "I don't know exactly how it works all the way yet—but I *can* see into here now, which means I can make you a portal. "

I wanted to assume the best of him—but I remembered what Rhaim had told me, and Filigro too. The fog-man seemed to sense my hesitation.

"I read about you in his journal," he added.

I was aghast. "How?"

"He gave me his castle, because he thought he was going away with you. "

I remembered Rhaim's last entry in it, that I'd read the night before the unicorn glade, written back when he'd still hated me, apparently.

"I didn't understand why he was doing all this, beforehand," the fog-man went on. "You seem perfectly nice, but who would do all this, for a mere human girl?" he asked. "Then I saw his most recent entries, written in haste, the ink hardly dry. "

"What did they say?"

The fog-man shook his head curtly. "I would not tell you of them; they are his words to speak. But I know he risks all for you, his little moth. So can you please just take one risk for him?"

And at being called "little moth" again, even by the wrong —*and not even human*—lips, all my doubts were swept away. "Yes," I answered.

"Good," the fog agreed. "I'll be fast, and keep it small—so hopefully we don't get found out—but duck your head down, very carefully. "

I did as I was told, and jumped through the cold-dark of the portal and onto sandy ground.

20

LISANE

I was outside again. At long last. With no roof and no veil, so I could see the stars—and in front of me, a familiar man was wringing his hands against the bars of a cage where a Deathless was trapped inside.

"Rhaim?" I whispered, as he turned around. His leather shirt was marked, his pants and boots too. His dark hair was only half pulled back, locks of it tousled down, and a collar made out of ominous black metal sat around his neck, beneath his scruffed square jaw.

I said what I felt was true. "You look how my heart feels. "

"You're here," he whispered, as if finally believing his eyes. I knew then, that however much I'd hurt him in the unicorn glade, I'd been forgiven. *But.* "I didn't save your life just so you could throw it away again!" I said, running up to him.

He caught me though, spinning me once before setting me back on my feet, and catching something from the other mage. He thanked the other mage, and the man who'd been made of fog told him, "Good luck. "

Then he turned back to me and picked me up.

I didn't even ask where we were going, I just wrapped my arms around him, too.

He pushed us into a dark tent, and *I* was the one who cast light in it, seeing a desk in one corner, and a thick pallet of sorts on the floor.

He lowered us to this, keeping me near, and I caught his jaw in my hand. "Rhaim—what happened?"

My fingers sank for the metal around his neck, but he caught them, saying, "Don't. It would harm you. " Then he pressed my palm to his lips and kissed it twice before moving to smooth my hand against his bristled cheek, while he closed his eyes.

I waited for a long moment while he breathed roughly. "Will you also kiss the rest of me?" I teased him.

And when his eyes opened again, they were full of a heat and desire that should have consumed me, right then and there. "Yes," he answered at last, his tone low. "You are mine, and I will have every piece of you tonight. " He let go of me and went to work the latch of the collar with what I now saw was a key, until he'd freed himself from it and tossed both of the objects across the room. "But how are you here?" he asked much more softly.

"I used magic," I said and swallowed as his hands ran up into my hair. I closed my eyes, just feeling his touch. "There were Deathless in the camp, and I stopped them—"

"Who put magic in you?" he growled, and my eyes snapped back open. It was the same man in front of me as always, but it was like I'd heard another, darker, voice.

"Finx. He bit me. "

Rhaim shook his head. "I will pull out his fangs—"

"No, I needed him to. Otherwise I wouldn't have been able to do anything while I was there. " My hands found his, pulled them down, and twined our fingers. "No Ker came for me, Rhaim. " I hadn't exactly been set free. . . but I also hadn't been thrown into anyone's chambers. "Nor you, it seems," I said, then let go of him to shove his shoulders roughly— which was exactly like shoving a wall. "I was trying to save you!"

"You've been saving me already, little moth," he said, as his gaze drank me in. "Ever since the day we met. "

"Rhaim. " I whispered his name softly, and suddenly my cheeks were wet. Every moment I'd feared I wouldn't see him again, every time I had to be brave when I wasn't—all of it rushed to the surface, and I didn't want to pretend anything around him.

And I shouldn't have to. Wasn't that the whole point of being in love?

"Shh, moth, shh," he soothed me, pulling me into his lap with him, stroking me with infinite care. I leaned my body into his, pressing as close as I could, just needing to know we were together.

"Everything I said at the unicorn glade was a lie to keep you safe," I whispered against his chest, thinking on how many nights I'd spent wishing I could take each word back.

"I know. And somehow you managed to," he said, kissing the top of my head as his hands ran against my body.

I pushed back from him a little. "The only reason it worked though, Rhaim, is because they already assumed the worst of you. They think a beast is all you are. "

A sardonic smile quirked the corners of his lips up. "Is it not?" he asked, but then he didn't let me answer him, instead his mouth came for mine. I tilted my head and ran my arms around his neck again, giving myself over completely. He made a pleased sound as his tongue pressed in, and between that and the way he was holding me and what I knew was coming up—I whimpered and relaxed, as he pulled back, dragging my lower lip between his teeth, while snarling like a dog, me going weak in his arms.

"So dizzy already, little moth," he teased, pulling only far enough away from me to whisper, then coming back to kiss the edges of my mouth.

"Yes," I whispered, need racing through me.

His lips found my cheeks and neck, and with each caress, my whole body ached. "Someday I would like to know what you taste like without tears," he murmured, reaching around behind me to unlace the back of my dress. "But today is not yet that day. "

I fought my way back to reality. "Why?" I asked.

"Because," he began slowly, pulling away the last ribbon from its bow behind me. His eyes were hooded with desire, but I could still see a cruel glitter lurking inside of them. "I like it when you are strong, little moth. But I also like it when you are brave enough to be weak around me. "

"You want to make me cry?" I asked with a mixture of fear and fascination.

"No, little moth. I want you to know that you need to cry—and then I want you to trust me to make you. "

"But what if I don't need to cry?" I asked, while feeling the heat of my pulse—*and my pride*—between my thighs and at my throat.

"Then I would say to you that you're wrong. "

I knew then that whatever happened next between us would be like going through a one-way portal—once we'd entered it, there'd be no going back to the other side.

And I knew that I would suffer anything to be with him—as long as it wasn't his absence again.

"Don't leave me again, Rhaim," I whispered. "And don't make me leave you. Whatever happens, from here on out, we face it together. "

He closed his eyes and sank back with a dissatisfied sound. "I cannot promise that, little moth. "

"You must. Or I will stand up right now and leave through that door. " I glanced back at the entrance to his tent behind me.

"If you leave, it will kill me," he said simply, once I'd turned back around.

"Then it's a good thing I learned how to be cruel from you," I told him, setting my jaw. "I would be bound to you, Rhaim. "

His eyes widened, and I could have sworn I felt something in him sink, as he went entirely calm, like the stillest of still pools. "Little moth, I am more than bound to you already. "

I licked my lips. "Truly?"

"Oh, Lisane. " He made a sigh of my name, pulling me close and running a hand through my hair again to grab and hold it like he liked to, like I loved, and made me look at him. "As true as words could ever be. "

And I believed him. His words were like nails hammered into my soul. "Because you are mine, and I am yours," I whispered, just like in all the books I'd read, and the *Wedding of Sweet Lirane.*

"Because I am yours, and you are mine," Rhaim echoed back, without any hesitation. "Even though I am the opposite of highborn, and there is not a unicorn in sight," he teased, while smiling brightly—like he'd looked when I'd managed to save the worker at the castle, only more so. I brought my hand to his face, wishing I could capture his smile in my palm—and he tried to bite it, with a laugh.

"I don't ever want to pet one again," I told him solemnly.

And the sound that he made then. . . "Then let us see to that.
"

I wriggled to get the top of my dress off, and Rhaim's hands moved to help me as I untucked both my arms. "I would tear this off of you, but you might need to wear it later," he said, until there was a pool of fabric around my waist. He wound the fabric in one hand, using it to hold me close, as his other pressed my back toward him, making me present my breasts for his attention.

I watched him take a nipple in, breathing heavily, and I wondered if his lips could feel the beating of my slightly panicked heart.

I wasn't sure what was coming next.

I only knew that I wanted it very much.

He made a growling sound as he sucked hard, roughing my nipple with his tongue, making sensations shoot through me, as I ran my fingers through his hair to keep him there. Wetness flooded the space between my legs. . . and I *hungered.* I rocked against him without thinking, begging him for more, watching him with a dropped jaw, making quiet, helpless, moans, as a tremendous thunderstorm started outside.

There was a flash through the tent, then a loud clap, and I jumped, as Rhaim pulled off of me to snort. "It's just Sibyi—

the mage who brought you here. Weather is his gift. He means to help hide us, I'm certain. " He let go of me and pushed me back. "Stand up, little moth. " I did as I was told, and Rhaim took the hem of my skirt, lifting it up for me to hold. Thunder clapped again, and he gave me a wolfish grin. "That means you can be loud," he said, as his hands rose up to grab the edges of my underwear and help to pull them down. He saw my naked feet when I stepped out of them. "Why don't you have on shoes, though?"

I gave a soft laugh. "It is a long story. "

He took my hands and pushed them higher as he moved to kneel in front of me. "You can tell it to me some other night, then. " One of his hands cupped the ass he'd once welted, while the other rested against my belly, his thumb pulling up the slight mound between my legs, as his tongue dove in. I put all of my skirt in one hand at once, and pushed the other through his hair again, trying not to sway, as I spread my legs wider for him.

21

RHAIM

Once again I was on my knees, licking my moth's honey from her.

My tongue was pressed between her thighs, and she couldn't give herself over fast enough to me. I rumbled with satisfaction and heard her give a contented sigh, as her fingers curled against my scalp.

And all the rain outside was no match for Lisane. She was so wet for me already, it was hard not to feel like I could rush because every minute we had together was stolen, but if this was the only time we had before our fates caught up with us. . . I wanted to act like we had forever.

I wanted to start off by being gentle with her. . . before I wound up being rough.

Her hand tightened in my hair as the tip of my tongue tucked under her perfect spot and I heard her take an excited inhale. "Rhaim," she whispered as I kept rubbing her there, moving her little clit up and down, back and forth. I moved both of my hands to grab her ass and tilt her hips toward my mouth to give me more access—I wanted to taste more of her, and more deeply. She whined but rode my face readily, even more so as I picked up one of her legs and dropped it over my shoulder. Then she began taking deep, steadying breaths that increased in pace as her hips rocked against me. I could only see flashes of her above me, until her hand that held her skirt tucked it under her arms, pulling the fabric above her stomach taut, and the light that she cast—the light that my wonderful, elegant little moth was still casting, without thought, like any real mage might—showed her full lips parted, the nipples of her pert breasts perked, and her eyes closed in heavy concentration just like when she was trying to use her powers.

Her standing leg started to shake, and had a hard time balancing as her body wound up, so I wrapped her lower back with an arm, keeping her aloft, licking, sucking, and drinking her as she bent over me and began to moan my name.

"Rhaim," she groaned, and a thunderclap rattled the tent around us.

"Let down on me," I growled up and into her, as one of her hands fisted in my hair, and the other clawed my shoulder.

"I want to," she whined. "Please make me," she said, finally opening her eyes and seeing me below her. "Rhaim," she whispered, pulling her hips in heavy draws across my tongue. "Please make me, please make me," she repeated like a prayer, as I sucked on her. Then I saw her eyes widen and felt her ass clench. "Rhaim—oh—*oh!*" she shouted, and then bucked against me like a wild steed. "Sir!" she shouted as she threw her head back and gave a whining sound, as another thunderclap struck. Juices flowed from her faster than I could lick them up, and I felt her cunt pulse like it was trying to grab me, light shudders running through her as quick as the raindrops outside.

Then she took a deep inhale and her skirt that she'd tucked up fluttered down like dropped flowers. I felt her sag, wanting to collapse, as though she'd just done great magic, and perhaps she had, because she'd made me love her even more.

I caught her and carefully lowered her to the ground below me. "Sir," she whispered, looking up from beneath heavy lashes, reaching up a hand to run along my cheek, still breathing roughly.

Half dressed and open-hearted, Lisane was entirely vulnerable to me in a way that I realized I had never been for her.

All of my bravery had been done knowing I had power.

Whereas she had done all hers knowing she might never gain it.

"Will you finally take me?" she asked.

"Yes," I said, and softly nodded.

I rose up and pulled my shirt off, then kicked my boots aside, and unlaced my leather breeches. My cock swung out, as if the piercing at the end were a magnet, and my little moth was true north. Eager fluid was already beading at its tip, and at the thought of shooting myself inside her—I took hold of my sheath and rocked it back, ready, but then paused.

"Come here, Lisane," I told her, reaching for the rest of her dress, and helping to pull it off her. She moved only enough to help me with it, and then lay back down, looking up at me, at first hopefully, and then confused, as I lay down beside her.

"Sir?" she wondered, giving me a curious look, as I reached for her.

"Come ride my cock like you just rode my mouth," I said, pulling her above me.

She laughed, a melodious counterpoint to the wild storm raging outside. "Rhaim—you can't be serious," she said, but I kept pulling, and while it took a bit to get her to straddle me, soon she was up around my waist.

"Utterly so," I said, arching my hips up slightly, while pushing her back by her thighs.

She planted both her hands on my chest to stop me, then scooted one hand over to cover my mage mark, like she couldn't help herself.

And then she pouted.

"It is no different this way than the other."

"But it isn't how I imagined it," she complained.

"I know. I wanted to take you in the moonlight, on a mountain-top," I said with a sly grin. "But reality can be better than imagination, you'll see." I grabbed her and lifted her up, setting her back down across my hips. She kept her thighs tight though, like she was riding a fast horse, and wouldn't touch me. "This way you will get to choose how quickly and how roughly," I explained, rocking up on my elbows. "Until I take away your choice, again."

Her full lips were still pressed thin, but then she lowered herself until my hard cock was nestled against her folds. I made a thoughtful sound at feeling her settle there, and then a deeper one, as she started to rock against my shaft. "See?" I asked her, and perhaps she took me literally, because she did look down. We both watched the head of my cock appear and disappear as she stroked against me, her actions squeezing more of my clear fluids out.

"Is that metal going inside of me?" she asked, and I remembered that I'd taken it out before I'd claimed her ass.

"Did you want it to?"

I saw her make up her mind like she always did, with fierce and extreme stubbornness. "Yes. "

"Then it will," I said and groaned, rocking back as she took another slick drag over me, absolutely coating my cock with her wet heat.

I watched that empower her, as much as any blow. She leaned into her hands on my chest and ground against me with intent.

"Does that feel good?" she asked me.

A smart *I think you know the answer* rose unbidden to my tongue, but then I remembered we were both dealing with firsts here: my moth losing her virginity, and my first time fucking anyone with whom I was in love.

"Yes," I answered truthfully. I only put one hand at her hip, I didn't trust myself with both of them—I planted the other atop her breast to pull her nipple. "But being in you will feel better," I confessed.

"Better than this?" she asked, rocking against me again, with a wild delight in her eyes at her power over me, and I chuckled.

"I should have fucked you the other way—don't torture me, Lisane. " All my blood was in my cock now, I was sure of it; I was so hard, and equally certain my balls had never been so heavy.

"Me? Torture you?" she protested, as though she didn't know the meaning of the word.

I stilled her hips with both my hands, gathering her attention. "As I have been tortured every day in recent memory, without you near. "

My little moth gave a soft gasp. "Rhaim, it's just—I don't—"

I took one of her hands in my own and put it between my legs to hold me. "You will figure it out. "

And I got to watch determination flood over her again— which somehow made me harder. Her smaller hand moved mine away and went to circle my shaft, as she awkwardly bent forward to line me up, letting my tip feel her soft folds just begin to part.

All I wanted to do at that moment was grab her hips and shove myself in to feel her sucking heat inside. Then she made a thoughtful sound, and all of my attention was on her again.

"You're very big," she said, looking down at where we were only beginning to meet and sounding uncertain.

"I am," I agreed, but then caught her chin so I could see her eyes. "But little moth—you will make room for me."

Her gaze stayed locked on mine as she slowly lowered herself down.

22

LISANE

This was what I'd wanted, almost all this time, this stretching and pulling, the strange sensation of someone else's ingress—and the knowledge that after it, I couldn't return to how I was.

The lower I got, the tighter Rhaim's hands held me, now both on my thighs, and his expression turned more serious.

Did he know just how special this was for me?

And was it anywhere near as special for him?

I let my hips drop a little bit more, and felt a sharp sting, like his piercing was piercing *me* inside. "Rhaim—" I hissed, in surprise, but he only nodded.

"It is because I am your first," he said, letting go of a thigh to trace his hand up my body. "It will not hurt for long."

"How do you know?" I asked him, then feeling foolish as I realized the answer. "You have been others' first, as well. "

His eyebrows rose along with the corners of his lips. "I've been alive for eight hundred years, Lisane. Would you have wished me celibate all that time?" He sounded amused when he said it, which made everything even worse for me, but then both his hands found mine and squeezed. "Little moth," he said in a deliberate tone. "I am in love with you. I have never pledged myself to another, so in that, you are my only. " He carefully smoothed my hands against his chest again. "And I would spend the next eight hundred years with you if I could have them. "

I tilted my head and squinted down at him. "And what if after five hundred years I were to get tired of you?"

A wicked smile crept across his face. "I can promise you, you wouldn't," he said, and he sent his hand down my belly, to rub his thumb where his tongue had just been. "I swear will never get tired of watching you come, Lisane, and I will never get tired of fucking you. So let me spear you, and have us both be done with your virgin blood, so then we can begin all that is on the other side. " He reached up to run the knuckles of his other hand against my cheek. "I want all the rest of my firsts with you. "

I felt him mean it as he said it, and not just because he was inside of me. I turned my head and nuzzled into his hand like a cat. "Yes. "

"Hmm. Yes, what, little moth?" he coolly asked. His tone was superior, but the look he was giving me then was like I was something divine.

I curled my hands against his stomach in determined fists. "Yes, sir," I corrected myself, and slammed my hips down on top of him.

I cried out—I would have even if there hadn't been virgin things up inside me—he was so big and he reached up and swept me down, pressing me to his chest, kissing the top of my head in a crown.

"My brave moth," he said quietly as I made a sad noise above him, and thunder clapped again outside. I hurt; it felt like I was going to split in two, he was taking up so much space. Whatever had I been thinking?

"And surviving all this time," he went on, brushing my hair away from my face. "So cunning. "

"You're trying to distract me. It won't work," I said.

"No, it won't. You're much too smart for that. " I pouted up at him, and saw him giving me a rather tender look down. "Do you still hate me?" he asked.

"No," I said, pushing myself a little up. "It's just that your piercing is in my liver. "

He laughed at that. "Your mind always amuses me. And I like it when your tongue is sharp. " Then he sobered. "Am I truly hurting you?"

I shifted experimentally. "No. . . it's. . . just. . . " I said, feeling him in the space he took up. I held my breath and rocked, sliding up and down him incrementally. The friction where I was wrapped around his base was good—as was the place deep inside he hit.

"Yes," he said slowly, before echoing me. "It. . . is. . . just," he said, moving with me, his pupils getting wider by the moment. "Keep going, little moth. "

I dug my knees into the ground and rode up and down him, and I'd bled enough even I could smell it in the air—but beyond that. . .

"Yes," he encouraged me, in an even darker tone. One of his hands sank to grab my ass and guide me, and the other wound into my hair and pulled my head back. "I can't wait until I can fuck you like I own you, little moth. "

"And when will that be?" I asked, as he shifted beneath me to begin thrusting, when I was trapped, held helpless by my hair.

"Your body will tell me. " I bobbed back and forth on him, pulled by my hair and pushed by his cock, as he let out a groan. "If I had known you'd feel this good, I never would've waited. "

"I tried to tell you," I said, doing my best to sound surly, even as I was spreading my knees wide, and lowering my hips to take him.

"You did," he agreed, letting go of my hair at last.

I sat up then, freed, and felt him ram home inside of me. "Rhaim," I grunted, riding his hips forward. "Oh—" I protested, trying to handle every inch of his cock. I both hated it and needed it, much like the man below me. "Rhaim, stay there—*Rhaim*—" I begged of him, as I started to grind.

The stretching went from good to pleasurable and where the head of him and his piercing rubbed inside me—"Rhaim," I hissed.

"Little moth," he agreed. His jaw was dropped, and his hands roamed my body, his fingers pulling at my nipples and rubbing at my clit as he held his hips high enough to pin me.

I ground against him, shifting myself by clenching my ass and putting my hands on his stomach to help me ride him.

"I'm so fucking deep in you now, Lisane," he told me. "And if there was more of me," he said, rocking me with a thrust, "you'd be begging to take it. "

"I strongly doubt that," I protested through semi-clenched teeth. "If there was more of you, I'd die. But as for what is in me. . . " Everything he was doing felt good. I'd gone from a lifetime of being empty to being filled to bursting. And surely there was nothing left in me that was virgin anymore. I gasped and moaned as I felt things tighten, and suddenly, I felt ravenous—like my whole body needed more. "*Rhaim*," I whispered in a high pitch, asking him to help me.

He growled and grabbed my hips then started pounding. To my ears our slaps sounded louder than the thunderclaps outside, and we were more wet than any rain, my juices sluicing where we met. "Rhaim," I whined for him, my body curving for a second time, as he grunted and shoved. "Rhaim —Rhaim—Rhaim—" I called out for him, in time with his thrusts. I gave myself over, falling on top of him, letting him use me for his pleasure because it pleased me. His hips thudded into mine relentlessly as I was spread wide and it was everything I wanted, until one of his hands swept up to catch in my hair again, making me look up at him, and see his lips curved in cruel concentration.

"I no longer care if you catch on fire anymore, Lisane," he growled at me, and for a second I wanted to give my life up; nothing had a purpose anymore, until he finished, half a snarl. "So long as you take me with you."

I clenched my hands into fists, bit my teeth into his chest, and screamed.

My moth was coming. I was sure half the continent could hear it, and I didn't care. Her hips spasmed against me, and inside her, her cunt wrapped and pulled, her sex demanding mine. I rolled on top of her without thinking, like an alligator taking down its prey, and my beast, which had been denied for so long, rose up in me, with her trapped below us.

If I let him control me now, when she was about to trapped to me—

I should have kept the collar on.

"Close your eyes, Lisane," I said, in an unforgiving tone.

She gave me a wide-eyed look, her cheeks flushed, her wrung out body shaking with each of my ruts into her, but then she did as she was told, closing them tightly at my behest.

"No matter what," I commanded.

"No matter what," she repeated, nervously biting her lips.

It wasn't safe to knot her, I knew that—but I also knew I might not get another chance.

I wanted to have that with her.

She was mine now.

Maybe my beast would know that?

The same beast that'd bitten her to blood.

But soon my body was going to take all choice away from me, because each time I plowed into her soft tight heat, I *needed* to come.

Just like I knew she'd needed me, I needed her, to take it all, to take every drop I had to give. My cum, my soul, my life, everything was one.

"No matter what," I warned her again. It made her tense; she grabbed me even tighter, and that was it for me.

I tried to pull out of her, but then my beast was there, riding me the same I was riding her, changing my body, changing my bones—

My knot flared, and the bastard tried to shove it in.

"Rhaim!" she cried out, her eyes still closed as he tried to make her fit him. I would have tried to tell her something comforting, or to run, but it was too late. He plunged forward another time, and somehow she managed to take it, the place we met opening just wide enough to let my knot push through, then seal tight behind it.

I howled then, as a beast or as a man, I didn't know, I wasn't sure what I was anymore, except that I was coming, shooting myself into her, and it felt endless. I couldn't pull out and I couldn't push in—because I was where I *belonged.*

My balls lifted and pulsed, again and again, my hips still shaking hers, the both of us locked, and I could feel the haze of my beast's presence, trying to claw his way out from deep inside, to take over me entirely.

"Feel it," *he* growled at her, with *our* throat. "You are mine. "

This was what *he* wanted—*her* trapped on him—so that no matter what *he* did next, *she* couldn't get away, and his teeth were at her throat, where her blood pulsed so sweetly.

I had to control him; I couldn't let him hurt her, even if we were still thrusting mindlessly, giving her the dregs of our cum.

Then my little moth panted, her eyes still screwed shut. Her legs wound around me tightly, squeezed once, twice, and then she called my name. "Rhaim!" she cried out, squirming below me in a way that made me want to bite her to make it stop, but then her cunt grasped at my knot like a hand, and I stilled. "Rhaim," she cried again, her hands curled up into fists against her face, as if to help her not to see me, as she fell into shudders, crying out, and I growled without thinking as her cunt gave another squeeze. Each of her waves began where she held me and traveled through us both, setting our bristly hair on end like electricity, as the cum that we'd spent in her overflowed, pushed out by her orgasm, spilling out to trickle down our sack and her ass.

And it was her coming while we were locked to her—that sensation of not just claiming her, but being claimed—that somehow forced my monster down.

"Rhaim?" she wondered, with her eyes still closed, slowly lowering her fists.

"Do not look," I told her. "But I am here. "

She nodded as she made a small helpless noise and breathed roughly. . . and then she tentatively reached up to touch me.

It'd never occurred to me that when we were locked, I would also be trapped by her.

There was no place for me to run to, or hide, and she had to know just what was above her, but I still twisted my muzzle away as her fingers found my cheek. "Rhaim," she whispered, tracing a finger down the short stiff fur she found there, before stroking down to touch the edge of my lip and begin to trace the teeth that had once cruelly bit her. Then she raised her other hand up to place it on my shoulder. She stopped when she touched my bristles, then slowly lowered till she was able to stroke through the softer fur beneath.

The Beast and Lisane by Calico Moss

"I know what you are, Rhaim. Can't I open my eyes?"

I ground my fangs together. I could feel my beast receding, but *he* wasn't gone, and what if seeing me over her made her gaze at me with the look that I'd seen when I Ascended? I knew there was no denying my time, and yet I hoarsely whispered, "No. "

She nodded again, patiently, and brought her hands through the thicker fur around my neck, as the things that were beastly in me finally relented, leaving me holding myself above her just as a man again.

"My little moth," I whispered, with my own throat, and I watched her copper eyes flutter open.

"And you love me?" she asked, her fingertips now twined in the hair behind my neck.

"Yes. " I had never meant just one word more. "You are my everything. "

Lisane bit her full lower lip and rocked it out in slow thought. "Does your beast agree?"

I lowered myself down to my elbows above her and felt her hips rise up to accommodate our lock. "My beast would tear the moon out of the sky to get to you," I said, placing a chaste kiss atop her breast. "But as for what he would do to you after that. . . " I closed my eyes and braced myself to ask, "Did he hurt you?" because I needed to know—because if *he* did *I* needed to take the blame.

She was silent then, her eyes taking me in, one feature at a time. She went to trace the scar she'd given me on my face—and I realized it was the same path she'd pulled through my fur earlier. "Not any more than I've hurt you, I don't think," she said, watching her finger, before looking me in my eyes again. "Is it bad that I'm not sorry about hurting you?"

"Not in the least," I promised.

"And that I thought of me having hurt you as a point of pride?" she went on, her eyes still on mine.

"Considering how many times I have hurt you, no. " I shook my head. "But you should know, Lisane, I carry many more scars than that from you, on me. In my mind, across my heart, and upon my soul. " I glanced down at myself, where the mark of her orgasmic bite was fading. "And apparently on my chest. "

She snorted, her lips curving into a grin. "Everything was so intense. I started seeing stars. I didn't want to slip away. "

"Slip away to where?" I asked her lightly.

"To wherever it is that people go when they are very happy. " A flush rose up her cheeks. "I just needed to hold on," she said, and then added a quick, "Sir. "

"Ah, a sir, at long last," I purred with a laugh. "When it is expedient for you. "

My little moth gave me a delighted smile. "I'm sorry, sir," she said, with an innocence my cock knew she no longer possessed.

If I didn't know that she, too, was a mage, I might have taken pity on her body, and let her rest, regaining strength—but as it was, and because we might only have one night...

I took both of her wrists into one hand and planted them above her head. "Perhaps not as sorry as you should be," I said, in a demanding tone. I watched her pupils widen, her nostrils flare, and felt her already wide hips open fractionally more to seat me. "Would you like me to give you magic, little moth?" I asked, tugging my still engorged knot against the entrance of her pussy.

I wanted her to know that if we started this, she would not be able to get away.

She swallowed, her heart already racing in expectation, I could see her pulse bounding at her throat. "Yes," she whispered.

I let her assent roll over me, almost as delicious as what I knew what was coming next, and fell to the curve above her breast, and bit her, fairly hard.

24

LISANE

I cried out again, in surprise, and then fought him, trying to get free, not because I wanted to be, but because I wanted to know how badly he would deny my release.

I wanted him to prove to me that he was never going to let me go again.

Rhaim growled and shook me, biting me anew, this time on my opposite breast, and sucked hard, leaving a red and purple mark behind—and I felt my magic, my soaring power, thudding home in to me, the same as he was, his hips landing against mine.

"My beautiful bruised little moth," he growled savagely, "and her tight fucking pussy."

The knot that he'd shoved into me did bad things deep inside. Kept me stretched around him, and it seemingly kept him hard.

"Are you going—" I started to ask him, then yelped as he bit my shoulder. I heard him snarl in my ear as he looped his free arm beneath one of my knees and hauled me up.

"To fuck you again?" he harshly whispered, finishing my question. "Yes, Lisane," he said, showing me with his body. "Now and forever. I will never tire of coming in your sweet cunt. "

My head rolled back as he leaned up and bit the underside of one of my arms, the soft white meat of it, as he began to fuck me wildly, his knot pulling against my entrance like he was fit to pull it out. He couldn't move far, but he didn't need to, because the more I felt trapped, the more I felt claimed.

"You taste so good, Lisane," he said, and bit me again, on the flat of my ribs beneath a breast. "It is no wonder my beast wants to eat you. "

I bucked the back of my knee against the arm that held it, trying to get away only to drive him to greater heights. He snarled, holding me down with more of his weight. "You will take what I will give you," he commanded.

"Yes, sir," was the only thing I could whisper in response, as he kept my hips held high, utterly pinning me. And if I'd thought he was deep before, I was wrong; this was it—he was hitting something deep inside me, and between that and his teeth—I felt magical inside and out, as though the stars were close at hand again, and surely he felt them too. "Please. Sir," I panted. "More."

But then he let go of my wrists and rose up, rocking back on his knees, pulling my hips up with him as he panted. "I wouldn't visit my beast on you again," he said, by way of explanation. I danced my toes out quickly, and arched my back up for support, until he grabbed my waist and helped to hold me there, my ass atop his knees. "And I wanted to see where we met," he said, his chest heaving as his jaw dropped, him looking down.

Whereas from this position, looking up, I felt like I couldn't see anything *but* him.

This was where I wanted him.

Always.

Above me, and also deep inside.

"Do you like it?" I asked him, not meaning just what he saw, but everything else—me, him, our bond—what we were to one another now.

He spit down at my cunt and I shivered in surprise. "It is perfection," he said, bringing his thumb in to rub where his spit hand just landed, then his gaze slowly scanned all over my body. "You are perfection. Come one more time for me, little moth. Take all the magic I've put inside you, and make me proud. "

"Sir," I whispered, finally looking at myself. I was covered in red welts from his teeth and purpling bruises from his kisses and I had maybe never felt so beautiful. I was mad that everything was healing, much too soon—

Because if I couldn't have a mage's mark, I wanted his.

I wanted something to prove that this had happened between us, for forever.

For however long that was.

I took a very deep inhale, as reality rushed back.

"Are you all right, little moth?" Rhaim asked stilling his hand.

I was going to lie, and then remembered I wasn't supposed to. "No," I said, and put my hands to my mouth in horror. "Rhaim," I gasped, shaking my head. "My father—they're going to kill you—and hide me in a cave. " He carefully picked me up and held me to his chest as I straddled his lap with him still speared inside. I clung to him, burying my face against his neck. "I love you—I can't lose you. " I wasn't sobbing yet, but I would be. "It's not fair—"

He nuzzled his cheek into my hair as the dam broke, and my tears slicked his chest. "Little moth, shh," he said gently, soothing me with his thumbs against my back, as he carefully held me through the worst of it.

"It's not fair," I repeated. Thunder clapped one more time outside and then the sounds of the storm began to lessen. "It's not," I protested, like a child.

Rhaim moved to blot my cheeks with the fingers of one hand. "And you thought you didn't need to cry," he whispered.

"How can you be so calm?" I demanded. It made me want to bite him again—this time in irritation. *And then I realized why.* "You already know. "

"Know... what?" he asked.

"How—how you die!" I hissed, squirming against him, wishing I could get free. "Filigro told me!"

Rhaim frowned darkly. "When he was supposed to be telling you not to use magic—advice that you were clearly about to ignore at your unveiling?"

I thumped my fists against his chest. "Yes, and I'm glad! Because why didn't you?"

"I didn't want to scare you," he said.

"You think that's more frightening than your beast, to me?" I hoped I looked as wounded as I felt. "Tell me how you die, Rhaim. "

The All-Beast shook his head. "Mages don't tell other mages their deaths, moth. "

"Why not?" I sputtered. "I love you! So I deserve to know. "

"No. "

"Don't stand on tradition now—"

"I'm not, Lisane," he said, with utter certainty. "I just want this one soft moment with you. "

"And then you'll tell me afterward?" I hoped.

"No. " I slouched and made an irritated sound, still trapped on him by his knot, which was entirely unfair because I wanted to go walk out the tent's door. "Not because I don't love you, or because I don't think you love me," he went on. "But because how I die is my business, little moth. Not yours. "

I inhaled to ask more questions, then swallowed them, because I knew he wouldn't answer. *Would he die by my father's hand? My brother's? Or by other mages that I didn't even know?*

And maybe Rhaim knowing how he died explained both why he'd first hated me, but also why he'd accepted me in the first place.

He'd always known his fate was braided to mine, even if he wouldn't tell me how.

"Just know that every moment I have had you in my life has been better than the last, little moth," he said quietly, imploring me to trust him with his eyes.

"That makes it sound like you know you're going away soon," I said, looping my arms around his neck again.

"I will have to, eventually. But never again by choice, Lisane. From here on out, whatever happens, happens. "

"And until then?" I asked him.

"We are bound," he said, running his cheek against my temple. "Don't you still feel me in you?" he asked, and then waited for me to nod. "It will ever be thus. Even when I am not, someday. But until then, little moth, grant me the pleasure of your choosing me. "

"What do you mean?" I asked, looking up.

He set his forehead close to mine. "I don't know how long we have—and it may be a very short time indeed," he began, and I bit my lips to stop from crying again. "But for as long as we can be together, look to me as I look to you. Because while our love has weight, it is neither a collar nor a bit. It is a thing we choose to have, to hold, to carry. "

And now, I was about to begin crying for very different reasons, watching Rhaim's face as he continued.

"Just because I have not loved anyone else before doesn't mean I have not tried to study it. To wonder what it is—*why it is*—how it makes people do the things they do. I have seen people fall into love, and out of love, and I was forced to think that it was some temporary state of madness, of people being ridden by their emotions the same way my beast rides me. But now?" he said, his voice lifting. I rose up in his arms as much as I could, ready to kiss him in an instant. "Now I know this is how I was meant to be. I am changed. The old All-Beast is no more, and the new one is yours, completely. And so I welcome fate, whatever comes, Lisane, because it was fate that brought me you. "

His lips came for mine and kissed me gently, right before I threw myself against him, lunging up as far as I could to claim *his* mouth and make him and all his sweet words mine. He laughed, held me tighter, and kissed me harder until he groaned.

"Did I hurt you?" I asked, pulling back quickly. It seemed impossible and yet my own lips were swelling from his kisses just as fast as they could heal.

"No," he breathed, then scoffed. "Well—yes—in that right now my balls ache."

"Why might that be?" I asked him, even though I thought I knew. I tucked a hand behind myself to stroke my fingers on his sack, and heard him huff a sigh, as he closed his eyes—and when I stopped, he made a noise of complaint.

It was my turn to laugh. "Torturing really is fun, Rhaim. I can see now why you like to do it."

"Difficult moth," he muttered, then licked his lips and started to use his hands to move me.

Still locked to one another in the position we were in, all he could do was rock me, and yet—I squeezed my thighs together to help me ride him, and he adjusted, tilting himself even higher up. I held onto his shoulder with one hand, and kept the other stroking him below, until he commanded, "Touch yourself," and so I did, moaning softly and bowing my forehead against his chest.

"Lisane," he groaned, pumping me against him with intent. I brought both hands up to his shoulders, now trusting in his friction to do the rest. "Please, come for me moth," he said, making me glance up at him. His eyes searched my face, as his lips twisted into a devious grin. "I might die if I don't come inside you."

"You're not funny," I complained, then hissed with need. "Rhaim—"

"Yes, little moth," he agreed in a dark tone. "*Yes.* "

I clasped him between my thighs and ground myself against him. "I'm so close," I whispered, growing frantic.

"I know. I can feel you. " He sounded awed. "Wrapping me. Grabbing me. Pulling me in. " He made a grunt with each abbreviated thrust. "You're going to come so hard, Lisane— you'd push me out if I didn't have my knot in you. "

But he did, and—*and*—**and**—he made a guttural sound as the stars flowed through me. I cried out his name, feeling every inch of his length and girth as everything inside me clenched and I rode up and down on his lap. "Rhaim!"

"Yes," he growled, and it rumbled through his body, as all of me pulsed again. "My little moth," he said, with a grunting shove. "My princess," he groaned, bowing his head as I still writhed against him, gasping from another wave. "My chosen mate," he breathed. "Look down. "

I did as I was told, and saw a dusky red sliver of his hard shaft pumping forward as his hips did, knowing it was filling me. I moaned softly at the sight.

"I can't believe I have you. I can't believe I'm in you. I can't believe you want me," I heard him say above me, in time with his slowing thrusts.

"Rhaim," I said again, and looked up, straining against his knot to throw my arms around his neck to kiss him more. His mouth caught mine and his hands helped keep me there as I felt the hot liquid he'd just shot in me spill out between my thighs. "I love you," I told him when I could speak next, brushing his hair away from his eyes. "And I will always love you. You will always have me. "

"Truly," he agreed, taking us both carefully to his pallet.

25
RHAIM

I wanted to stay hard in Lisane forever, just like this.

But she wasn't wrong—my most likely death was at her father or her brother's hand, with her terrified at my side. And even though I knew my fate was inevitable, I would do anything I could to postpone it—just like a thousand-thousand mages before me, I was sure.

Even so, I kissed her contentedly until my knot faded. Whatever happened to her after I had passed, I always wanted her to know my love for her. Once I could slide out of her though, I knew it was time. I got dressed, then went and got a rain-damp cloth to wipe her blood and my cum away.

"I'm sorry it's cold," I apologized as she watched me be tender toward her with glittering eyes.

"Can't we just go back to your castle, Rhaim?" she asked, opening her legs for me without shame. "No one else will want me now. "

"Because they are fools," I told her. "But that doesn't mean we are free. "

I couldn't have anticipated this turn of events, but now that she was in my arms again— there were plenty of desolate places in the world that only I knew. We could go from one to the next, I could protect her with my magic— *or she, me, with hers!*—and we would have as long as fate allowed us.

I saw her thinking then, her gaze tracing over me, before looking past me, to the front of my tent, outdoors. "Is that what I think it is, in the cage?" she asked.

"Yes. A Deathless. "

"And you caught it? And. . . it didn't kill you? Or die itself?"

"No one is more amazed by that than I. " I caught my hair back and pulled all the loose strands into a tie behind me, so that I might think more clearly, as she wriggled back into the dress I should have torn off of her on principle alone.

She shrugged her sleeves back on, then looked at me. "Are you close?" she asked with hope.

"To defeating them? No. " I closed my eyes and shook my head with resignation. "I don't think anyone will ever be. Not in a permanent sense. "

"Do you want to hear how I managed them in camp?" she asked, twisting to present her back to me, with all the laces I'd undone. And as much as I wanted to just take her into my arms to portal, I supposed I ought to let her dress first.

"Tell me," I said, running the first of the untied ribbons through its embroidered hole.

I listened to Lisane tell me a fantastical story as I worked the laces up her dress. My little moth had burned the tent they'd trapped her in, and then gone to where they'd had her unveiling, and pried unicorn horns free from her throne to fly at them with her mind. "Unbelievable," I said when she was through.

"Not really," she said, twisting back over her shoulder to give me a tight smile. "I hate those things. "

"You have more reason than most. " I gave her final set of laces a tug, bowed them off, then stood to offer her a hand. Lisane took it, and let me pull her up. If we were to escape, the first thing my moth needed was shoes. . . and I was just about to ask her where in the world she wanted to go, when she looked up at me.

"You can't even imagine what it was like, Rhaim. "

"I have fought them before," escaped my lips, then I realized I'd been a fool when I saw the sorrow in her eyes. "In your chambers, you mean. "

"Yes," she said, very slowly.

"You may tell me," I said, wrapping my arms around her, "but let us wait until after we portal. "

"So we're running?"

"I don't know how else to keep you—but that is all I want in life. "

"Where will we go?" she asked, looking up.

"Far away from here. " I knew of a hunting cabin in the Ashen Mountains—it was empty when I left it because I had killed all the hunters myself. I should have just taken her straight there, and not bothered with this tent. "Will you come with me?" I asked her.

"Of course," she said quietly, squeezing me.

"Good," I said, and swept her up into the cradle of my arms. "Let's go. "

I t was already daylight on the trail near the cabin. The forest we were in was beautiful—but not as beautiful as Lisane, and the way she smiled with total abandon the second the sunlight struck her face.

"Is there a bath wherever it is that we're going?" she asked, turning toward me as she beamed.

"There's water nearby. We can heat it with a fire. " I moved to hold her closer to me. "Finish your story, little moth. " I wanted to dispel any clouds from her memory—and to start making new ones with her as soon as possible.

She tucked herself against me and nodded against my leathers. "All right. You have to try to imagine it though, Rhaim. You can't just listen, okay?"

"I will try," I promised.

She made an agreeable sound and continued. "So—pretend that you never got to go outside, and see all this. That all you know are your chamber's walls. And that there was this one day a year that was special to you—because that's when you always got the best presents. "

I frowned a little, listening to her, angry at her father anew for keeping her hidden—then it occurred to me I did not know when her birthday was.

"And your brother just got to go up into the castle," she went on, "and he's left you mostly alone, so all you have left is your mother and your books, but you know on Darkest Day, everyone will have to visit. So you stay up all night, thinking about it, looking forward to seeing everyone, and just when you're about to fall asleep. . . that's when you hear screams. "

"Darkest Day?" I repeated her, stopping. We were at the edge of the clearing with the cabin in it—it was small, but well-made, and the forest hadn't reclaimed it yet.

Lisane nodded strongly and gave me a strange look. "Yes. "

"No. "

"What do you mean, no?" she asked, pushing away from me. I set her down—we would be on grass all the way now to the cabin's front stair.

I shook my head lightly. "The Deathless didn't attack Drelleth until—" I thought back to all the records I'd learned, and ticked attacks off in my mind—"three weeks after that. Your father's castle was the fourth incursion," I said, and watched her eyes widen. "Not that it wasn't devastating, I'm sure," I said, then instantly wishing I could take my words back, as she gave me a look of sheer disbelief.

"Do you think I don't remember when my own mother died?" she asked, her voice arching as her expression went dark. "Are you calling me a liar?"

"No," I breathed. A dreadful realization was sinking through me, and I dragged my eyes away from her to the cabin beyond, to see if I could keep it to myself.

The cabin was everything I ever wanted. Endless hours with her, in front of a warm fire, on a soft bed.

And I could have had it, too. . . if she hadn't been looking at me like that. "Lisane, who all died at your castle?"

She licked her lips and swallowed, still looking hurt. "My mother, obviously. And two of my favorite maids. " Then she squinted at me in anger. "Why do you ask?"

"Did you ever see their bodies?"

She put a hand to her mouth immediately. "What kind of question is that?"

"One born of cruel necessity," I said, gently catching her wrist, so I could hold her hand in mine. "Answer me, moth. Please. "

I watched old pain blossom on her face and hated it. "Only my mother's. I—I saw the Deathless down her. Right before she closed the door. " She was lost in her own memories for a moment, and then she started trying to read my face. "Why do you ask?" she pressed again.

If she was right—and there was no reason she shouldn't be —then the first Deathless attack had been in Drelleth's women's chambers. And her father, and others perhaps, had gone on to cover it up.

All of the records I'd ever seen had claimed that Pelakia was the location of the first eruption—an island made from an old volcano—and men and mages had trod its rocks to sand, looking for any clues as to why. I'd even made Sibyi take me there, during the Deathless doldrums, to see if there was something I could find myself.

But if Drelleth was the first, and Drelleth seemed to have gained the most by hiding it. . .

"Rhaim?" she pressed again. "What are you thinking?"

I ran my other hand against her jaw to steady her before speaking. "That your mother was the Deathless' first casualty. "

Her eyes widened, her lips parted, and she began to pant. "No. " But then she refuted herself before I could. "One of my maids ran to get the guards. I never saw her again. My other maid who died was sleeping. " Her gaze traveled up into the trees behind me, as she talked to herself, wracked with memories. "I never stopped to wonder how they died. The one who got the guards—she should've been safely in the hall—how would the Deathless have killed her?"

I nodded on her behalf. I had no doubt that maid was dead, though. Murdered to keep her silence, because, as a maid, she could leave the chambers and talk.

Unlike my poor Lisane—who had witnessed horrors, but who didn't count, as no one would ever take her seriously. Even if my moth had been given to a pleasant Ker—should one such exist—he likely would have never given her story a second thought, as insulated as he was from thoughts of the Deathless at all times, by his throne-sworn.

And very much unlike me, the one mage who had promised to put an end to them entirely.

"And no one else knows?" I asked her.

"Helkin. And Castillion," she said with a nod. "I heard their shouts of surprise on the far side of the door. And my father, of course. "

"Of course," I repeated mildly.

She squeezed the hand I held. "Does this change things, Rhaim?"

Do you want it to? I longed to ask her, praying that she would answer she did not, as she continued. "Does this mean you can figure out how to stop them?"

I watched hope unfurl in her eyes like a flower with copper petals and knew it would be the end for me—because I could deny her nothing.

"No, little moth. There are no guarantees. " Not where the Deathless were concerned. But hiding in a cabin was no guarantee either. I took a deep inhale. "But it might help if others knew, too," I answered her honestly, with resignation. "I should at least tell Sibyi. " Seeing as I'd gone and left him with the damned thing.

"Which. . . means going back," she said, finally looking around. She spun slowly, taking in the grass beneath her feet, the dense trees, the shaded cabin, and then gave me a sad smile when she was finished. "It's beautiful here, Rhaim. "

"Not as beautiful as you," I said quietly, and opened us up a portal back to the darkness of my tent. We stepped through it together, and then I let it go, watching any hope of a different fate for us close behind her.

26

LISANE

It was still dark when we returned to Rhaim's camp.

He briefly left me in his tent, then returned with boots, and Sibyi, the weather-mage, that I hadn't been properly introduced to.

"Don't even look at her," Rhaim told him, while I knelt to move mounds of fabric away and pull my new boots on.

"You do realize when you say that, it just makes it harder not to?" Sibyi complained.

"Do all mages have hungry eyes?" I asked, bouncing up—the boots Rhaim had found for me were too big, but they were better than nothing.

"Yes," Rhaim said firmly, moving to block Sibyi's view of me.

"No," Sibyi disagreed, stepping aside. "I've just never met a woman who could do strong magic before. It has nothing to do with the rest of it," he said, waving a dismissive hand at me, while Rhaim began to growl.

I grinned at him, in spite of myself. "That is how I felt when I saw your storm-form!"

"Yes!" Sibyi said, smiling back. "Half the fun of meeting other mages is finding out what they can do—"

"My moth is not a toy—"

"I also want to meet the girl with magic," said a deep voice, as the front of Rhaim's tent parted.

"You're. . . a tree," I said slowly, my jaw dropping.

"See?" Sibyi said, swinging his hand between me and the new mage. "It's hard not to look!"

"Not all the way, yet," the tree-mage answered me. "Though I feel our curses run a similar route," he said, giving Rhaim a nod.

Rhaim put his fingers to his temple. "Magic mocks us all," he muttered, and then more loudly said, "Fine. This is Lisane. Lisane, this is Sibyi and Wyrval. "

"Do you have a moniker yet?" Sibyi asked.

"She does not," Rhaim answered for me. "And she doesn't need one," he said, giving me a strong look. "Because no one else needs to know how her magic works. " I caught his hint with ease.

Sibyi squinted at me, unwilling to let it go. "I heard about the unicorn horns—and the fire. So the real question is—did you cause the fire, or did you pick it up, and float it toward your tent, like the unicorn horns? Can you start fires, or are you merely telekinetic?"

"Tele. . . what?" I asked, and looked to Rhaim.

He moved to stand in front of me. "We didn't come back here for this. "

"I'm surprised you returned at all, honestly," the tree-man intoned—and I remembered mages could oftentimes feel other mages' portals.

"Why did you come back then?" Sibyi asked, looking between us.

I waited for Rhaim to discuss the discovery of my father's lies. It would be easier hearing it from his tongue, than it would be for me to confess it all again.

"We're here because we need to take our captive Deathless to the war camp," Rhaim said—surprising even me.

"What?" I asked him.

"There's a connection between your father and the creatures, moth. I don't know what it is yet, but I know I need to get a Deathless close enough to him to find out. " He looked to the others. "I will tell you more later—for right now, we need to put wheels on the cage, and I will summon beasts to pull it. "

Wyrval made a contemplative noise that sounded like wood creaking. "That journey will take several days. "

"Three, with no sleep," Sibyi said.

"I can create trees of the appropriate size for wheels—and vines for ropes—" the tree-mage went on, already planning.

"And you'll have to take me back. " I said it aloud just as I thought the words. Rhaim's attention snapped to me.

"No," he growled, heavily enough that it made the other two mages step away.

"My father hates you, Rhaim—I can't imagine his opinion of you would be improved in any way by this, your first legitimate kidnapping," I said, trying to make light of things, even though they hurt me. "My presence would be a distraction, and if I go in with you, everything you do or say will be suspect, or they'll use you taking me as a pretense to fight you, and any good that might come of this would be lost. "

"We already know they want the yllibrium, All-Beast" Wyrval said. "There's not much to stop them from trying to take it again—we shouldn't give them cause. "

Rhaim ignored the other mage. "I am. . . pledged to you," he said with great difficulty, as I realized his beast was rising just beneath his skin. "You. . . told me we would not part again. "

"I know I did," I said, putting my hands out to calm him. "And this makes my heart hurt too. " I looked out between the tent flaps, where dawn was coming. "But if I don't go back now none of your plan will work—and if you can truly solve the Deathless, Rhaim, then maybe we will be free of all this mess. "

Rhaim was breathing heavy, his body beginning to strain the confines of the leathers he wore. "Get the collar," he commanded all three of us—and Sibyi took him up on it fastest, running across the tent to pick the dull black metal hoop up off the floor.

The weather-mage started cursing the moment he picked it up, tossing it from hand to hand like it was heated, before offering it out to Rhaim by his fingertips. Rhaim snatched it up and opened it, slamming it around his neck with a silent scream, before stumbling to his knees.

Watching him fall made my world stop. I dropped to my knees beside him, grabbing his shoulders as he panted, bowing his head away from me so I wouldn't see him in agony. "My beast would not let you leave again," he explained once he could breathe, both his hands holding onto the collar, one thumb hastily spinning its lock.

"And your man?" I asked quietly.

"He has more sense than that, but not by much. " Rhaim lifted his head to look at me. "No matter what happens when we're parted, little moth, no matter what difficulties either of us face—know this is not the end. "

"This is not the end," I repeated back to him, in a promise.

He lunged and grabbed my face, pulling my lips to his, kissing me longingly and deep, until I forgot everything about where we were and what was coming up. And then when he pulled back, leaving me breathless, he whispered "This is not the end" one more time, before helping me to stand up, and passing me off to Sibyi, who'd already opened a portal back to the darkness of my prison tent.

"Three days, little moth," Rhaim said hoarsely, wiping his mouth with the back of one hand, and the fire in his eyes. . . even with his collar on, I wasn't sure it was entirely human. "Wait for me—and when I see you next, we will never be asunder. "

"Never," I agreed, and nodded and kept nodding, until the weather-mage pulled me through.

27
RHAIM

"You could have summoned oxen first, is all I'm saying," Sibyi complained, walking beside me in the mud his rain had made the prior night. Wyrval was right, ropes and wheels were easy, but hauling a solid metal cage through several inches of mud by hand was not.

"I was distracted at the time," I said, leaning into the ropes just as much as he was. "You might have noticed. "

"Aye," the other mage said, shooting me a look. "Distracting is definitely one word for her. "

I gave him a growl so low it had begun in my balls. "It's a good thing for you I have this collar on. "

Sibyi snorted. "Except for the part where you can't summon us oxen. "

The Cloudmaker had a point. But I didn't dare take the collar off now—the second my beast knew Lisane was leaving again, he'd never come on that strong inside of me, not without me doing great magic first. I wasn't sure just what he'd do to get out after that, if I let him.

Or what he would manage to do once he did.

He was entirely capable of portaling.

It'd taken the rest of the morning to get things ready to go, but now that we had, I wouldn't sleep or eat until we got to Jaegar's camp.

And while I'd told the first group of scholars and soldiers who were helping us the truth—that I didn't have an answer, but that I thought I knew how to figure it out. When they'd told others, and more still, now we were apparently part of a triumphant brigade, hauling our trophy back to the war camp.

I didn't want to dissuade them—because most of them would take turns pulling on the vines, and happier men pulled harder.

I just hoped I didn't make a liar out of them.

And I hoped, knowing that I'd see Lisane at least one more time before I died, that telling her "this is not the end" didn't make a liar out of me.

"Finally!" Sibyi exclaimed, as we reached dry wagon ruts, and the wheels behind us freed themselves of mud.

I grunted with a nod. "Keep going. "

LISANE

I stepped out of Sibyi's portal back into solid black, and I didn't turn around to see the portal close.

Because then I might see Rhaim again, and then what?

Be tempted to throw myself back into his arms?

This was for the best, and it was temporary—it had to be.

I used a little magic to cast a light around and saw that nothing inside the closed-off tent had changed since I'd last been there.

Except for me.

I turned off my light and put my hands to my heart, letting my feelings flood me in the dark.

I was loved.

Exquisitely.

There could be no denying it with all the ways that Rhaim had shown me: his kisses, his caresses, his bites, and his groans. He had seated himself and his love deep inside me, and he was right. No one could steal any of it back.

It was mine, and through it, I was bound to him for life.

I took a dizzy turn in the darkness, and then sank to my knees, curling up on the tent's floor, replaying every moment I'd had with him inside my mind, until I fell asleep.

I woke up to sudden sunlight, and a very angry shadow.

"Do you know what you've done?" someone demanded.

I threw an arm across my face—I'd been having the loveliest dream, Rhaim and I, inside the cabin that he'd shown me—and I blinked. "I'm thirsty," I said, rather than answer the question, and got splashed with water for it. I yelped in surprise and sputtered, kicking back on the ground. "Helkin?" I asked. I heard him curse, as one of the guards outside held the tent flap open, so there was light inside with me. I blotted myself with my skirts, not understanding, as he walked in. "Were you worried I was going to catch on fire?" I asked, sarcastically.

"No," he grunted. "I was pissed. " He squatted down in front of me on his heels, meeting me on the ground. "Do you remember Tuttle?" he whispered, so quietly I was afraid I hadn't heard him, before his voice changed. "You've ruined everything, Lisane," he said, in a growl that might have challenged Rhaim's.

"I—I don't understand," I confessed, to both things.

Helkin and I had had many arguments in our childhood, but the one thing we could agree on was that we loved Tuttle, a doddering old tutor we'd had, who once upon a time had been a spy. He was there to train Helkin, and I was only lucky enough to get to listen along, as he told my brother about wars he'd helped stop and the many he'd started. But more entertaining than any of his histories, was that he'd taught us how to send secret messages—which we'd used to call each other names, in code, in the margins of our workbooks thereafter.

So when Helkin threw a handkerchief at me in a dismissive manner, presumably so that I could clean myself up, I caught it, and was sure not to use it to wipe anything.

"I can't believe you!" he said, his upper lip curled in disgust.

I decided to play along—and earnestly hope that it *was* playing. "What is there to believe?" I fought back. "That I didn't want to be given away to a man I hardly knew?

Again?" I said it from my chest, as I hid his handkerchief in my skirts.

Helkin squinted, his eyes following my hand. "You don't know what you've done, foolish girl," he said loud enough for anyone outside to hear.

And I said back what I always did to him, when he acted like that. "We're the *same* age, Helkin! There is no difference between us!" I rocked up to my knees. "And I saved people! People who otherwise would have died!"

He closed his eyes, as if in pain, though his tone was still angry with me. "And in doing so, ruined all of your chances. "

Whatever fake argument we were having was well on the way to becoming a real one. "Better that now than some Ker finding out later," I spat, full of feeling.

"Helkin!" another familiar voice snapped from outside the tent. "Come away from there!"

Castillion—beckoning my brother off, like I was a chained dog to be wary of. My brother gave me another meaningful look before answering Castillion's call. The tent flap descended, and not long after that I heard the sounds of myself being sewn back in.

I waited until the needles were through to fish out the cloth Helkin had thrown at me, holding it up as I shone light through from the far side, illuminating the subtle stain he'd painted on its cloth.

I will come to you tonight.
Be ready to go.
Burn this—I know you can.
~H

I let out a long, low exhale, and then did as I was told, spending a tiny piece of the magic Rhaim had put inside me on setting the note aflame, then turning it carefully while blowing, so that the fire spread evenly, until there was nothing left of it but a tiny fleck of ash.

I had no idea where Helkin was taking me. . . but I wanted to find out.

RHAIM

I treated the men who hauled the Deathless's cage no kinder than other men treated animals, urging them on into the night. I would've whipped them too, if I'd had one.

"They need rest, Rhaim—as do you," Sibyi said, coming up, casting enough light for all to see. I was picking up a vine again—I would keep the cage rolling forward if I had to drag it with my teeth.

"That thing doesn't sleep," I said, pointing at the Deathless with my chin. It was still alive as ever, somehow surviving without food, without water, like its only source of power was the air. Most of the day it lay quietly moaning, but some times it would get up and lurch from side to side, with mysterious intent. It reminded me of creatures that could survive the entire winter, frozen, nose to tail-tip, only thawing out in spring—but it didn't want to mate, that I knew of, or eat, that I could tell.

"Once again, you are human," Sibyi said more firmly, taking the vine I held back from me. "And it is just a few hours until dawn. Let the men sleep while it's still dark—we'll start fresh the morning. "

"Bah," I complained, but it was too late—the others were already heeding Sibyi's words, eating the bread we'd brought and lying down on the ground.

I stalked away past Sibyi's light, wanting to feel the darkness on me—just like the tent Sibyi said they'd sewn Lisane in.

I'd been so close to being able to keep her. If I didn't know I'd see her one last time, likely right before my demise, not even the collar would've kept me sane.

I sat down and stared out at the stars.

"I loved a girl once, too," Wyrval's voice said beside me. I hadn't heard him walking near. For as big as he was, he was as silent as the wind. "She was my master's great-grand niece. He never moved away from his family's farm, he just took up residence in a hut nearby after he Ascended, and they mostly left him alone. "

I was surprised to hear it. Wyrval hadn't bothered to confide in me before. "What was his skill?"

"Twisting things. Hay into bales, hemp into ropes, but he also made nets, for fishermen, or wound reeds together, for baskets. I once watched him undo a brutal storm though, by twisting the winds the other way. "

I nodded appreciatively. Like I had often told Lisane, many mages were limited more by their imagination, than by their talent. "And were you ever worried about him twisting you, if you were caught with her?"

The tree-man broke into a slow grin. "No. We were careful. And it wasn't like I could get her with child, so..."

I snorted. "Yes, that had made me popular too, once upon a time. " When I was younger, still searching the world for challenges and proving my powers, I realized there was almost always a group of women looking to get you in trouble with their husbands, if you tarried in their towns long enough. I reached down to pick up a nearby stone and fling it forward. "Did she love you back?"

Wyrval seemed to contemplate this. "I think so. Or at least she sought me out as often as I sought her. My room was just above hers, and the floorboards were old—many of the knots had fallen out. And when I learned I could extend a vine from any part of me... " Wyrval's voice drifted, until his memories redoubled it. "She would stand on her bed and knock quietly on her ceiling—and I would crawl beneath my bed and set myself in a spot that both let me see below and set my organ through. "

And here I'd spent almost my entire life merely worried about my knot.

Wyrval turned to me and quietly continued. "I would watch her writhe by the moonlight her window let in, fucking her until she had to hide her face in a pillow not to scream, for as long as either of us could stand it. And when we couldn't anymore, I'd slick her with my sticky green, and both of us would sleep contentedly. "

My eyebrows were quite high now, and I was glad that it was night. "What happened to her?"

"The same thing that happens to all of them, I think. She grew older and wanted different things from life. That town was her home, and her mother's home—going back for generations. She had a place there, while I wanted to see the world. But even if I stayed, I believe eventually she would have had no use for me. "

"I would think someone of your magical caliber would've been more useful than a mage who merely twists things. "

"You would think, and yet," he said, laying himself against the ground, and a pillow of moss appeared beneath his head. "If I had stayed there, I would have stayed small. True power is defined by a certain discontent, and cheerful people don't make great mages. "

I snorted at that, unable to disagree. "But they have the virtue of being happy. "

"And the joy of being smug about it, usually," Wyrval said, giving me a grin. "So how great are her powers?" he asked, and I knew he meant Lisane.

"If measured by unhappiness, then very great indeed. " I twisted toward him in the dark. "How old are you, Wyrval?"

"Past you by several centuries, but younger than Filigro. If you're asking if I remember the old ways though, then, yes, I do. But I have no truck with fire—and neither does the weather mage. "

"You asked him?" I said in surprise.

"No. I just know it is not in his nature to burn things. He prefers to put them out. And I know it is not in my nature to want to be set on fire, or in your nature to set them. But your woman. . . "

"Yes. " Lisane's spirit was fierce; no wonder she channeled flames readily.

I wondered how she was, where she was. If she was fed and warm, or cold and hungry.

"You may rest for a time, All-Beast, I will keep an eye on the camp tonight. " Long grasses shot up in a wide circle away from his body, encompassing our group. "I will make sure all are up in time for the morning. "

I lay down on the ground, my head on my folded arm, but I knew I wouldn't slumber.

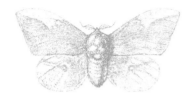

28

LISANE

I paced inside the tent, once I knew it was night—I could tell because the walls had cooled to the touch.

I couldn't sleep, not while I was waiting for Helkin's. . . rescue?

If that's what it would be?

I hoped that it was, and felt ashamed by the depth of that feeling. How nice it would've been to have a brother again, facing all of this, with me.

But. . . did he know of our father's lies?

He must have.

So did that make him complicit?

I paced until I'd gotten blisters from my borrowed boots, and then I sat down—until I heard the sound of the threads that sewed my door shut being snipped open.

I was about to say my brother's name, but was glad I didn't, because it was Castillion who walked in, holding a small light in his hand.

"Have you come to yell at me too?" I asked him.

He heaved a sigh. "A little. " He was wearing a vest, like he always did, but he'd also brought a satchel, which he set down and started pulling strips of strongly smelling fabric out of, trailing them around the perimeter of the tent, like a paintbrush dragging paint. "I've yelled more at myself though, honestly. "

I stood warily, watching him as he circled. "Why?"

"Because—I never should have taught you to hold light. " He gave the walls I was trapped in a meaningful glance. "And because, in a way, that makes all of this my fault. "

"Your. . . fault?" I repeated. The words to ask him about my mother's death were on the tip of my tongue. *How had it come about, and why had he **and** my father had decided to lie.*

"Yes," he went on, then grimaced at me, when his chore was through. "Which is why I've sent all the nearby mages and guards far away. " He dusted off his hands and then produced a striker from the pocket on his pants, and knelt in front of the door. "You already burnt your own tent down. So no one will be surprised when this one goes up too, and takes you with it."

"Castillion!" I shouted, and ran for him and his nascent flame. He threw his other arm in my direction, and a spear rushed out to stop me.

Sensing him using magic was the only thing that saved my life—I dodged, and his pointed metal clipped along my flank, ripping through my dress and skimming along my skin, leaving a bloody tear behind on my side. I clapped my hand against it.

"Just stand still, princess," he begged, as though what he were doing harmed him more than me. His other hand kept working the striker. "It will all be over shortly."

"Are you kidding me?" I shouted at him. "No!" And then I realized the game I had to play. "Castillion, you can't—" I acted like I was going to reason with him, taking a slow step forward—and the spear that'd hurt me, retracted and re-aimed—an event which I also dodged. . . barely. "You've known me all my life, Castillion," I begged. I couldn't tell if what was in me now was magic or sheer horror, but I knew I didn't dare start anything with him, until I was sure that I could finish it. "Castillion," I pleaded again, offering my hand out—and his next spear struck it through.

I gasped, pulling back without thought, and would've fallen to my knees and puked, had I not known violence prior.

Whatever magic was in me now would have to be enough, because I didn't dare get any closer to him.

"I cared for you!" I howled, as I raised the wicking fabric up behind him. I created a twisted loop of it while he worked the striker furiously, trying to get enough sparks to light. "I thought you were my friend!" I shouted—and made the noose descend.

His eyes went wide, once he realized what it was that I'd done. "No," he grunted, shooting spears out of his collarbones, looking like certain spined eels I'd seen skeletons of on Rhaim's shelves.

"Yes. " I denied him and reached my hand out for more, summoning all of the material he'd brought in to my cause, winding it around him just as fast as he could cut it, twisting it tight with my mind.

He had the foresight to stumble toward me at last, shooting spears at me rather than the knots I was wrapping him in, but I was faster than he was as I ran back and out of his reach.

"I don't want to do this," I told him, because it was true.

But I couldn't think of a way to *not* do it either, because if I let him live now, I knew he would kill me, and so I knotted all of the fabric that was left around him.

He took another stuttering step, spears shooting out of him at random now, like the last of his magic was turning him into a shooting star, and he grunted guttural things, trying to keep his throat open.

"Why did you make me do this?" I whispered at him as he fell down to his knees, his hands clutching at the ropes I had around his neck now, all of his own magic forgotten.

"This is not. . . how I die. . . " he whispered.

"I say it is," I told him, and kept twisting until I was sure of it.

The cost of that was throwing up.

I would have anyhow, but I'd never been possessed by such a need to vomit before. I fell to my knees, retching, again and again, not far from Castillion's corpse. All of my guts were in commotion, and any time I felt like I might be finished, no, a fresh wave of nausea began, until there was nothing left, but green bile and spit—

And a dead body, in my tent with me.

But beyond the mage, was an open door.

I held myself on all fours, feeling weak, and knowing I had no magic left.

What would happen if I ran? Would I ruin things for Rhaim?

And what the *fuck* would happen if I stayed?

If Castillion had been just a little smarter, or hadn't felt the need to make things personal—he could've easily doused my tent with something flammable from the *outside.*

I crawled up to his body, touching it, and it didn't move. And then I looked into the bag he'd brought. It was empty. . . except for something set in yet another pouch.

I pulled this out and unfolded the leather—and found myself holding Love's Lost Tear, Drelleth's teardrop shaped throne-stone, without the chain my father wore it on.

It was the size of my fist, tear shaped in all dimensions, its tip pointed enough to cut skin, while its faceted base had a round, pleasing weight.

What was it doing here—and on Castillion?

Then I heard the sound of somebody walking up outside. I dropped the stone back in the bag and flung it into the tent's depths, while turning my light down to hide the bag in the shadows.

The tent flap re-opened, framing Helkin with the night outside. "Where are your guards?" he asked, before taking in the scene. "What happened?" he exclaimed.

His horror seemed genuine—he hadn't been expecting to visit a burning sibling. "Castillion came to kill me. " I finally stood on shaky feet. "He was going to burn the tent and me with it. " I looked to my hand, which was now almost healed, and to my side, where my dress was torn.

"He. . . attacked you?" Helkin asked, then saw the striker near his feet and believed. "Lissy!" he exclaimed.

I put my hands to my mouth. "I know!"

And I lost all sense in the moment, running for him, like I would have when we were in trouble as children. He grabbed me, and for a moment I believed that not everything in my past was a lie. "I'm so sorry," he whispered, holding me close. "This isn't your fault, Lissy. None of it is. "

I extricated myself from his embrace, frowning. "That's what Castillion said, right before he tried to set me on fire. "

Helkin looked down at the mage's corpse and spat on him. "No—you did me a favor. The world is a better place, without him in it. "

"What do you mean?" I asked.

"That whatever evil thing it is that he and father have been doing—it has gone on long enough."

"The Deathless attacked our mother first," I blurted out, and watched him nod.

"I know. I was there," he said, then quickly corrected himself. "Not like you were, trapped in chambers. But I remember how it happened, and then what happened after."

"Which was?" I pressed.

"More attacks. Sometimes at random—but sometimes not. They're controlling the Deathless, somehow."

I had so many questions I wanted to ask, but one was paramount. "Why?"

"Because Drelleth was waning in power. You know how father's been?" he asked me.

Worried about Drelleth's destruction, obsessively. "Our whole life," I said, with a nod.

"He and Castillion concocted the Deathless somehow. To create a crisis that only he could control—and solve."

Which put my father's plans at direct odds with Rhaim's.

I took a deep inhale, shuttering my rising panic. "Why are you telling me this now?"

"Because you don't deserve to be here, Lissy. It's not your fault you learned magic. Father sent you to the beast, so you had no other choice. It's why you still have your honor, clearly—you learned magic to survive. "

"That's not true," I whispered quietly.

His brow furrowed. "It is—I read your letter—"

"The letter lied," I said, and Helkin's head tilted, unable to comprehend what I was saying. "When I wrote that letter, I was mad at Rhaim," I said, and paused trying to explain. "Did he whip me? Yes. But only because I asked him to. "

Helkin flinched back as though he himself had been struck. "Why?"

"To help me learn magic. There was no other way. "

An infinite number of horrors crossed Helkin's face in a moment. "I don't understand—"

"I don't think you can," I told him, realizing as I said it, that it was true. "So please, just trust what I'm telling you: I would have rather learned magic every day at the end of a whip, than spend a lifetime like this, trapped in a cage. "

My brother was silent for a long time, and I worried he was lost, until he next spoke. "I didn't want to leave chambers, you know. " I shook my head because I didn't, as he went on. "But I had to, Father made me. Said 'it was time for me to be a man. ' He had me fitted for armor, and instead of fighting with sticks like we'd played with," he said, giving me a bittersweet smile, "I was given a real sword. "

"Just like you'd always wanted, right?" I said, remembering his indignant complaints as a child.

"Yes," he agreed. "But it wasn't fun anymore, then. " He looked up and down me, then looked away, ashamed. "I got all of your letters. But Father told me to ignore them, that it would be better that way. "

My lips twisted to the side. "Was it?" I quietly asked.

He shook his head. "No. " I watched my brother take a deep inhale, and then look around the room again, as if for the first time. "There are guards who are loyal to me—they will help me dispose of the body, and then you and I, we will run away from here. "

I rose up on my toes, eager to follow, before rocking back. "I can't. I need one more day. "

"Why?" he asked, before realization dawned. "Because the beast returns. "

"Not just any beast, Helkin. Rhaim is *my* beast," I said, pressing a hand to my chest. "And?" I started, then finished before I could help myself. "We are bonded, so you must not hate him. " I needed to claim what Rhaim and I were aloud.

"He only killed Vethys because of me—I didn't want to go back—and my letter said as much! I wanted to stay with him, keep learning, and be free. "

Helkin's expression was incredulous. "You love him?"

"So much so that I came back here to save his life, at the cost of my own soul. " I inhaled to explain myself, then realized I couldn't, and flung my arms at the four walls I was trapped in. "I am like a flame, Helkin," I said, willing him to understand. "And Rhaim tends to me carefully. He would not see me put out, and he likes it when I shine brightly. But. . . here, with Father? Or were I to go with Vorsha, or any other of the Kers? All any of you want is to hide me away; extinguishing my dreams, hoping that my light might disappear. " I watched him trying to think and pressed. "Again, if you cannot understand me, brother, I pray you would just believe the words I say. "

Helkin appeared to consider things, then exhaled roughly. "All right," he said, then followed up with, "Does he love you?" before scoffing at himself. "Of course he does, he must, who else would go through everything he has for you? But we know he's coming, Lissy. Father means to kill the Deathless he brings, and then put him inside that magicless cage, as punishment for teaching you. "

I grabbed for his hands. "You cannot let that happen. You have to somehow help me turn the tide. "

"How?"

"When Rhaim gets here—come and get me, and take me to him. We will solve everything together. "

He gave me a disbelieving look. "I know you can make unicorn horns float—and fabric, too," he said, giving Castillion a meaningful glance. "But unless you can cast a whole army aside, it will be impossible. "

"He and I will manage something together. I know it," I said, squeezing his hands hard before letting them go. "You'll see. "

Helkin nodded deeply. "All right then. I'll send *my* guards back to watch this place, and keep you safe in earnest. " He knelt down and picked up Castillion's body, flopping it over one of his shoulders with a grunt. "They'll also bring water and food, before they sew you in. "

"Thank you, brother," I said, feeling like I'd finally gotten a reprieve.

"Don't thank me yet," he said, but I knew it was a tease as he exited the tent.

I watched the space he'd left for a very long time after that.

Even if Rhaim and I couldn't stop the Deathless. . . at least I'd gotten my brother back.

29
RHAIM

The second the war camp was on the horizon I knew I wouldn't tire.

Being so close, it was like Lisane called to me, and I was fated to answer.

And either the other men fed on this, or they were as excited to see our destination as I was, because we traversed the plain in what felt like record time, with the sun beating down, and wind at our backs, until we reached the outskirts of the camp.

Word of our arrival had already spread, and curious onlookers, soldiers and civilians both, had come out to greet and stare. We'd put a sheet over the cage holding the Deathless, but passersby could still hear him moaning, and while some men held their children over their heads to see us pass, other frightened fellows pulled their braver women back.

The circle of mages protecting the camp parted to let us through, and we took the main road into the center of the camp itself, which was where I wanted to see and be seen— and wanted everyone to hear.

"I am back, with a Deathless!" I bellowed, whipping the sheet off of the cage. The creature inside was standing, leaning against the bars with its eyeless face, and one of its hands reached for the sheet, making it look like it was stretching out for the commoners. Some men shouted, and one woman screamed.

There was the sound of a more coordinated procession coming up, boots and metal beating in turn, as Jaegar himself pushed through the crowd, surrounded by a group of soldiers. He appeared to inspect the Deathless from afar, then archly asked, "And?" He looked around, encouraging everyone present to feel his disdain. "I seem to recall you promising a solution to them. This doesn't seem like one— he seems quite alive. "

"I needed to bring it here, first," I exclaimed.

But the truth was. . . I wasn't entirely sure what would happen next.

As mindless as the Deathless were, I refused to believe that they didn't serve a purpose, like all other living things.

They had a *reason* for what they did, and why they did it, and somehow Jaegar was the key to that—so I watched the creature carefully, to see if it had a reaction to him.

It did not—but it was steadfastly looking to the east for some reason now, even though it didn't have eyes, and I was sure it had not been before.

"Kill it!" shouted someone from the back of the crowd, and there was a murmur of assent. I moved to block the cage with my body—if the thing died now, before I'd solved this mystery, everything was truly lost.

"I agree," Jaegar said. He snapped, and the soldier nearest him raise a bow, setting his sight between the cage's bars.

"Wait!" called a woman.

My heart leapt, and whatever in me that was still beastly growled.

Lisane pushed through the crowd in the same dress I'd ravished her in, only now it was more torn, and the Deathless appeared to be looking at her.

LISANE

The day of Rhaim's arrival I was tortured by thoughts of how everything could go wrong—and it was unfair that that pain alone was not enough to empower me.

I listened as best I could through the heavy fabric of the tent, waiting for Rhaim's arrival, for my father's cruelty, and most of all, for my brother to rescue me.

I had all but given up hope, kneeling down, wringing the fabric of my dress repeatedly on my thighs, until every piece of it was wrinkled, when I finally heard the sound of someone cutting open my door.

I tensed, in case I was wrong to be pleased—but then my brother appeared, just like he'd promised. He put a hand out to me. "Hurry!"

I took it, and let him pull me out of the tent.

We ran the same as everyone else was running, for the center of camp, to see. Helkin was dressed plainly, and I looked like —I didn't even know. My dress was torn, and stained with ichor and my own blood now in several places, but people let us through, thanks to Helkin's spirited shoving, until we were at the nearest perimeter of the group, and then my brother turned to me.

"This is for you," he said, holding an object out to me. My father's key—for Rhaim's collar. "May it free you from your cage. " I grabbed it, as he took my head and kissed it, before running back through the crowds the way we'd come, looking to escape, too.

People were already shouting for the Deathless's blood, and my father wasn't doing anything to discourage them—so I elbowed through the final few and shouted, "Wait!"

Rhaim saw me first and anyone could have read the look upon his face—it claimed me like a clawed hand.

I pulled up short though when I saw the Deathless in the cage behind him, and felt the horrible creature's full attention on. . . me.

Rhaim noticed it as well, appearing concerned, and reached to protect me, but I stepped away on purpose.

The thing that the Deathless possessed instead of a face, just a blank expanse of skin over a gaping maw, was mine alone.

It appeared to want me.

Or. . . *something I held.*

I reached under my skirts quickly and untied Love's Lost Tear from the portion of my poor dress that I'd hidden it in, and hoisted it aloft. The Deathless's attention was gained at once, the thing not slavering for me, but for what was in my hand.

"It wants the gem," I told Rhaim, showing him the thing I held, and watched realization bloom across his face. "It wants the gem!" I shouted, far more loudly, so everyone could hear, twisting my wrist so they could see my fingers wrapped around the stone.

Each of them had seen the Tear around my father's neck before—but with Castillion's help, and ability to portal, the Tear had been mobile.

"What have you unleashed?" Rhaim demanded of my father, coming up behind me. I found his hand and planted the key into it.

My father's eyes were for the Tear alone. "Give that back," he said in low warning.

"I will not!" I said stridently. "It does not belong to you! It belongs to Drelleth!"

But why had my country had something so poisonous within its borders—in its throne room, no less?

"You don't understand what you're holding, girl," my father intoned, and then looked to the nearest archer. "Kill the creature, the mage, *and* the girl."

"You will have to kill the *mages*," one of Rhaim's friends said, stepping up, as a storm began crackling overhead.

The archer paused in fear, as Rhaim lunged forward to protect me—without having taken his collar off yet—then Jelena jumped out of the crowd.

"The unicorn queen saved your lives! Give her time to explain!" she shouted. She had a bag strapped across her shoulders, and I was sure that Finx was inside it.

I freed myself from Rhaim and held the stone up for all to see. "I think the Deathless follow this, though I don't know why. And I think that Castillion the Spiked has been portaling around the continent with it, encouraging the Deathless to emerge. "

"And when defenses weaken, or protective magic runs low. . . they would come for it here," Rhaim said thoughtfully, looking at my father. Over his shoulder, the Deathless was reaching reached for the stone with one monstrous hand, pinning itself against the bars of its cage to get to it.

"It doesn't matter what you think you know—you must give it back! You don't understand!" my father said, grabbing the sword off of a nearby soldier to stalk forward.

"Then those of us who've been fighting for you would like answers," said Rhaim's tall, tree-like friend. Rhaim unfastened the bolt of his collar and tossed the black metal ring into the cage, so no other mage could get it.

"How do we stop them?" I demanded, shaking the Tear. I would have crushed it in my palm if I were sure that that would work. Silence fell around us as the storm above started up, everyone present awaiting answers. My father's face was as stony as the gem itself, unchanging, showing neither shame nor hope for mercy. "My mother died, because of you," I shouted at him. "Why?" I then realized that it didn't matter. "No. I don't care. Because there was nothing that was worth her death—or any of the other peoples' who died or were displaced by these things," I said, casting a look back at the Deathless behind me. "If you won't apologize, Father, then I will! It is a horrible thing that has been done! And I will undo it, as best I am able!" Rhaim stood close behind me then, resting a hand at my hip. I placed my own hand atop it meaningfully. "It came from Drelleth—and back to Drelleth it goes!"

"Are you sure?" he asked quietly, for my ears alone.

I licked my lips. "Yes. Please. "

"Anything for my beloved moth," he whispered—and then pulled me through a portal.

RHAIM

I brought us as close as I could get to Drelleth's castle, inside a gated pavilion, in front of a massive and ornate edifice, where all the former warriors and kings of Drelleth were celebrated in stone, and covered in bird shit. It was hauntingly empty, probably because most of Jaegar's people were off at his war.

"This was as close as I could get—I've never been inside," I told her, as she looked up at me.

"It's okay," she said, hitching up her skirt to tie, like when I'd seen her that one day in the river, beating laundry. She reached for my hand, and held the stone in the other, ready to drag us both up to the throne-room—but I held back.

If the stone summoned the Deathless, which I was sure it would—we'd be attacked, outside of the war camp's magical protection.

The only question was how long it would take.

And how long I could hold them back for her.

I took her face in my hands, blistered from pulling the vines for the cage to meet her. "I love you," I said simply.

I watched the knowledge of what I was going to do pass through me and into her and she gave me the look I had spent my entire life waiting for.

"Rhaim, no," she whispered.

"I love you," I repeated, and continued, "and my love for you has been my greatest triumph—next to teaching you magic," I teased and tried to smile. But tears were already streaming down her cheeks, and it killed me that I didn't have time to kiss them away. "This is how I die."

I felt the ground shake—we both did—the Deathless coming to claim the stone that was theirs, and inside of me my beast rose up, eager to meet the on coming challenge, knowing *his* time was near.

"I can't," she began, placing a fist to her stomach, as I shoved my beast down for the time I had left. "Rhaim—don't leave me. You promised."

"All mages know how they die, Lisane. But because of you, I have been lucky enough to know what it means to be alive." My eyes searched her face, memorizing everything about her, one last time. "So kiss me, my lovely moth, that I may die content."

Lisane flung herself at me, wrapping her arms around my neck as mine bound her waist. Her lips met mine, parting instantly, and it would've been foolish to say that I would remember the taste of her, the feel of her, forever, when I knew I had such little time left—but we were both compressing all the memories we would never get to have into one sweet moment in time. Our love, our hunger, our strength—everything passed between us, just as it was meant to be.

I was hers, she was mine, and as long as I knew that, then fate could have me.

"I love you," she said, when she was forced to pull away, because I was setting her down. The hackles on the back of my neck were rising up, soon the Deathless would be pouring toward the castle. "I will always love you," she whispered.

I caught her hands and placed one of them atop my chest, above my mage-mark. "I know you will, little moth," I told her calmly, even as I began to hear horrendous groans. "But if you see my beast again Lisane. . . do not give him a second chance to bite you. Kill him on sight. Promise it. "

"Rhaim!" she protested, stricken.

"Do it so that I may die in peace," I said, urging her with my eyes.

I watched her close her eyes and swallow. "Yes," she exhaled, when she opened them again.

I ran my hand up her jaw to stroke her cheek with my thumb one last time. "Then go catch the world on fire, Lisane the Flame," I said, before releasing her, to run to the castle's gates.

30

LISANE

I ran up to my castle's door, sobbing, unable to bear looking back, knowing that if I did I would be pinned to the ground I stood on, and once I got there I beat against it with both hands, one empty, the other holding the Tear.

A curious guard looked out. "It is me! Princess Lisane!" I announced.

It took far too long for recognition to spark in his eyes. "Princess?" he asked, in disbelief, opening the door.

"The Deathless are here! You have to evacuate anyone left behind in the castle—now!"

He looked past me. "Where's Castillion? Or your father? How are you alone?"

"Never mind that," I said, pushing my way inside. "Do as I tell you," I commanded him. "Or you will all die like my mother," I shouted, running past him.

I ran through empty hall after empty hall, my boots echoing on the stone, through rooms I'd barely ever gotten to see, because they had tall windows. There was the banquet hall where I'd gotten to make rare "appearances" as a child, and the room where my father did official things, where statues of warriors with golden weapons were meant to look imposing, but none of which were as ominous as the throne room, which lived at the top of the castle, so that anyone looking out its windows could see Drelleth's lands on one side, and the Sorrowful Sea on the other.

I reached the throne room and drew up short. It took up the castle's entire upper floor, and I instantly felt small. I had been here least of all as a child, but it had left the greatest impression on me, because of the way my father looked sitting on the throne, so imperious and commanding, and because of the statue that loomed behind him, a woman's face, symbolizing our country, with the emerald tear on it that I now held.

Now, she was still crying, but there was a gap on her cheek, where Love's Lost Tear should be. I crossed the room to her, mesmerized by her presence, and steeled by my love, knowing Rhaim was fighting the Deathless outside. I prayed I had a chance to save him.

I ran past the throne to reach up. I put my fingers on her face, and paused because I could see there were words carved inside the stone's setting:

If you can see me, cry.

I stopped to contemplate that—and it was a moment too long.

Incredible pain shot through me, from back to front. I looked down, and saw red spurting out of myself, from where I'd been pierced with a metal spear.

The spear retracted, and I clasped my hand to where it'd been, trying to hold my blood and guts in, and I turned, without thinking, my current goal lost in the pain, to see my father standing beside his throne with Castillion, who looked like he'd crawled out of a shallow grave.

"I told you that wasn't how I died," he sneered, sending out another metal spear. I felt it catch on ribs, as it also pierced me through.

This indignity seemed to have some effect on my father, at least. "Lisane," he said wearily, slowly walking up. I still held the stone in one hand, its shining facets dimmed by my blood's darker red. "I would have rather this never happened to you," he said, coming up to me like I was a wounded animal, with one of his hands out, and the other on his sword.

"Why?" I asked him, meaning not just why was he killing me now, but why had he taken everything from me?

And because I needed to know how the stone worked, if I were to ever have a chance at fixing things.

"The stone you hold is ancient magic. It grants wishes, but at great cost. "

I clutched it tighter for a second, willing it then to answer me, to bring back Rhaim, and my mother, and my very own life, which I could see spilling around me on the floor.

But none of that happened, and I saw my father's sad smile as he took the stone from my hand. "You have to put it into the setting to reset it. So I'll do that now, and wish that no one remembers what you discovered or said, and then things will be back to the way they were. "

"But. . . why?" I asked again, feeling like a child.

"Because the last king of Drelleth who used it was shallow-minded. He asked to be prosperous, for a mere millennia—and our time was coming up. But with the help of the Deathless, sowing chaos and destruction and making our star rise, I will see us prosperous, forever. " He settled a hand upon my shoulder. "I wanted this future for you, too, Lisane—not just for Helkin. I was going to make you a Queen of Rabel, the First country, and I would have made Vorsha suffer if he had dared to put his hands on you, before I killed him. "

Another spear pierced me through, making me stagger.

"Castillion, that's enough!" my father snapped.

"She heals like a mage does!" Castillion snapped back. "Lucky for me, you haven't Ascended yet though, girl—or you would've already seen your death, by my magic, right here. "

I stared at him blankly. There was a flicker in my vision, but I didn't trust it, because everything was going gray—gray like the clouds I saw through the windows, rushing across the sky outside—and then I saw it again, a tendril snaking across the window's glass, crazing it like it was stained instead of clear.

There were other mages outside. Helping Rhaim.

Helping me.

"She's clearly the price of my next wish," my father growled.

"Yes," I agreed, finally letting myself feel all the magic Castillion had filled me with. "My life has been the coin you've spent, all along."

31
RHAIM

I pulled myself up the castle's closed gate then leapt over it, rather than kick it open—all the better to give Lisane more time.

All around the castle's grounds, in a moat of meadowed parkland before the confines of Drelleth's largest city, the ground was opening, letting hoards of Deathless drag themselves up, and I was beset by a clarity of purpose, such as I had never known.

This was what it felt like when fate interceded. When decisions were made and there was no going back again.

I knew I was going to die, but I would make sure that my death had *such* a cost.

I ripped my leather shirt off, and howled back at the foul things that were beginning to come, then I fell to all fours and slammed my hands to the earth.

I, too, could pull things out of the ground.

I summoned a herd of rhinos, rising and kicking themselves free of the dirt to charge, bowling the Deathless down, slamming back and forth with their massive bodies and horns— and once they were set loose, I summoned tribe of gorillas, the same size as I was, but with arms twice as strong, willing them into the fray to pull the things apart.

"Rhaim!" I heard someone say, but I didn't dare turn, I couldn't let my concentration break.

"We're here!" a sonorous voice announced. "And we brought the spider!"

"And the girl carrying the spider," I heard Lisane's little dark-haired friend complain.

Sibyi and Wyrval. I knew it—because above the field of animals wrestling creatures, I could see the beginnings of a storm, and greenery lash out of the ground to begin pulling Deathless apart.

Finx ran up to accost me from below. "Where is the princess?" he demanded, flailing several sets of legs up.

"Inside!" I shouted out through gritted teeth, loud enough for all of them. Finx ran off at once. "Go help her! I'll manage here!"

I could already feel my beast scratching at my insides. *Stampeding bulls would be next.* I concentrated and *willed* it to be so, making the earth unveil them in an arc around me, sending them in to replace the rhinos that the sheer numbers of Deathless had downed.

"You'll—" Sibyi began in disbelief. "Come on now," he complained, running up to me, sending his lightning bolts surging, as rain began to pelt.

"I mean it, Cloudmaker," I growled without looking up.

There was a close thunderclap, and then I heard Sibyi say, "Oh," in a knowing tone.

"Yes," I told him, confirming everything.

I felt him put his hand on my back, while I concentrated on keeping my animals intact and the Deathless at bay. "Fighting with you was a joy and a pleasure. "

"I feel the same," I grunted. "Now—GO!"

Alone on the field of battle, I was fractured into as many facets as Drelleth's gemstone. I could feel my hands ripping, my horns piercing, my hooves stomping—I could taste the ichor of the Deathless across what seemed like an infinite amount of tongues, I could feel the grease of their decomposition slicking hide and fur, and I could hear the sounds of battles engaged in all around, from a thousand different ears.

But it didn't matter how many of them I killed.

They wouldn't stop coming.

There were already some behind me, shaking the castle's gates, climbing up on top of one another, and soon they would clear them entirely.

I once thought of my magic as a fuse that I burned through, knowing once it was gone, I would only be my beast.

Now I realized it was my life that was a fuse, instead. Lisane had sparked it the moment I'd first met her, and it'd been steadily burning, ever since.

And... now?

It was almost gone. My jaw ached to birth fangs, my hair freely sprouted, and each of my fingers were tipping with claws. My beast howled, wanting to join the field of battle, ecstatic *his* time had come.

These were going to be my last human moments, until the darkest embers of what I truly was finished burning away my life.

I closed my eyes and saw Lisane's face one last time. Terrified —not *of* me, but that she was *losing* me.

But I wasn't dying by accident.

This was a sacrifice made freely, with willing intent.

I loved her.

I loved her.

I.

Loved.

Her.

I clawed my hands into the earth, summoned another wave of creatures to fight, and then let go.

32
LISANE

Before my father could step past me to slam the stone into its setting once more, covering up the warning carved inside, the entire castle shook.

I'd thought the growing shadows on the ground were due to my own blood loss, or the oncoming storm, but in actuality the vines across the windows had grown wilder, thickening until the glass broke and came crashing in, setting loose a rockfall of stones from the ceiling above, exposing the whole throne room to the cloud-filled sky.

Castillion shouted in surprise and then agony, as massive stones from the ceiling pinned him, but that didn't stop my father. He was lunging past me to slam the Tear into place when—something stopped him.

He stared at his hand, fighting something I couldn't see.

"Stop that!" he ordered.

I stumbled sideways—and realized his hand had been trussed by silk—from Finx, who was crouching atop the throne.

"Give it to me!" I commanded him instead, yanking it out of his palm.

I turned back to the statue. All I had to do was replace the Tear—then be willing to pull it out again and wish to change things.

"You don't know what you're doing!" my father shouted as Finx lassoed him again and again, tacking down all his limbs with his toughest webs to the throne's rough stone.

"I know all I need to!" I shouted back at him, turning back to the statue, while the storm raged above through the hole in the ceiling, spattering all of us with rain like cold tears.

And then a metal spear pierced me again, from back to front, taking a different path than prior, and I knew Castillion the Spiked had wriggled one of his hands out from beneath the masonry.

This one was in a vital part; I could tell by the way it was changing things inside me, the metallic tang of the blood rising in my throat, the way it made me catch my breath.

But it didn't matter.

There was nothing anyone could do to me now.

I was possessed by fate.

"Don't waste it on love!" my father commanded me, right before Finx's webs muffled his next demand.

"I'm not," I told him, holding a hand to my bleeding breast, wrapping the spear there with my free hand as lightning crackled above us all and thunder clapped. "The man I love is no more. " I wiped the back of my other hand across my lips, and saw it kissed by streaks of red. I took a step forward, and another one, feeling the metal slide against bone and flesh, walking up its length for the statue with the Tear in my hand. "I am only here for what he fought for me. "

I put my blood-stained hand against the statue's face for balance, stamping it like a mage-mark as I settled the stone into the socket to cover up the dire warning.

And once that was done, I focused all my will and magic upon the gemstone.

"I am not choosing love," I whispered to it, as I pried it loose again to make my wish. "I'm choosing to get a choice. "

Then everything went bright and thunder clapped, right on top of me.

33

LISANE

"Lisane!" I heard an unfamiliar voice bellowing my name, but I could only barely hear it over the sounds of fire, crackling all around me, a roar coming from sheets of flame . . . on me.

I was burning alive.

Just like Castillion had wanted, just like old wives tales had promised, and in my own never-shared fears—I was enveloped, in light, in heat, but most of all, in pain.

It took my breath away, and then my skin, my bones, my soul —there was no part of me that it was not combusting. I felt my hair vaporize, my eyes melt, every piece of me blackening to ash and then blowing away.

I was destroyed, and that destruction was so whole and thorough that I was obliterated, all of me cast on the wind, to everywhere, all at once—and because of that, for one shining moment, my essence was inescapable.

Then I coagulated again, that was the only word for it, and as I finally took a breath I had a vision.

"Lisane!"

The voice was louder now. Nearer, too.

"Princess?" I heard as something furry ran beneath my hand.

I opened my eyes and found myself kneeling in a watered-down puddle of my own blood on the floor of Drelleth's throne room.

And I was whole . . . even if the wet dress clinging to me was not.

"Finx?" I said, finally processing the spider-cat's presence. I still held the Tear—but I threw my other arm across my face to cover my nose from a terrible stench.

"Yes!" he crowed. "You were hit by lightning!"

"I was?" I wondered, standing. But I must have been—some of Finx's hair was singed, and my father . . . the front half of him was burned away. What was left of him was sagging forward, held up only by Finx's webs. I put a hand to my mouth to hold back a rush of bile at the sight—and realized the spear that'd been in me was gone now. I looked to where it must have come from and saw Castillion's limp hand emerging from the rocks. If lightning had hit me—he must've felt it, too.

"And your throat!" Finx went on.

"My . . . throat?" I said, setting my other hand to it. It felt raw. All of me did. I felt that I had won . . . but at what cost? "Rhaim," I whispered—and it was as if me saying his name had summoned him.

His beast had clambered up the outside of the castle, and now he flung himself inside through a broken window, landed on all fours, and rushed at me.

I dropped the Tear and heard it shatter as he grabbed me and lifted me up with a howl.

"Lisane!" he both growled and shouted and I trembled in his arms to hear it.

"Rhaim?" I asked, my voice breaking.

Hot breath from his muzzle rolled over me in bursts as he held me even with his eyes—eyes that I *knew* I recognized.

"You were supposed to kill me!" he said with a shake, setting me down, but not letting me go.

Tears of joy sprang to my eyes. "Did you . . . want to die?"

"Not again," he said, his new voice rough with emotion, and then he took in the rest of me, the way my dress was shredded and full of holes, thanks to Castillion. "My little moth, what has happened to you?" He knelt down so that we were still even, touching me carefully like he couldn't believe I was here.

"It doesn't matter now," I said. "We're alive. "

And as if to confirm that fact, he thudded his head against my chest and pressed me to him, while I threw my arms around his broad and furry neck.

"We're alive," I whispered again, as reality sank in.

Finx ran in a happy circle around us, shouting, "Yay!"

RHAIM

I'd gone to a place where there was only nothingness. I felt it greet me like a friend, and hold me like a womb.

No more strife, no more fear, no more curiosity.

It was a place where silence was satisfying in and of itself.

And I would have gladly stayed there for the rest of—if not my life, then my eternity.

A place of solace and solitude, distant from any mortal concerns.

Except . . . something was tearing my beast away, bit by bit.

I knew it because he was coming *here* with me.

Like a part of my greeting was him joining me, slowly gaining form, solidifying into a separate creature entirely, instead of the one that I'd always held within.

And I both watched and felt—while somehow knowing what was happening was impossible to understand—as he went from a few brushstrokes of thought into something *real* like me.

Or rather, like I had been.

I stepped up to him, floating forward in my incorporeality, until parts of us were driftingly connected.

He could have murdered her before.

He could have been so much more cruel.

But I remembered him carrying her into my castle after she'd closed the ground to the Deathless, after suffering his bite.

I remembered him feeling the same desolation as I did without her, at the unicorn glade.

And *she* had not been pledged to me alone.

He had also known her, knotted her, and needed her.

And he was protecting her now. The creatures I'd summoned were lost, so he was immersed in fighting, trapped in front of the gate by an impossible number of the Deathless, more than anyone had ever seen. Feeling their teeth and their claws, tasting their ichor, performing acts of wild savagery and violence heretofore unknown, determined to slay them all at any cost.

Not for himself, but for *her*.

Even though I had just told her to kill him on sight.

A thing we both knew she would never do.

"Don't stop," I urged him, coming nearer, feeling his battle through our still shared soul. "Save her. No matter what. "

And I knew he either would—or he would gladly die, trying.

He may not have been good.

But he wasn't completely evil, either.

"Let me help you," I told him, offering him my hand for strength.

He took it and—

34
RHAIM

I found myself in his form, in a field, where it looked like giants had danced, so much of the earth had been moved.

But there were no more Deathless.

My little moth had done it—and I was alive.

Like this.

Covered in fur.

I strained, to change my form, but couldn't—and then I tried to listen for creatures, and I couldn't do that, either—but none of that mattered right now. I loped for the gates of the castle and soared over them, racing on all fours towards a strange tree that was now there. I used it and the elaborate carvings to haul myself up the building's side until I could burst through an open window to see Lisane standing in a pool of blood, in front of a still-smoking corpse.

And when she looked up and saw me, I expected to see horror in her eyes—but didn't.

I stormed her at once, was upset at her for not listening, and then once I started holding her, I realized I would never have to let her go.

She was mine now, forever, no matter what. And I knew she was feeling and thinking the exact same thing from the way she clung to me, her arms only barely wrapping around my neck, as her happy tears stained my furred cheek.

I didn't know how much time passed, and I didn't care, so long as I was with her—but I did need to keep her safe. I pulled back, looking up at her briefly before I stood, looming over her in this much larger size. "You Ascended, didn't you, little moth?"

"I did," she agreed, her whole face lighting up with a pleased smile. "How could you tell?" she asked.

"Your mage-mark," I said. "It's here," I told her, and then wrapped my hand over it, where it lay above her throat.

Her brand was the same size and shape as my paw.

LISANE

"Yay!" Finx said, running around in excited circles, cheering us both on. I gave Rhaim a look, and he laughed, his whole body shaking with the motion as I fell into his arms again. All of his fur was sticky, and he stank, but I didn't care, because he was here again.

With me.

"Brilliant little moth," he said, holding me tight. He picked me up and spun me in his joy. "But—how?" he asked, setting me down.

"I don't really know," I confessed, reaching a hand up for his toothsome jaw. "I thought you were dead, so there was nothing left to wish for, except that nothing like this could ever happen again. " I turned to look around at the vast destruction behind me. "I just wanted to have a real choice in my life. So I wished for that," I told him, watching his brow rise.

"You wished for it?" he asked, somehow managing to give me an incredulous look, even though he had a muzzle.

"I did," I said lightly, with a laugh. And then I heard the sound of someone shouting from below.

"Can I get some help?" I heard Jelena—*Jelena?*—calling.

Rhaim was as startled as I was. He stepped away from me, toward the window, then paused, as Finx surged past him.

"I'll go the long way!" I shouted, running for the halls and stairs.

I heard a surprised shriek echoing up, but by the time I arrived, Rhaim had convinced Jelena of his usefulness, and they were both pulling on a rope inside a well. Rhaim wound it around his arm until a bald man emerged on the far end.

"Lisane!" Jelena shouted, running for me, once Sibyi's rescue was handled. "I decided to take my chances with the mages. "

"You didn't want to be a noblewoman anymore?" I teased.

She stopped before hugging me, looking me up and down with a laugh. "No—but there's no way I'm doing that laundry. " I grinned at her, as Sibyi quickly untied himself.

"I'm . . . alive?" The very wet mage looked at himself like he couldn't believe it. "I'm alive!" he whooped and did a little dance. Finx joined in at his feet, mimicking him.

"Whatever were you doing in the well?" I asked him, as Rhaim set the rope down and came back to hold me.

"I had to keep drinking water to make the storm work—it was the only thing I could think of to do," he said, then gave Rhaim a crazed look. "But that *was* how I died, Rhaim," he said, pointing back, and sounding firm. "I'm not complaining, but—how?"

"I can't explain it either," Rhaim said from behind me—then he looked to the tree that'd overgrown half the castle's side. "Wyrval?" he said with alarm.

The mage was far more tree than man now, although I could still make out a face-like shape on the tree's trunk. Rhaim was stunned, and I was completely uncertain.

"Are you okay?" Sibyi walked up to the tree and demanded.

The tree laughed with a voice like breaking wood, making its leaves shake, and a tide of tiny rocks came cascading down. "This is as a good a place as any to finally set down roots," Wyrval said, and then the features on the wood went away.

"Wyrval!" Rhaim shouted—but the tree-mage didn't answer him.

"What's going on, Rhaim?" Sibyi asked in confusion.

Rhaim looked to him. "Try to call up a storm."

"Ugh, no, I'm dry—"

"Try it," Rhaim commanded with a growl, and Sibyi groaned but did something with his hands.

Only the sky above was clearing.

"I can't," Sibyi said, looking at his fingertips like they'd betrayed him. "Why not?"

"Because," Rhaim said, looking wisely down at me.

"Because . . . I wanted a choice," I reasoned out, pacing away before turning toward them. "My father threatened there'd be a cost—that's why my mother died when he made his wish, I'm sure of it—along with all the others the Deathless killed. And while the only thing I wished for was to have a choice in my own future, the only way that was possible was . . . " I put a hand across my mouth in astonishment.

"If no one were able to perform magic again," Rhaim said, squinting. "Including yourself?" he asked.

I briefly tried, then nodded. "Including myself. "

I'd wanted to change the world—and I finally had.

"It makes sense," Rhaim said. "Because as long as fate only propelled certain people in the world, others had no say in their own destiny. But now that fate is gone, the world will be what people make of it. You've given many more people a choice than just yourself, little moth. "

Sibyi tsked. "Wait, so I'm normal again?" he complained.

Jelena whirled on him, having taken all of this very well. "Some of us never got the chance to be special. "

"Yeah!" Finx said from near my feet, jumping in to take her side. I laughed and knelt to pet him.

"If you'd still been a creature of fate—you would have drowned," Rhaim told him, jerking his chin back at the well. "Lisane saved your life," he said with pride, and then looked to me with a sly grin across his muzzle. It was funny how easy it was to read his moods on this beastly version of him —perhaps because now he felt free to express them. "Filigro warned me you might bring about the end of the world. "

I slowly stood again, as my jaw dropped. "And you didn't tell me?"

Rhaim held out open hands, with clawed fingertips. "I was a man of science. I wanted to see what would happen. "

"Oh, I'll tell you what's going to happen—I'm going to yell at you a lot," I said. Jelena laughed, Sibyi snickered, and Rhaim only grinned wider, showing more and more teeth.

"It's all about perspective," he explained. "To a mage, the end of the world is losing magic. So the future with you in it, the one that ancient mage feared, was utterly accurate, though not for the reason he assumed. "

"And now everyone's vision of the end's been canceled out?" Sibyi asked.

"I suspect so," Rhaim said, shrugging. "The rest of us will have to wait and die like any man. "

Jelena clucked the mages back from their philosophy. "Don't get me wrong, I'm happy to be alive, but—how are we going to explain any of this?"

Rhaim held his furred hand out to me while answering her. "We're not. That's not our job anymore. I, for one, would like to go back to my former life and as much as I am able ignore the rest of everything," he said, smiling down at me. "Unless you wanted to stay and rule?"

"Absolutely not," I told him, letting him pull me to his side.

We started walking for the gate, and I saw the webbed ladder Finx must have created for Jelena hanging down, as Rhaim moved to crush the gate's lock open with one hand. "Don't deny all your heritage though, little moth," he told me, after he'd tossed it aside.

"Why not?" I asked.

He gave me a wolfish grin. "Because from here on out, you will be the queen of my heart. "

Jelena groaned. "Ooooh, that's a good one," she said, looking at me. "And I'm a connoisseur of these things. But how are you going to kiss him with all those teeth?" she finished up, in an intentionally not-very-quiet whisper.

"I'll figure something out," I said, beaming at him as Sibyi drew even with Jelena's side.

"You know, you could probably still be pretty special," he said.

Her eyes rolled back instantly as she laughed. "Aye, and where have I heard *that* before?"

"Well, you did save my life, so technically I'm in your debt," Sibyi said, smiling brightly at her. "Also, I suddenly find myself with no other goals or plans. "

"Hmph. And I suppose someone will have to show you how to be a mere mortal again?" she asked, putting her hands on her hips.

"I am a studious man," Sibyi promised as Rhaim herded me a little away, wrapping his arm around me and pulling me close as we both walked, him shortening his stride to match mine. We listened to their conversation, and Finx zipped this way and that way ahead of us, inspecting each new pile of dirt we walked by, as I slowly realized . . . I was outside.

Where I would be, for forever, and there was nothing that would change that.

"The air, Rhaim!" I said, running out in front of him. "And the ground, and the sky!"

I spun to show him.

He laughed and bounded after me on all fours for a moment before catching up, grabbing me and hoisting me aloft.

"I am glad you didn't burn, moth," he whispered in my ear, as he carefully set me down.

I closed my eyes and leaned against him. "Me too. "

EPILOGUE
RHAIM

Drelleth's capital was in chaos, which worked greatly in our favor—the army of Deathless attacking the castle hadn't gone unnoticed, and while the threat was gone now, everyone who was even remotely mobile was trying to leave the city too.

This meant that it was easy for Jelena to spend her coin—Lisane had apparently given her gems in quantity prior to vacating her former tent—and get us a few things for the road before shopkeepers also locked their doors and disappeared.

Lisane and I hid in darkened alleys with Finx while Sibyi and Jelena got what was needed—me because I was afraid I would frighten people, and her because she was worried she might be recognized. I didn't know how to tell her that there was no way anyone would peg her as a high-born girl now, between her torn dress, her knowing eyes, and the mage-mark laced around her neck, but I also wasn't sure she would take that as a compliment and so I kept it to myself. And when supplies were gained, we headed off, following the surge of people out into the countryside, keeping together, and keeping to ourselves. Jelena had gotten me a piece of fabric to wind about my waist, which I supposed made me a little less threatening, and Finx was in her bag again, though I could still see his outline when he squirmed.

As if by mutual agreement, none of us said anything until we were sure we were alone, and after we'd outpaced all the rest of them—or everyone else had thought better of running and had begun to head back—and finally it was just our small party traveling on the empty road by the light of the moon. Jelena let Finx out to scurry around our feet, and we felt safe comparing notes.

Jelena's story was the shortest—she'd demanded Sibyi bring her, and Finx had made a silk rope ladder for her and Sibyi to escape over the wall surrounding the castle and so they did. He'd gone on to create the storm of a lifetime for us, almost drowning in the process, saved only by Jelena's quick thinking and good timing. Finx had helped save Lisane, and when I heard what had happened to her, I quickly stood.

"We need to be alone," I said, offering her my hand, so I could draw her away from the road and off into the nearby trees.

"What is it?" she asked when we were separated from the rest.

"Take off the top of that dress. I need to see you."

She made a sound of surprise. "Rhaim—"

"You just told me you were pierced by spears, multiple times. " The vision of Castillion hurting my moth haunted me. My beast had always been right about him; we should've killed him long ago.

"How can you even see?" she asked, twisting her arms behind herself to undo her laces.

That took me aback. "I . . . don't know. I just can. " I hadn't questioned how much better my eyesight was now, even in the moonlit dark, as my beast—in the same way I hadn't questioned how much easier it was to smell everything, for good or bad.

Lisane laughed softly. "Well, if you can—here you go," she said, presenting herself to me. "He got me here," she said, finding a spot beneath a breast, "and then here," she said, fingering another, "and lastly here, too. " She pointed to a spot right beside her sternum.

I ate her with my eyes. She was lovely, without even a scar on her, and more importantly than that, she was whole. I reached a clawed finger out to trace the path she'd made and heard her gasp as I set it upon her.

"How much of you is beastly now, Rhaim?" she whispered, after licking her lips.

I felt my blood race and my flesh become eager. "All of me. " Her hands dropped to help finish freeing her from her dress, but I caught it before it could fall. "No, pretty moth," I said, and watched her pout by moonlight. "I cannot take you without seating myself in you—and just because we're away from your castle doesn't mean that we're safe. "

She took her dress back from me reluctantly. "And you're sure?" she asked . . . and the tone of her voice thrilled through me, because I already knew what she would do next.

"Very," I said—at the same time she dropped her dress and turned to run.

I counted to three—it was all I could stand—and then chased her instinctively, hitting myself against the trees she dodged. She squealed and laughed ahead of me, racing into the dark, knowing that I would catch her— and knowing that she wanted to be caught.

"I am coming for you," I promised her, gnashing my teeth as I listened to her pant, breathing in the light scent of her sweat and the heavier notes of her musk, snarling after her and playing her game until I couldn't take it and I burst through a set of branches to pounce and pull her to me. I took the blow of our landing on a shoulder, as she breathily screamed my name.

"Rhaim!"

"You think you can taunt me?" I growled at her in play, letting go of her to flip her on her back.

"I could've gotten away if I'd had better shoes," she said with a laugh, still kicking away from me.

"Like I will ever let you leave again," I said, grabbing her knees and pulling her to me on night-damp grass.

"Rhaim!" she protested again, before laughing, as I settled myself on my stomach between her legs. "Fine!" she started, the very voice of feigned irritation, but when she felt my tongue swipe her whatever she was about to say next fell into a soft moan. "Oh," she said, quickly rocking back and giving herself over.

I chuckled evilly against her, licking all of her, up and down, and whatever joys I thought I'd had tasting her before were beyond redoubled in this new form. I kept licking, then grabbed the bottom of both her soft thighs and pulled her legs up for her, until her heels were kicking against my back.

"Rhaim," she whispered, between pants, and I lifted my head.

"I may not be able to mount you out here, little moth, but did you think you'd be unsatisfied?" I asked, before pushing my tongue in deep.

She moaned again and I snarled to hear it as her hands reached down to grab the fur below my ears. I fucked her with my tongue, my formidable teeth pressed against her clit, and she was fearless in the way she ground down and tried to ride me. And when my tongue was coated in her juices and her pussy about to clench, I pulled back and lapped at her clit like I was drinking water, torturing the both of us until she couldn't stand it anymore.

"Rhaim," she gasped, her heels digging, as her back arched.

"Come for me, little moth," I whispered with my new rough voice, urging her forward. "Come for the beast that captured you."

She cried out then, rocking wildly beneath me, calling my name, and of course I was hard—not getting the chance to fuck her, it was a miracle I wasn't rutting the ground. The second she was conquered, I rose over her on all fours, balanced myself on one hand, and used the other to fist my cock, pounding myself wildly as she lay below me, breathing hard. I knew the sounds of flesh hitting flesh were echoing into the night and I didn't care. My clawed fingers tore into the earth beside her head as I chased my satisfaction, and my knot flared, sending me shooting onto her. I grunted and rocked into my hand, ropes of my hot cum spattering her, gleaming in the moonlight and making her smell like me.

And when I was finished, my cock still hot and hard, I smeared my cum all over her body, first with the pierced head of it, and then with my hand.

"Mine," I growled, and I wasn't playing anymore.

Lisane gazed adoringly up at me, pale in the moonlight, but no place so white as the fresh mage-mark about her throat. "Yours," she dreamily agreed.

A fter that, things were easy, though denying her was hard.

We'd decided to travel back to my castle, and if I'd realized how far away we were, I might have made different choices when I'd settled it on the ground. But because I knew Sibyi wouldn't be able to fly the thing, I'd chosen someplace I'd have wanted to stay myself: remote, but surrounded by good land with both deep woods and running water, plus a scenic view from the topmost floors.

Once we were on the open road, Sibyi had graciously "ceded" my castle back to me, as long as I promised to call it the Lightning Palace thenceforth.

Oddly . . . I agreed.

"You're joking," he said, squinting at me. "You're even harder to read now, with beast eyes. "

"That's not true, don't listen to him," Lisane said, readily coming to my defense and sticking her tongue out at him.

So for the next three months, Jelena's coin eased our passage across the continent, buying supplies to camp with or nights in inns in turns. For some reason, innkeepers thought better of me with Lisane at my side, and soon everyone seemed to know there was no new magic in the world, so the story of who I was—clearly a poor piteous mage, now trapped in this form for good—made them sorry for me rather than fearful. It helped now, too, that we'd fashioned a loincloth for me and a robe of sorts to wear, and now that I was in charge of this body, I was able to smile in a fashion and definitely able to laugh.

So the four of us plus Finx spent nights around fireplaces in warm, sturdy buildings, listening to stories from other people while hiding knowing smiles, or passing a pipe around the campfires we started outdoors and chatting, and for one entire season, I got to watch Lisane blossom.

Every day of freedom was new for her, every experience we had together was fresh. She laughed readily, ran through meadows of wildflowers, learned with abandon, and threw herself into living her own life with passion—the same way she threw herself against me.

We were at an inn and in her absence, I'd turned on the lamp in our shared room the old-fashioned way, with a stump of a candle borrowed from the innkeep. If you'd asked me to live without magic before, I would have been horrified, but in some ways, it made me as newly born in the world as Lisane, which was good for us both.

She returned from a bath in trader clothing, her fragile dress long since left for rags. "How far away are we now, Rhaim?" she asked like she did every evening, as I blew the candle out and set the lamp down.

As we were traveling quickly and there were flat lands ahead . . . I did quick mental calculations. "No more than a month. "

"A month," she complained, like she always did, even though it was one day shorter each time—and as though I didn't lick her delicious cunt clean every night.

She sighed and took off the silk scarf Finx had made for her that hid her mage-mark, and looked between me and the bed. "And you're sure?" she wondered.

I grinned at her, as I sat down by the door. "If we broke that bed, we'd definitely have to buy it. We shouldn't be so quick to spend our coin. " And very few beds at inns had looked sturdy enough to also fit me.

"What if I met you down there?" she said with a grin while looking at the floor.

I couldn't deny that I wanted that—but as if to grant me strength, we heard a commotion in the main room, right below us, through the thin floorboards. She heard it too and gave me a resourceful look.

"What if," she supposed, turning her back to me, kneeling on the ground. She took off her shirt and hitched her pants down far enough to present herself to me. "We met half-way?" she suggested, over one shoulder, leaning on the bed with both her elbows. "And I promise to be very, very quiet?"

"I do not believe you," I whispered, going to all fours.

"That I am pressing the matter, or that I can be quiet?"

"The latter," I said, coming up behind her, "because I can already scent your wetness from here. " I pushed my loincloth aside, revealing myself and my familiar piercing, sliding it between her tight thighs. She moaned at that, feeling it rub against her in its passage. "See?" I asked, and she turned to roll her eyes at me.

"It's not wrong to want my pledgebond, Rhaim," she whispered.

"No, it is not," I told her, licking the shell of her newly bathed ear, where she tasted clean. "As I want you all the time. Spit into your palm. " My little moth did as she was told, eagerly, and then looked to me for more instruction. "Now press me to you," I said. She sank her hand to do as she was told, and I began to thrust.

She instantly opened her thighs a little wider, to give me room—I couldn't go inside her yet, but this was good enough, stroking myself against her dripping valley while she ground against my cock. She was panting in an instant, so well trained, already expecting pleasure from me. I wrapped an arm around her, palming one of her breasts with all my claws, and whispered, "Be glad it's not a boot," which made her whine.

I stopped. "What did you promise me?"

Eyes that were already pools of darkness fluttered open, thinking. "That—I'd be quiet. "

"And will you be?" I asked, thrusting again.

She nodded very quickly. "Yes. "

"No matter what I do to you?"

I watched her slowly come back into her body at that. We'd furtively played in the woods some on our travels this far, but I hadn't done anything cruel to her because I didn't want to hurt her. She was my most precious possession.

But sometimes it was good for precious things to break.

Because sometimes, in the breaking, it lets them be reborn.

"Yes, sir," she softly breathed, knowing everything she was giving over in that moment.

"Good, moth," I whispered, then carefully pressed my claws against her, and thrust.

Her pants turned to gasps as she bit back moans. I laid my teeth upon her and carefully pinched her, leaving little red welts behind, feeling her flinch and tremble. I pulled my hand away from her breast and stroked my claws in reverse against her stomach and upper thighs, before switching directions to do the same, leaving even red lines. Her body was hungry for mine, and because of that, I could play her like an instrument. The hotter she was, the longer I could torture her, which let me further turn up her heat. It was like I was twisting giving her and taking pleasure from her into a tightly wound golden thread, that any moment now I would be tempted to strum.

I kept thrusting, her juices slicking the length of me, so much so they might've been pooling on the floor, as she pushed the thick head of my cock up against her, making it rub up and down her clit. My fur would smell like her now for days, and I licked my lips at the thought.

"Rhaim," she whispered hungrily.

I made a low growl of warning. "Do not let them hear me pleasure you, little moth," I said in time with my thrusts. "Be ever so quiet. None of them deserve to hear your song. " She swallowed and nodded, breathing hard. "Move your hand, Lisane. "

She quickly did as she was told, and I reached down to smack her cunt.

She yelped, and I growled at her. "Did you forget your promise to me?" I said hoarsely in her ear, as I used the pads of my thumb and forefinger to pinch her swollen clit.

"No, sir," she whispered apologetically, her expression aching with barely suppressed lust.

"Good," I said, and then smacked her again.

She whimpered at that, and I seized her. "If you cannot be quiet, I will make you be quiet," I warned, wrapping my other hand atop the mage-mark on her throat, as I went back to rubbing her, which made her arch her hips harder back into me. The lamp I'd lit cast our shadows on the wall, making me look even more fearsome than I was—and then the shadows showed me her hand reaching up, right before she took hold of my lower jaw, wrapping her fingers over my teeth, trying to claim me in return.

"Moth," I growled at that, bowing my head over hers. I needed her, this beautiful creature who trusted me enough to let me hurt her, to come, and I no longer cared if it made her scream. Her other hand was wound in the thin bedding, her neck bent forward, as her body longed to curve.

Her thighs trembled and her ass shook. "I can't be quiet," she said, sounding pained.

I chuckled darkly in her ear, around her fingers. "All right, moth. Then be loud," I said, releasing her throat, and right after that she almost howled, her hips bucking in my hand as she held onto me by my teeth. Her orgasm flooded through her, making her cry out, again and again—to riotous cheers from below—and when she let go of me and I pulled away from her, she turned, and I saw she was pink with shame, from her cheeks down to her rosy nipples.

She put her hands to her face in embarrassment, then saw me through her fingers, my hard-on pitching up my loincloth like a tent. Her eyes went cunning in a moment, and she whispered, "Fair's fair," before coming for me with her mouth.

I didn't even bother trying to be quiet as her lips found me. "Fuck," I growled low, running my fingers through her hair so I could watch her. "Yes, moth. Lick yourself off me."

Lisane made an accommodating sound, and tried to take me as deeply as she could—it was enough. I moved to push her back, but she fought, and I gave up quickly—if I couldn't come in her cunt, her mouth was the next best thing. I made an animalistic sound, shooting into her, and kept pulsing, until my balls were dry, my knot was taut, and she'd swallowed every drop.

I gasped as she pulled off of me, still hard but satisfied, although it always made her unhappy to see me so. "Can you not taste my pleasure with you?" I asked her when I saw her worried look, after pulling up her pants.

"I can," she said, wiping her mouth delicately with her fingertips, before picking up her shirt and pulling it on quickly. "But I just want to *be* with you, Rhaim. Fully."

I reached out a hand for her, which she took, and she let me reel her into my arms. Once she was there though, she started pushing me to the ground, and I let her win, as she nestled up against me, like we were still sleeping outside. "You should've wished for patience, moth," I said, brushing her hair back with a claw, and breathing a kiss as much as I was able against her cheek.

"That would've truly been impossible," she said, smiling at me as her eyes closed and she drifted off.

LISANE

A season later, I was practically a new person. My skin had gone red then tanned brown, I knew how to cook, and I had learned words to very naughty songs. I could recognize a hundred different flowers now, and every night Rhaim made a point of teaching me the stars.

The four of us plus Finx had taken our time on our journey, seeing as there was really no need to rush, but when we finally reached the nearest town to wherever it was that Rhaim had set his castle, Jelena came up with a reason for her and Sibyi to stay there for a time. I knew after having had to listen to the sounds from our tent for the past few months, she was just trying to give us some privacy . . . but there'd been quite a lot of sounds coming from their tent, too, and maybe they also wanted a little time alone.

"He's not a nobleman," Jelena had told me one night, giving Sibyi a sly look, while the other former mage sat obliviously across the campfire, discussing future plans with Rhaim. "But I don't need one, now that I'm a noblewoman," she said, patting her nearby bag still full of jewels. Then Sibyi caught her watching him, and his entire face lit up. Jelena tilted her head so that she could talk to me from behind a veil of her long dark hair. "He makes me laugh," she said with a secret smile. "He'll do. "

So they promised to catch up with us in a bit, Rhaim drew them a very detailed map, she kissed my cheek, Sibyi gave me a hug, and we took our leave of them.

Finx came with us though, of course, and I let him out of his bag the second we were outside of town.

"When will we be there?" he asked Rhaim.

"Not you, too," Rhaim said and laughed.

The place Rhaim had abandoned his castle was lonely indeed—and now that there weren't portals or airships, it was clear how many places on the continent were quite spread out. I mentioned as much to Rhaim on our third day of hiking, and he nodded. "Borders will rearrange and languages will shift."

"I put a lot of people out of business," I said, with some remorse.

"Better than sending them off to war."

"There will still be wars, Rhaim," I said, and he snorted.

"Yes, but hopefully less magical ones."

I paused, to shrug my bag higher—Rhaim carried the weight of all our newly bought supplies, so I was carrying our belongings. "I can't quite believe that we're safe now." But we'd managed to go through several towns that had never seen a battle, for whom the Deathless might as well have been made up.

"More than that, moth," he said, pulling up, and looking down at me, before jerking his muzzle forward. "We're home."

I squinted. We'd just come around a bend, and the topmost floor of Rhaim's castle was clearly visible above the trees.

"What . . . if?" I asked him, meaning what if bears had gotten in and ransacked the place, or worse yet, people?

"I will be horribly disappointed if the Lightning Palace has been harmed, and when you next see Sibyi, you can tell him I said so," Rhaim said with a grin, striding forward.

Rhaim had locked the castle's lower doors shut from the inside before his final portal out, so he'd had to climb to my window and pry away the boards he'd tacked up in haste prior to leaving, so that he could get back in.

"What's taking so long?" Finx asked, around the same time I'd begun thinking it too.

He'd adored his entire trip in the countryside, and we'd taken turns carrying him so he could sleep during the day, allowing him to prowl around at night, having nearby adventures and keeping us safe. But he seemed to be looking forward to seeing the inside of the castle again as much as I was.

"I don't know," I told him as the door opened up, showing Rhaim.

"I need an hour," he announced, as Finx zipped inside with proprietary glee. "But I brought you a book to read," he said, handing one out.

"But I don't want to read a book," I said, taking it nonetheless—only to have him shut the door on me. "What if I've forgotten how to read?" I shouted through it.

"You haven't!" he shouted back, and then I knew he was gone, inside . . . and I was out here, trapped between fuming and laughter.

"Rhaim!" I protested, banging on the door once with a fist. "I just want—" I began to shout, not even knowing where to begin. A real bed? Access to the rest of his library? A bath? A view?

And time with him.

I blew air through pursed lips, sending strands of loose hair fluttering, and rolled my eyes. Rhaim didn't have whims, though, he had reasons, which were usually far more annoying. And in any case, I'd already come this far . . .

I set my bag down and leaned against it, opening up the book he'd given me—and I realized what it was in an instant.

The book I'd seen that one night in his bedroom, on his lectern, where he'd written of me.

I wanted to skip to the end, but I made myself start at the part I'd last seen, when he'd been angry, then realized it hadn't been *at* me.

He was mad at the *idea* of me.

And what I represented to him.

Back when he didn't know me at all.

But after he did . . . the rest of the pages were filled with his neat script. Him cursing himself for ever lying to me, his fears that he would never see me again, and his hopes for what he would do to me if he did. I traced my fingers on the pages like I was running them against his very skin, as word after word there filled my heart, and at the end was this:

I will get her back.
Or I will gladly die trying.

"The rest of my journals we might as well burn— that is the only one that matters," he said, having reappeared. I was so intent on his journal I hadn't even heard him open the door.

I jumped up to both feet at once. "I love you," I exclaimed—I'd been crying softly for who knew how long.

"And I, you," he said. He'd taken off the shirt he sometimes wore, and while his fur melted into the inky blackness behind him, I could feel the warmth radiating from his eyes. "Can I welcome you home, little moth?"

"You'd better," I lightly threatened with a grin. I took his offered hand, and wasn't surprised in the least when instead of letting me walk, he scooped me up into his arms, his journal still pressed against my chest.

"Without mage light, the stairs are dangerous," he explained.

I knew they were, seeing as I'd cut myself on one, once upon a time, but I nuzzled into his chest. "Oh, yes, that's the entire reason you're holding me—you're concerned for my safety. "

"Intensely," he said, rumbling, as Finx raced back toward us along the stairway's rock wall—there was a light coming in from somewhere behind him.

"There's so many bugs for me to catch!" he exclaimed.

That concerned me far more than the stairs. "I don't want to hear that!" I shouted, and Rhaim paused to laugh.

"Don't bother us for a while Finx—"

"How long?" Finx asked.

Rhaim gave me a sly look before answering the spider-cat. "Three to four days. "

"And what if I get hungry?" I asked him, as he kept walking us up towards the light. "Or thirsty?" I teased.

"When have I ever not taken care of you?" he asked me, in all seriousness, and I felt a flush rise beneath my tan, from my head down to my toes.

I squirmed a little bit in his arms though, to call back over his shoulder, "Make sure you get them all!" to Finx, before relaxing again as Rhaim walked from the stairs, through a doorway to toss me on top of my old bed, where one of the windows was missing entirely, showing sunny afternoon sky.

"Here?" I asked him, absolutely sure of what was coming next, more so as he removed his loincloth too.

"Here," he agreed. "My bedroom is too dark with the shutters closed—I made you wait so I could sweep the glass out of this one. "

"Mmm. I thought you just wanted me to read a book about how much you were in love with me. "

"I did want that," he said, with a pensive nod. "Because I know I'm not the same man you fell in love with."

I pushed myself up on my elbows in bed. "I know who I'm in love with, Rhaim. " His head tilted expectantly, while I let a pause linger. "There was this man in a tavern," I said with as much conviction as I could muster, and put a finger to my chin. "Three towns ago?" I guessed, and Rhaim laughed again.

"Wait here then—I'll be back when I've killed him," he said, reaching for his loincloth as he made for the door.

I squealed his name and he came back in, grinning. "And you say you're not the same," I teased.

"I am," he said, looking down at me on the bed, the light behind him filtering through his dense black fur, giving it a ruddy tint, "and yet. "

I sat up with more intent now. "The only difference between that Rhaim and this Rhaim was that one was easier to kiss and shut up—which is what I would like to be doing right now. " He gave me a lopsided smile and crawled onto bed with me, reaching for the buttons of my shirt. "You use buttons and you're worried you're a beast," I tsked.

"If I bit you out of this, you'd have to sew—I'm only protecting your precious fingers," he said, finishing my shirt for me, as I kicked off my boots, and he went to help me tug my pants down so I could finally be as naked as he was.

And then we were finally together, in his castle, safe, where we belonged. I blinked my eyes quickly. "I'm not crying this time."

"Liar," he said, and swiped his tongue across my breast.

I ran my hands into the fur at his neck in an instant. I loved the feel of his rough tongue on my body—and I knew he loved licking me. Given the chance on the road, he would've done so for hours—but I'd been waiting for one thing for so long.

"Are you out of patience, moth?" he asked, rising up and gently stroking a hand full of claws down my body. His hard-on was already in full view, curving up against his belly, the piercing gleaming at its tip, his heavy balls swaying as he moved himself between my legs.

"Yes," I whispered, and heard him make a satisfied sound over me, trapping me in his arms as he lowered his body down, while pushing his hips up.

"Me too," he said, setting his teeth against my neck as he parted me.

RHAIM

I'd been waiting to sink into her again for months, torn between doing what was "safe" and "right"—not endangering my moth by being locked to her on the road—versus what my entire body wanted me to do, which was take her.

There was no pretending the urges I had were some other creature's anymore, I knew what I wanted, from the moment I woke up and found myself pressed against her, hard and ready each morning, until the moment I went to bed again, having been pleasured, but leaving something still achy and hot in my soul each night.

And this was what I wanted—to sheath myself inside her again, to stopper her with my knot, to claim and to feel claimed.

She ran her hands through the fur at my neck, clawing her fingers against my skin, as I stretched her—and she was so eager for me, she was already wriggling her hips for friction, her eyes closed as she made soft, high-pitched noises. "Stop that," I murmured, pinning her down, as she whined. "Don't tempt me to fuck you before you're ready. "

Her copper eyes whipped open at that and she glared. "I am ready. "

"Hmm. " I lifted myself up off of her a bit, so that I loomed above her, and spoke in my lowest voice. "Little moth, perhaps you have not noticed how much bigger than you I am now. "

She looked up at me, grabbing hold of the fur on the tops of my shoulders, and kicking me with her heels. "Or," she began, everything in her bearing challenging me, "perhaps you have not noticed how badly I need to be fucked. "

My nostrils flared and I lifted my lips to show all of my teeth to her. "By your beast?" I asked her.

Her own lips parted in anticipation. "Yes. Sir. Please. "

I reached down to grab her hip with one clawed hand and tilted her up, looking at the place we joined, where I was only halfway in. "Beg me again. "

"Yes, sir, please," she said, the words flying off her tongue, and I fed her greedy pussy more of my cock with each one. She moaned. "Yes—please. " She kept going. "Sir—" she hissed, as the heady scent of her sex filled the air, and I shifted to stroke without going deeper, just feeling the hot and tight place she held me within. Her words had drifted away to contented sighs in time with my thrusts.

"Is it everything you remembered, moth?" I asked her, licking a line up from her breast to her cheek and making her shiver.

"More," she said—at first I thought answering me, but then I realized she was asking.

"I don't want to overfill you," I said, stroking the line of my nose beneath her chin.

Her hands fisted into the fur behind my neck. "Consider how long I've been empty. "

I sped up and pushed deeper into her. "Never again," I swore, as she stared into my eyes. I could feel all of her wrapped around me, her juicy cunt stretched wide, and when I thought about everything we had gone through to get to this point, all the danger, all the sorrow, all the death—she stilled beneath me and brought a hand up to cup my jaw.

"If I'm not allowed to cry, you certainly cannot," she said, laughing warmly.

"I just still can't believe you're here," I said, twisting my face into her palm. "And—I kept you in a dungeon," I told her, with a little disbelief.

Her eyebrows shot up. "Yes," she said back. "You were an asshole. You still are an asshole, sometimes, Rhaim. Only you're my asshole now, so it's suddenly okay. "

I grinned down at her and then squinted thoughtfully. "I don't remember that being part of our pledge vows. "

My little moth laughed again, and trailed her hand down my back. "I think it's the part that goes unsaid. " And then she wound her legs tighter around me. "Yes, please, sir?" she asked, while flashing me the eyes that would make me take on an army for her.

"Yes," I agreed, in a low tone, reaching beneath her head to grab her hair and make her show her neck to me. She made a helpless sound and I could see her pulse speeding up. "Anything for my moth and her tight little pussy. " I put my muzzle by her ear. "No one on the continent can fill you like me, Lisane," I whispered hoarsely. I was thrusting more freely now, my shaft slicked by her arousal. "I told you you could take more of me—I told you that you'd beg for it—and I was right. "

Her full lips fell into a tiny pout. "I hate that. "

"It doesn't feel like you hate anything to me. " I swung my hips against hers again, getting even more of myself inside her. "Rather the opposite in fact," I said, chuckling darkly, as she gave another whine. "And when I'm all the way inside of you, I'm going to give you such a—" I threatened, as it happened, and I found myself hilted deep. I groaned rather than finish what I was saying, relishing the feeling of being buried inside her.

"Give me?" she wondered, after a soft moan.

"Everything," I answered, and did so.

LISANE

I was so full I lost the ability to speak; it was like his cock had pressed all the words out of me. But I knew it was the same for Rhaim—he was breathing just as hard as I was—and all our teasing stopped as he started to stroke in earnest.

Everything felt good.

Not that it hadn't felt good all the times he'd made me come on the long road to get here.

But being here, with him, him filling me up, it just felt intensely *right*.

Part of me wanted to lie there and let him give me the satisfaction I had so patiently earned—while the rest of me wanted to pull it out of him with a fight. I clawed my hands into his fur again, and heard him make a low growl as his hips sped up. "I like it when you have to hold on, moth," he said.

"I like it when you make me," I whined.

He reached down and lifted my hips with one hand to make it easier for him to fuck me, and I could feel the indents of each of his claws against the meat of my ass.

"Touch yourself, moth," he commanded, and my fingers flew to do as they were told, fumbling my clit as his hips smashed them—and then he started taking me in bolder, grander, strokes, pulling out so that I could feel the fat head of his cock against the walls of my swollen pussy, and then shoving it back in so I could feel its plunge and where it landed. I made a guttural sound at the first of these, and then cried out, again and again—it felt like he was making a home in me, like he was making me fit him, and that was what I craved—and then he pulled out and I was so stunned I couldn't believe it at first until his face was between my legs.

"Rhaim!" I protested, reaching down to punch his shoulder. "What the fuck?"

"If you come around me," he said, starting to lick me and then talking between them, "you'll bring me off for sure—"

"I thought that was the point?" I asked as he reached in his hands to stretch me wide with his thumbs and kiss me carefully with his tongue. "I'm so mad at you right now. "

"I know. I can taste it. "

"Fuck you," I groaned, as my head rolled back, but it wasn't fair. He knew exactly what to do; he'd done it to me so, so, many times before. I reached back and grabbed hold of my pillow as I arched my hips against his face. "Fuck!" I shouted, almost a complaint, thrashing as my orgasm roiled me. "Fuck—Rhaim —fuck!" I whined, while he snarled and kept licking me until I couldn't take it anymore and I was closing my legs and pushing him away—but he didn't stop snarling, he just rose up, breathing hard, showing himself to me again, so that I could see his thick, ridged cock, with the clear fluids that drooled out from its tip, following the metal of his piercing before dripping onto the bed, and then on my stomach, as he neared.

"Turn over, Lisane," he said. "Your beast wants to mount you. "

The way he said it made me want to come again until I thought things through, and I frowned. "This isn't because you don't want to be locked to me like this, is it?" I asked, gesturing between us, face to face.

Rhaim paused, one eyebrow lifting. "Can't a man just want to watch his woman's ass jiggle when she's fucked?"

"Yes," I answered quickly. I did as I was told, going onto all fours, spreading my knees wide as he wound my hair around his hand. He reached between us to drag his cock up and down me, and even though I knew what was coming I still wasn't prepared. "Rhaim," I moaned, as he shoved himself inside me. I sank my head, or tried to, only he was pulling on my hair. "Oh, fuck," I whispered.

"Such a tongue on you now, little moth," he said, grabbing my hips and planting himself deep. "I'll have to put my cock in your pretty mouth next, and see how much you can say when you're choking on my cum. "

I moaned again, bracing on the bed, and then walked my hands up until I was bracing on the wall. Rhaim made a sound of deep satisfaction at that.

"Keep yourself pinned there," he said, letting go of my hair to spread me wide and watch himself rock in and out of me—before smacking my ass with the flat of his palm. I yelped but didn't move. "Good moth," he groaned. "Good, beautiful moth, who knows where she belongs," he said, with a series of thrusts and more spanks, until he pulled himself out and leaned over to bite where he'd just hit me without piercing the skin. I cried out again, and he soothed his hands up and down me, before shoving his cock back home. "My moth, who I adore," he said, leaning over me, covering one of my hands with his own, and reaching the other down between my legs to pull at my clit for me, as his hips sped up. "My moth, who needs to come for me, so I can knot her and fill her up," he whispered low.

I made a whining sound, a sharp counterpoint to the messy wetness where we met between my legs where I was gushing. I could hear Rhaim's heavy breathing behind me, feel his fur on my back as his hips rode mine—and then I felt him put his teeth where they'd been when he'd bitten me before, on my shoulder and neck, only this time I felt completely safe, and I knew that his beast had been wrong.

I didn't need to be a tamer of beasts, as long as this one loved me.

"Rhaim, I'm going to—" I warned him, and heard him growl in response and shove himself deep as I came.

I howled, trapped between his teeth and his cock, my whole body pulled tight and breathless, my eyes seeing white, before I screamed again, riding him hard with each of my pulses, until I sagged and he caught me, moving his hand that'd been between my legs to hold my waist.

"Moth," he groaned, thrusting wildly. "Stay still—oh fuck— stay still," he implored, as he took us to the bed, meeting my hips with his. He gave a triumphant howl as his body covered mine, and even though I knew it was coming and I'd felt it before, I still squeaked as his knot stretched me wide, and kicked up my feet behind me with pointed toes in surprise.

"Rhaim," I panted.

"It's going to be okay," he promised with a growl, as his knot took up all the space inside me, pulling everything inside me tight.

"How do you know?" I whispered.

He paused for a second, breathing hard by my ear. "Because you're not hitting me. Also, maybe don't be so literal when I'm trying to comfort you. "

I looked back over my shoulder at him as I swallowed. "Lies aren't comforting," I said, but then I laughed, and he licked my shoulder and groaned, pulsing his hips against mine again.

"Fuck, Lisane—I feel like I'm still coming. "

I could feel his cock twitch again inside me, as his knot jerked and pulled at my entrance. "Maybe you are," I told him, and he made an anguished sound behind me, snarling and giving me another shove. His hands moved to clasp my hips and I could tell he was trying not to dig his claws into me.

"You just feel so fucking good," he said, with another shudder.

I gave a sigh of pleasure and exhaustion, then reached back to hook a finger around one of his fangs and pulled his head to me. "Mine," I said, like he liked to say to me.

He laughed, smacked one of my ass cheeks, then grabbed it to shake. "Yours," he agreed.

RHAIM

I was soaring for minutes after knotting her, which made me even more glad I had never dared to do it on the road—*but now*—I picked her up and rearranged her, so it was almost like she was sitting on my lap, with her back against the bed, one of my arms beneath her head, and her legs kicked over mine so I could breathe into her hair and hold her to my chest.

I liked being this close to her, and I loved still being inside her—I didn't have to see her face to know that she was smiling. I stroked the claws of my free hand through her hair and trailed them down her body. "That was good, Rhaim, but I'm going to be so sore," she said.

"Some of the herbs I left in storage should still work. "

She rolled her head back and made a sad sound. "No magic means no healing tub. "

"Definitely not. In fact, after three months, it's probably full of algae or flying fish. "

She giggled. "I guess I can drink murky teas if it means more of this," she said, squirming a little.

"I can be more careful," I promised.

"Only sometimes," she said, as she picked up my hand and pressed my palm to her heart.

I lifted my head a little. From here it was easy to see the mage-mark on her throat, and now I understood why she'd found mine so endlessly fascinating for a time. I slid my hand up to her neck and rested it there readily.

"When we were in the castle, how did you know not to kill me, Lisane?" I asked her, watching her eyes flutter open.

"I didn't have any magic," she said, with a lazy smile.

"Did you know, then? Did you even try?"

Her smile slid to a knowing one, as she reached up and ran her fingers along my cheek and up to rub against my ear. It would've been embarrassing to admit how much I liked it when she scratched me there. "I had a vision when I Ascended. Same as any other mage. "

"Oh," I said, and wondered quietly.

"Ask me and I'll tell you what it was, like people who love one another are supposed to," she teased.

I gave a moment's thought to being strong, then knew my curiosity would get the best of me. "What was it?"

She scooted to look more at me, my knot tugging her entrance tight. "It was of you, like this, Rhaim. A beast, but with vast tracts of gray in your hair—and you were still with me. That's how I knew. " She licked her lips and beamed at me. "And even though I'm going to be able to read all your books now—I'm sure that's the best vision anyone's ever had. "

The last true vision of the last true mage, and the only woman I'd ever loved. "I've already read all my books, and I'm sure too," I told her, nuzzling my face into her hair.

Love the series, want the hardbacks?

Pick up all three special edition hardbacks available ONLY on Cassie's store: cassiealexander.myshopify.com

And make sure to keep reading for more Rhaim and Lisane news!

PS: Cassie here —

Not ready to give up reading about Rhaim and Lisane
just yet?

Me either!

. . . so what if I told you you didn't have to? Keep reading!

Take Her: The Moth and the Monster Book One is a completely new alternate universe story featuring Rhaim and Lisane in a contemporary setting. They'll have the same dynamic you're familiar with and many of the same tropes, but the overarching story will be a dark mafia billionaire age gap romance, with high drama, high angst, and buckets of debauchery.

I'll be going **all** out—and you can read the very first chapter, all in Rhaim's POV, if you just turn the page...

TAKE HER
THE MOTH AND THE MONSTER

The very first thing I noticed about her were her ankles—because the shiny catsuit she was in was an inch too short to cover them.

They were a stark white in the darkness of Vertigo's debauched basement rooms where anything—and anyone, to some degree—could be bought.

I'd been sitting at the well-stocked bar sipping wildly over-priced whiskey and idly watching the door for company, because despite paying my membership fees, it'd been a long time since I'd bothered to come down here. The bouncer still remembered me, as did some of the other patrons, and I gotten more than one welcoming nod plus a few hopeful stares. But the people who still knew me knew what I liked best.

Being alone.

It wasn't that I was a voyeur—on the contrary—but that I didn't enjoy any of the burdens being a committedly good dom required. Building a relationship, trust, having a flair for public exhibitionism, a tolerance for aftercare—I was just as aware of my own flaws as I was of everyone else's currently in this room.

Which was why when she came in, in her too-short shiny black catsuit and her strappy black heels, I would've bet a stack of hundreds that her fetish costume had come from the Halloween store.

It wasn't that she wasn't beautiful—she was; the catsuit left no doubt of her figure, which was just curvy enough to grab while being taut enough to bounce a quarter off of—but she was anxious, and I didn't recognize her, so that meant that she was not for me.

I wanted a sure thing, with someone who already knew I was an asshole.

That didn't stop her from trotting up to me at the bar, like a nervous yet still sexy-filly. Her long, dark brown hair was in a high ponytail, and it splashed in waves down around her shoulders, giving her a somewhat pony princess look.

All she would need to complete it would be a bit in her mouth, hoof-boots instead of heels, and a propensity for crawling.

"Hi," she breathed, flashing me a smile.

I took a moment to stare her down before responding, hoping that it might quiet any further attempts at conversation. "Hello," I said, and turned away from her, observing the rest of the room while shielding myself with my drink.

That didn't stop her from tapping me on my shoulder.

"Is this seat taken?"

The music was loud enough I could pretend to ignore her. Or I could show her my true nature and just get up and walk away—I owed no one my time.

She tapped me again though, more insistently, not catching the hint. "Um, this seat—was someone else—" she asked.

I looked back with a sigh, caught her shifting slightly as she anxiously pulled down the sleeves of her suit, and I realized her predicament. Her store-bought catsuit was too tight—the only safe place she could get away from the torture of her heels was beside me, at the bar, with its higher stools she could lean on—because if she sat down in that get-up, there was a good chance it would rip.

"I suppose it's free," I said, gesturing to it with the drink in my hand.

Her smile—showing off the best teeth Daddy's money could buy, I was certain—somehow turned even brighter. "It's my first time here," she confessed.

"I had guessed," I said slowly, then remembered the club's rules and narrowed my eyes a bit. "Where's your minder?"

Only friends of friends could get into this place, and you had to sign off on whoever you brought, at least for the first time. It helped keep the community safe.

She fluttered a hand over her shoulder. "He went to talk to someone."

"And abandoned you?" I questioned the man's judgement at once.

She gave a soft laugh. "It's not like there's murderers down here."

I cocked one eyebrow up at her. "How can you be so sure?" Her eyes widened, and it was my turn to laugh. "I apologize. That was a sorry attempt at a joke. Have a good night," I said, standing and picking up my drink for a location change.

Her expression spun on a dime, looking a little stunned. "Would you like to know a secret?" she quickly asked, over the thumping base.

And apparently I had invited this on myself, by being kind. "Not really," I said, begging off.

"I don't have a minder," she said, pressing quickly on.

"Well, then I'll have to be speaking to Vertigo's membership coordinator about that, because I'm not paying as much as I do to be having conversations here with casuals." I took a step back, attempting to extract myself. She was pretty, but I had a suspicion the whiskey in my glass was older than she was.

"I just knew the password," she said, and then added at a slightly louder volume. "Do you want to know what it was?"

"No," I said simply, turning around to walk away.

"It was, 'I'm gorgeous and I like to get spanked,'" she called after me, at a pitch where everyone at the bar could hear.

I paused at that. It was clear she wanted my attention.

And while I didn't want to give it to her . . . she still had it.

"Ignore him," said another man's voice from behind me. "He doesn't play well with others—but I can show you a good time."

I slowly turned, and saw Clark—a trust-fund type, far closer to her in age—circling in on her like a shark. Her warm brown eyes were filled with panic, until she noticed me noticing, and then she kept her gaze on mine like I was her savior.

And I realized that was why she was here, and what she wanted—the same as most people in the place.

Saving.

And it'd been a long time since I'd been in a situation where I could save anyone.

"Oh, come on, Rhaim," Clark complained, as I strode back. "Everyone here knows you're rusty—"

"Fuck off, Clark," I said, without taking my eyes off of the woman. "Daddy issues?" I guessed, and watched her cheeks flush even in the club's dim light.

"Yes," she admitted, the tip of her tongue furtively peeking out to give her full lips a nervous swipe.

"As long as you cop to them," I said. "What's your name?"

"Uh—Lisa," she said, after a moment's panic more.

I knew what it was when she said it. "That's your real name, isn't it?" I asked her, mystified.

"Was it not supposed to be?" she asked.

Her password story might actually be real at this rate. "We usually leave our real names upstairs. For instance, the guy who sells weed on the back deck calls himself Madman23—and I've never met his older brothers one through twenty-two, or his younger brother, twenty-four."

I was making conversation with her now, pretending to be personable, a little to piss off Clark, who was still watching, but more to calm her, and she gave me a slow smile in return.

"What should I call you, then?" she asked, swinging her mane of a ponytail over one shoulder provocatively.

I cast an appreciative eye over her entire body, before staring her down again. "You *are* gorgeous," I agreed. "But did you mean what you said?"

She rose up on her toes and nodded hopefully, so I downed my drink and set the glass on the bar behind me, before offering her my arm. "In that case—you can call me sir."

L isa took it and we walked through the rest of the floor at a stately place. Vertigo had installations in certain rooms that they took pride in, sometimes holiday themed, others just represented common kinks, but they went to elaborate lengths to make them special for scenes, all the better to draw crowds in when a theme changed.

I'd already walked the premises earlier in the night out of curiosity, which was why I knew exactly where I was taking her, in her silly catsuit, and on her teetering heels: a throne room.

It was done up to look like it was from that ridiculous dragon show on television, and it contained someone's massive, beautiful antique chair that'd they'd sacrificed at the altar of sexuality. It had all sorts of blunted swords artfully laced to the back of it, with winding layers of suspension rope wound around the front, a comfortably padded seat, and wide leatherbound arms—real leather, unlike the outfit she was in—with two women playing on board.

"Oh," Lisa gasped as we entered, and I suspected from the way she'd been looking around en route, she hadn't made it past the bar.

I should've wondered why—I was good looking; but not magnetically attractive. I'd kept myself up—for a long time I'd had nothing to do but work and work out—but I was well aware God hadn't blessed me with the same charisma he had others. My boss liked to tell me that my gruffness was part of my charm, but if it was, he was the only one who thought so.

Nero Ferreo liked me because I was his living pit bull, both in person and on paper. He enjoyed having the plausible deniability that came from having someone else do all your dirty work, and I enjoyed pretending like it was all his fault that I had to do it, like I didn't enjoy it in the least.

I'd started off with him twenty years ago, when we were both much younger men, on the cusp of our "industry" evolving, away from the docks and into finance. And when wetwork shifted to deskwork, I was one of the few men who worked for him capable of making that change. You'd think a bunch of bookies would be better at doing math, but no . . .

But I still sometimes I need more avenues to pursue my long denied baser nature, which was how I'd found out about Vertigo myself, years ago, first as someone else's friend, and then as a member, once I could afford it.

I had no idea how *she'd* really gotten into this place, but since she *was* here, I was going to give her an evening to remember.

I waited for her to return her focus to me after surveying the room. The women on the throne weren't wearing much more than electrical tape and glittering diamond chokers, riding something purple and silicone between them, with one of the club's photographers nearby.

Lisa's jaw dropped once she parsed that. "They take pictures here?" she said, gawking at me, before practically hiding behind my back.

"Yes, but you'd have to pay extra." I chuckled, but gave her cover nonetheless. "Some people want to commemorate the occasion, and they may only get to come here once a year. Which is also why we're patiently waiting our turn for them to finish." She believed me enough to creep forward again, watching the couple on the throne before giving me a guilty look, which I waved away. "They wouldn't be doing it in public if they didn't want people to see, so go ahead. I'll be right back," I told her, briefly leaving her to negotiate with the other members who were watching the show in line.

I didn't expect her to last more than ten minutes, and while I had no idea who she was, many people would've known me here in real life, no matter what name I gave them, so I'd never bothered to lie about it—and outside of these walls, I was the kind of man you wanted to owe you favors.

So it was nothing to gladhand a few fellow pervs, allowing us to cut—and I was happy the show was still going when I returned, because Halloween-store Lisa and I needed some time to talk.

"We'll be next," I informed her, coming back to stand by her side.

Her lips parted at that, and she took in a thoughtful breath, nodding deeply, like she was preparing herself to go on a frightening rollercoaster ride. Her eyes were still on the women, who were chasing after pleasure, which gave me the freedom to look at her. Her ears were delicate pink shells, closely set against her head, and the angle of her neck was swanlike.

"Have you ever done anything like this before?"

"No," she breathed, without turning.

"How do you know you like it, then?"

Her amber eyes flickered up at me. "College is a time for experimentation," she said, with a hint of a tease, before sobering. "But this seems a bit more real."

"It can be." The thought of someone else her own age trying out things on her they'd only seen in porn disappointed me. *Why would you take a thoroughbred to a children's party?* "So let's both do our homework."

At that, I had her attention again, and if I were honest, traitorous parts of myself liked it.

"I want you over my knee, but I only intend to touch you from here," I said, indicating a height beside her hip, "to here." I sank my hand down to outside her mid-thigh. "Will that be all right with you?"

She bit her lips and then nodded.

"Words, please."

"Yes," she said, and swallowed. "You can touch me."

It was my turn to nod. "Did you have a safe word you wanted to use?" I asked, and when she didn't respond quickly enough I added, "Like a code word in case you'd like me to stop?"

"I won't want you to stop," she said brashly.

One of my eyebrows rose perilously high. "May I touch your chin, then, before I give you incredibly stern advice?"

She gave me a questioning look. "Sure."

I took it in between my thumb and crooked forefingers to make sure she could see nothing else but me. "Anyone who says that, in real life, and especially in here, is a fool. Are you a foolish girl, Lisa?"

Emotions ran rampant across her face again, especially at the mention of her name, then she squinted. "Maybe I need to be punished?"

I shook her head for her with the hold I had on her chin. "Don't play act yet. We're not done with the rules—and if you're too impatient for rules, then I'm walking."

She straightened her shoulders and became serious quickly. "I'm sorry," she said, then added "Sir" as an afterthought.

"Good. Back to our discussion. What's your safe word?"

"Mmmm . . . Lambo?"

"As in the car?" I asked.

I felt her nod again, and let go of her. "All right—if you'd like. Just one last question, then: what do you want to get out of tonight?"

That made her blink with surprise. And then she inhaled, as if to say something, but then fell back, swallowing whatever words had been on the tip of her tongue, as her gaze jumped everywhere but at me. "I—I don't know."

"Don't know—or would rather not say?" I pressed.

"Can't say," she answered quietly.

"Brave enough to get spanked in front of strangers in public, but too scared to tell me why?" I asked with bemusement.

"Something like that," she said, looking down briefly at her pedicured toes—before raising her chin back up defiantly. "What is it that you want?"

"For you to call me sir," I said simply.

She groaned at that, as I hid a grin. Then she sighed heavily, before asking, "And what is it that you want, sir?" in a falsely congenial tone, like each of the words pained her.

I gave her a Machiavellian look—the same kind of look I gave suited men in boardrooms before I stole their companies from them—and instead of taking a highly appropriate step back, she took a challenging step forward, so brazen she almost made me laugh while giving me a hard on.

She was the exact type of woman I shouldn't have been playing with. She ran hot, then cold, she didn't know the rules, but was determined to win the game. I considered lying to her, but seeing as I had already had a more interesting night with her than I'd expected, if I were honest with her and she backed down now, then either I'd sorely misjudged her, or it wasn't meant to be.

"Well?" she demanded, staring up at me, completely fearless, so I decided to reciprocate.

"What I want, little Lisa, is to make a pretty spectacle of you." The women on the throne were moaning louder, and the scent of sex was heady in the air—so I took her chin again and leaned down and in, so she could hear me, and I would only smell her honey-scented shampoo. "I won't tell you how beautiful you are, because you surely know it," I said quietly into her ear, "but I like the idea of you strewn across my lap, your heart-shaped ass in the air, you mewling with each stroke as I spank you, preferably until you cannot breathe, and possibly until you cry." My desires became more cogent as I gave them voice, and then they outstripped rational thought entirely. "I want you to dredge through whatever brought you here tonight and leave it behind as I beat it out of you, until there's nothing left of you but the pride that you've survived me."

I heard her breath catch in my ear. "Are we playing now?" she whispered.

"Yes."

"Then . . . . I want that."

"Which part?"

"All of it," she said, before adding, "Daddy."

I made a dissatisfied sound as I rose up, releasing her. "I'm not sure whether or not that makes me feel old, or like a monster," I said, giving her side-eye with an arched brow.

But then she was there, her eyes wide and her expression begging me for something I already knew I couldn't give her. "Why not both?" she said, with absolute sincerity.

The acridity of cleaning products cut through the air. The women on the throne were through, and some of the club's new members were doing their service hours, quickly preparing it for our show.

And Lisa was still . . . hoping, I thought, was the best verb.

Wanting me to be something for her that I could never be. My only consolation was knowing that no other man in the room could manage it either—so it was just as well that she was with me.

I heaved a sigh. "Fine. I can call me that. You cannot call me that. And this is just one scene. Nothing real. After that, I don't owe you—and you don't know me," I said quietly.

She nodded quickly. "I understand," she said just as quietly back.

"All right." Everyone in line knew we were next, and the throne was empty.

Waiting.

I centered myself, ignoring everything else in the room, settling my full attention on her like a heavy cloak, and I watched her accept it, frighteningly receptive to me, ready to respond to all of my cues. She was like some kind of filly indeed—one who'd been searching for the right rider—and so I gave her a somewhat wicked grin. "Lisa, would you like everyone else in this room to see what a good girl you can be for me?" I asked her utmost indulgence.

She gave me the sweetest, most trusting smile I'd ever seen, one that made me feel like an asshole for sins I hadn't even committed yet. "Yes, please," she said, beaming.

I offered her my hand, and she took it.

· · ·

I let her lead the way to the throne, so that I could watch her ass—might as well pre-game some, since I was back here—and so that everyone else would see her acting of her own volition.

I had dragged women through rooms here kicking and screaming before—consensually, of course, with all the rules carefully hashed out and written down, practically notarized —but this wouldn't be like that.

No, because somewhere along the line I'd apparently decided to be a good person . . . well, maybe not good, but I'd decided to give her what she wanted for the evening. I couldn't put my finger on exactly when it'd happened, but no one was more surprised about it than me.

I mounted the dais the throne sat on and took my seat, careful to arrange myself—and the hard on I was sporting— for maximum comfort before crossing my legs. I could've spanked her lying flat across my lap, but I liked the idea of her being a little topsy-turvy, and having to brace herself against her own abuse by placing her hands on the carpeted floor. She made to kneel down, and I tapped my upper thigh meaningfully when she paused.

"It's just that," she said, trying to move and wincing, as all the lines on her catsuit became uncomfortably tight.

I resisted the urge to chuckle. "If your suit tears, you'll be giving the couple over there the best show of the evening," I said, tilting my head their direction. "But if it does, I swear I'll give you my coat to take home, to cover yourself with."

I had no business breaking up a bespoke Fioravanti suit, but I would if I had to.

If I didn't, my dick might never forgive me.

"Okay." She nodded and ungracefully climbed over me, like she was crawling into a tunnel. Her hands reached the ground and she shimmied, wriggling until my thigh caught her beneath her hips, and my cock was pleasantly trapped between my stomach and her ribcage.

"Remember your safe word," I reminded her. "And tap my leg twice if you can't speak."

"Okay," she said again, looking innocently over her shoulder at me, one side of her face framed by her hair. "Go slow?" she asked—her first true hesitancy of the night.

I slowly put one hand down over her right ass cheek, the one furthest away from me, to palm it while I could see her expression.

"I would never hurt my little girl," I promised, as her face went even more flush than it had been prior from being so close to the ground. And then I added "Much" and raised my hand.

F ive spanks in, and there was a strong chance I was going to hell.

I'd always assumed that if there was one, I was, because where the hell else—pun intended—would have me?

But the longer this went on—and I wanted it to last a very, very long time, far longer than I'd asked the others in line behind me for permission—the more certain I became.

I'd started slowly, rubbing her between blows, my callused hands taking their fill of her beautiful half-moon curves, sliding over the mere millimeters of cheap fabric that kept me from her skin.

Then she'd pitched her hips up higher, practically begging me for violence, and I felt myself inclined to give it to her . . . and I knew she'd let me, if I asked her right.

I sank back into the throne a little bit and jutted my hips forward, contemplating the perfection of her ass, as the shine of her costume was being slowly dulled by my handprints.

"You do realize you're the most perfect girl here, don't you?" I said, stroking a hand across her lower back.

I felt her whole body tense—her stomach muscles against my thigh, her arms straighten against the ground. I even heard her give a little gasp.

"There I was, sitting all by myself at the bar, wondering what I was going to do with the rest of my night," I said, as rhythmically as possible, like I was charming a snake, and I moved my hands from stroking to palming, kneading the places on her I'd already hit, that I was sure were sore. "And then you came in, and I knew."

That . . . wasn't precisely accurate. But we were in a scene, and I was well aware it was what she wanted to hear.

"You did?" she said softly, twisting her head back quickly to look at me over her shoulder.

Lucifer was handing me his business card.

Beelzebub was opening a gate.

"I did," I lied, and somewhere in the distance I heard Asteroth throwing away a key. "You were meant for my hand from the moment I saw you," I said, running one of my forefingers down the seam stretched against her crack. The action made her close her eyes and shudder, and it was all I could do not to evilly laugh. "Can I spank you harder, Lisa?" I used her name because I hoped she would know it was a genuine request, but as soon as her eyes opened, and before she could rationally answer, I switched tactics like the asshole I was doomed to be. "Do you think you can take it for Daddy?"

She twisted more fully toward me at that, panting harder than the pain required. "I can take anything," she breathed.

And in that moment . . . I wanted to give it to her.

It'd never occurred to me that perhaps I was the one who needed a safe word.

"You don't mean that," I told her in a low growl. "We discussed this."

Her eyes blazed and she shook her head. "Don't tell me what I don't mean."

"Then maybe you do need punishing after all," I threatened.

"There's nothing you can do that can hurt me," she proclaimed, and I quite literally felt her insubordination as she physically braced for whatever onslaught she was taunting.

But I was older than her, and wiser than her, and extraordinarily used to getting my way.

"No?" I asked her rhetorically—and then roughly slid my hand between her thighs.

Her whole body tensed as she gasped.

"Technically this is within the priorly arranged touching zone," I said, twisting my wrist to gain a little freedom—enough space to run the pads of my first two fingers against the fabric trapped against her pussy.

She took a long and shuddering inhale, before protesting, "You wouldn't."

"You clearly don't know me," I said, leaning over, to look her directly in her eyes. "I absolutely would."

It was nothing to find her clit—I highly doubted she was wearing underwear—and once I was there, I thought the only thing that would stop me would be her saying the name of an overrated car brand. I traced lightly against it, getting her used to the idea of me touching her intimately—and the expression on her oval-shaped face was an exquisite combination of turned on and betrayal.

"Are you okay?" I asked her softly.

Me asking made her melt against me and she quickly nodded. "I think so," she said, then nervously added, "You're not really mad?"

Daddy issues indeed. "How could I be?" I told her, then gave her my best impression of a warmhearted grin as I stilled my hand. "When everyone here is going to watch the prettiest girl in this room come for me?"

Her gaze lingered on mine, as she bit her full lower lip and then slowly released it as her thighs squeezed to pull my fingers in.

"Such a good girl," I praised her, sitting back up. She gave me one last longing look, and then braced one hand on the ground and clutched the other against my calf. I pushed my hand in deeper, for better leverage as I stroked her, and her thighs parted to let me.

I ran a figure-eight pattern over her clit, before pulling it between my first two fingers in a gentle V, feeling her rock against me. I had no idea how much time had passed, but if anyone else in line complained before I got her off, I would kill them personally.

"So beautiful, so passionate," I crooned on. "So smart enough to pick me," I added, and felt her laugh. She pushed her knees a little wider, giving me more space, and I rubbed my thumb against her pussy, which made her moan. "Did you like that?" I asked, so quietly she probably couldn't hear —but she might feel the soothing rumble of my voice. I circled her entrance, pressing hard against the fabric that separated us, while working against her clit with my fingertips and knuckles. "Is my little girl going to come for me?" I asked more loudly.

Her hand around my calf grabbed tighter, and her hips rose in response, grinding against my hand, and riding up and down the shaft of my trapped cock, too.

I had sudden visions of what I would do to her if no one else was there. I would stay on the throne of course, but I would rip her out of her silly catsuit, wind my palm with her long hair, and make her ride me. I would come in her pussy, her mouth, and her ass, and after I'd satisfied myself with every hole, I'd stripe her tits with my cum just because I could.

And then she gave a needy whine, pulling me back from my reverie.

"Mmmm," I purred, leaning forward to capture her hips between my lap and my chest as I put my elbow between her knees, and turned my hand into a fist, so I could bring all the muscles of my forearm to bear, rocking against her pussy's edges with the knuckle of my thumb, feeling the muscles of her cunt quiver with anticipation. "Does my little girl need me?"

She was panting harder now, it was easy to see the movement of her ribcage beneath her catsuit's shine. "Yes," she hissed.

I changed angles and took a long moment to just trace the folds of her pussy and stroke at her clit, and no matter where my fingers went, her hungry hips chased me. I would've laughed, were I not so breathlessly hard. "Yes what?" I asked.

"Yes, sir," she begged, arching into me. Her entire body was tense, her toes pointed far harder than her precipitously high heels required. I could tell she was on a cliff, all she needed was to be pushed over.

And for this one instance, this singular moment in time, I was a man who could not resist temptation. I ground into her pussy and rubbed her clit roughly.

"Yes . . . what?" I asked again, more meaningfully, and the second she realized what I was giving her permission to do her fingers clawed me, her hips hitched up, and I came as close as I could to fully fucking her with my hand.

"Yes—yes—*Daddy*," she cried out, arching against me, coming beautifully, the muscles of her stomach pulling tight against my thigh in waves as her orgasm hit her, passed through, and then roiled back again. She kept crying out as she came, making pleasing, helpless sounds, absolutely lost in the moment, utterly forgetting that we were in the middle of a crowd.

"Mmm, good, so good," I promised her, stroking her back as I followed her through, my hand riding each of her spasms.

"What a good girl," I swore, petting her until she stilled. "You needed that, didn't you?" I kindly asked, like I was doing everything for her sake, like she hadn't just given me enough material to jerk off without porn for the rest of the year.

Her hips slowly sank, and she released me to reach for the ground with both hands, pushing herself up, to collapse to the ground on the other side, sliding off of me to scattered applause.

I watched the realization that we weren't alone flood her, as her lips parted with surprise, but she didn't take her eyes off of me.

"Are you all right?" I asked her, and she nodded.

"A little lightheaded," she said, bowing briefly down so her blood pressure could even out, all fears about her catsuit's seams forgotten.

"Yeah, you came pretty hard," I said, as she attempted to gather herself, and I realized I liked her just like that.

Wrecked by me, and kneeling.

And because unlike certain people, I hadn't gotten the chance to come—which apparently meant that all of my sensible blood was in my cock—there was nothing left to check the urge to say so.

I took her chin in my hand again and raised it, making her look up.

"If we ever play again, I'd want you to lick my shoes and worship me."

Her eyes went wide, and she nodded slowly—and as my own blood redistributed itself, I let her go.

"You were brilliant, Lisa," I said, hopefully summoning both of us back to reality with the sound of her name. I stood and offered her my hand. She took it, standing upright shakily, and I carefully moved us away, making sure she didn't trip on the step down, pulling us to a darkened corner of the room before releasing her. "How do you feel?"

She patted her herself with her hands like she was unfamiliar with her body. "Dizzy," she said, "but good."

I made eye contact with a circulating server who came over with two flutes of champagne, and took both, offering one over to her, which she took.

"These are on my tab, seeing as I don't believe you actually have one. But thank you for an excellent scene," I said, and made our glasses clink. "You should probably take some Aleve tonight, and sit on an ice pack in the morning."

She stared at the glass and its contents like they were alien things, and then she looked at me. "Did you have a good time?"

"Yes. Of course. I only do things I enjoy," I said, brushing her question away.

She nodded her head and smiled at me. "Then . . . can we talk?"

And here it came. The part of the evening where she would try to make plans with me, to create some nebulous future out of nothing more than sheer endorphins. I cursed silently. "No. You are not mine, nor do I want you." Lisa blinked, rocking back on her heels.

I'd been in this exact same situation a hundred times before, and learned that abruptness verging on rudeness was the only cure.

"I say a lot of things in a scene, and I'm willing to suffer a fair amount of carpal tunnel to get a girl off," I admitted, before taking a sip of my drink and giving her a look of pity. "But somewhere out there I suspect you have an actual father, and I suggest you get over him."

Little Lisa stood much straighter as her sudden shame sobered her up.

And then she threw her drink at me.

I laughed half a second after the cold champagne hit my face, licking away a trail of bubbly alcohol and blotting it off with my tie before it could burn my eyes.

"That's too bad," I said, polishing my own glass off with a grin. "It was very expensive. You would've liked it."

"Fuck you," she said.

"You almost did," I taunted, and watched her nostrils flare and her eyes burn. She was so spirited—no wonder I wanted to break her.

Not for any dire purpose—*no*—for the same reason people pulled apart daisies.

Just because I could.

Which was why I shouldn't be with *anyone.*

I knew because I'd made that mistake before.

"Get home safely, little girl—it's probably past your curfew," I said, taking her empty glass from her as she sputtered, putting both our glasses on a nearby table. "And think fondly of me tomorrow, when you see my handprints on your ass."

I gave her a low wave, then turned around, walking to the coat room to collect my coat, my phone, and summon an Uber.

Did I fuck my hand that night?

Yes.

Fuck yes.

I spent half the ride home hard, and luckily my coat hid my hard on from the doorman, and then I was tempted to stroke myself in the elevator, but remembered they had cameras in time—so I made it to my own door, first, until it was locked behind me, and I'd stumbled to my couch.

I should've taken pity on my dry cleaners, but they were used to me, and besides they were already going to be getting out champagne. It didn't matter, I'd pay them a fucking hazmat fee—I just needed to stroke myself to completion, imagining myself buried inside her cunt.

I was so hard and ready and because I'd already wanted to blow more than once tonight, it didn't take long at all—just remembering the perfect curves of her ass and her wriggling body and—I was gasping and groaning in moments, covering myself with my own cum.

I rocked my head back like the rest of my body was a traitor —because it was. I had only the most tenuous connection to it: I punished it in the gym, I forgot to feed it for days at a time, and I worked straight through for weeks without sleep.

And then here it was tonight, making demands—already getting hard again, like it'd never heard of a refractory period.

"She's not even here," I complained. But it was like my body didn't know that—not when if I breathed in deeply enough I could convince myself I could still smell her hair.

"Fuck," I cursed, and the rest of me agreed.

I let my hands do what they wanted to, closing my eyes, and this time, I imagined her riding me.

By Monday morning, I'd fully recovered my inner asshole—and working most of Sunday helped. Nero had texted me on Saturday saying he needed to run a proposition by me, but said he wouldn't till we met in person next, which told me that it was too dangerous to put in writing, so I wanted to get caught up.

I made it a point to go to the gym early and finish up my run on time, so I could shit, shower, and shave and be in my office, exactly where he wanted me to be, at eight-oh-one.

And eight-oh-three.

And eight-fifteen.

I was used to him by now. Nero Ferreo was the human embodiment of a cat. Easily distracted, with the potential to be ruthlessly cruel. As the head of Corvo Enterprises it wasn't his job to be on time—and ever since I'd first been the driver in one of his cars for him, back when I was fourteen, well before I had a legal license, I'd always known waiting was part of the job for me.

So I carried on—he'd find me when he needed to—greasing all the wheels of our assorted legal industries, making sure that all of the money we made via illegal means was bleached, washed, and starched, going through an entire screen's worth of excel tabs one by one, until my assistant, Mrs. Armstrong, rapped twice on the door like she always did.

"Mister Selvaggio? Mister Ferreo is here."

I glanced at the clock. *Ten-oh-five.*

I would've told her to let him in, but it didn't matter, he was already opening the door. Nero was of the opinion that nothing should be locked to him in the entire building, because he owned it all—which everyone knew, as he was fond of reminding us.

But I couldn't truly complain. I remembered where I'd come from and where he'd found me—and he'd made sure I was well compensated over the years.

And every once in awhile he would throw me a bone like for old times sake. Like when his coke dealer had cut his stuff before an important party a few months ago.

So many bad things could happen to someone in international waters.

It was really just a shame.

I stood as he walked in, ready to shake his hand, offer him a drink from my bar, and get down to business.

"Bestiola!" Nero bellowed, because he only had one volume, using the only nickname I'd ever had on this earth—little beast—despite the fact that I was now forty-four—and I would've complained about it like I always did, only I noticed someone else walking in right behind him.

And this time she wasn't in a catsuit—no, she was in a caramel brown pencil skirt, and a shiny, loose off-white, long-sleeved blouse, and her hair was in a bun.

"You remember my daughter Lisa? Little Lissy?" he went on, as she walked in, surveying the room coolly, before she looked at me.

"Rhaim Selvaggio," she said pleasantly, holding out one hand, like the hand she'd be shaking wasn't the same one that'd spanked her on Friday night before making her come. "Of course I remember you."

"I remember you, too," I told her with a complete flat inflection, as Nero went on, oblivious, grabbing her shoulder and shaking it roughly, like she was one of the boys.

"Lissy just got her MBA. I want you to teach her everything you know, Rhaim—because someday soon this place is going to be hers."

"Thanks, Daddy," she said, with a sweetness that didn't reach her eyes—I knew because she was staring fire right at me.

Daddy's little girl hated me.

I.

Was.

Fucked.

Take Her releases in Spring 2024, but you can preorder it now!

And don't forget to join Cassie's newsletter -http://www. cassiealexander.com/newsletter -for free bonus content, character art, Cassie's latest news, and plenty of cat pics!

ALSO BY CASSIE ALEXANDER

Check out cassiealexander. com for content & trigger warnings.

The Dark Ink Tattoo Series

Blood of the Pack

Blood at Dusk

Blood at Midnight

Blood at Moonlight

Blood at Dawn

Blood of the Dead

The Longest Night (Bonus Story)

Edie Spence Series

Nightshifted

Moonshifted

Shapeshifted

Deadshifted

Bloodshifted

Transformation Trilogy

Bend Her

Break Her

Make Her

The Prince of the Other Worlds Series (Written with Kara Lockharte)

Dragon Called

Dragon Destined

Dragon Fated

Dragon Mated

Dragons Don't Date (Short Story)

Bewitched (Bonus Story)

The Wardens of the Other Worlds Series

Dragon's Captive

Wolf's Princess

Wolf's Rogue

Dragon's Flame

Standalone Stories

AITA?

Her Ex-boyfriend's Werewolf Lover

Her Future Vampire Lover

The House

Rough Ghost Lover

ABOUT THE AUTHOR

Cassie Alexander is a registered nurse and author. She's written numerous paranormal romances, sometimes with her friend Kara Lockharte. She lives in the Bay Area with one husband, two cats, and one million succulents.

Sign up for Cassie's mailing list at cassiealexander.com/newsletter to get free books, bonus scenes, even more character art, and cat photos!

 facebook.com/CassieAlexanderReaders
 instagram.com/authorcassiealexander

Printed in the USA
CPSIA information can be obtained
at www.ICGtesting.com
LVHW060810140124
768916LV00041B/1588